I0583060

THE BEL ALGORITHM

by ANDREW PARTINGTON

The Bel Algorithm

2nd Edition - no cuss words in this book.

Copyright © 2018 Andrew Partington

Submarine Media Pty Ltd, Lockridge, Western Australia

This novel is a thriller with elements of satire.

CONSPIRACY: mid-14c., from Anglo-French conspiracie, Old French conspiracie "conspiracy, plot," from Latin conspirationem (nominative conspiratio) "agreement, union, unanimity," noun of action from conspirare (see CONSPIRE); earlier in same sense was conspiration (early 14c.), from French conspiration (13c.), from Latin conspirationem.

CONSPIRE (v.): late 14c., from Old French conspirer (14c.), from Latin conspirare "to agree, unite, plot," literally "to breathe together."

CHAPTER 1 - EASY AS PIZZA PIE

DOOMSAYER'S DAY

Lead-lined gloves, of course, are a necessity.

But despite their bulky nature it's easy enough to keep them out of sight when you intercept the pizza van, especially once you know the addresses they are delivering to. That's the advantage of having a back door into any computer without a warrant. Makes it a breeze.

But its not really a breeze on a breezy day, for the wind sends the tumbleweeds tottering and tumbling and it reminds you that life is a pointless round, 'cause your hair flaps in your eyes and your trousers flap back and forth like some sort of a cut-off fishtail still struggling, and you feel clumsy climbing in the back of the pizza van with the Plutonium fragments clasped inside the enclosed cup tongs, opening up the box – peering over your spectacles to make sure its the right pizza – but when the pizza company are organised enough to tape the receipt on to the box, you feel grateful, 'cause then you can be certain you are putting the Plutonium fragments on the pizza that is going to that particular address, why, and then, it really is a piece of yellowcake, pun intended.

Or a piece of pizza pie, you could say.

A fatal piece.

PHEONIX, ARIZONA

Some people are addicted to alcohol or cocaine, or over-eating, or porn, or gambling.

Hacking was Natasha's addiction. An adrenalin rush; that moment she got through all the protections and firewalls into the inner sanctum of someone else's life was like the moment an addict stuck the needle in.

She had done well for a long time, avoided hacking for quite a few years, but events last year had turned back the clock and she had returned to the habit she thought she had left behind. Her Anglo-Indian parents would have been appalled.

The wind whistled down the alley past her room and a rotten odor filled her nose, blown over from some rubbish dump somewhere. It reminded her of where she was at.

To make things worse Natasha had just bought a new computer, a Metabox even more souped up than her previous machine, with two internal four terabyte hard drives, sixty four gigs of RAM and a lightning fast multicore processor.

The wind whistled even louder and at first Natasha thought it was saying, "Wow!" but then she realised it was saying something more like, "Big deal, in five years it will be outdated."

She shoved those thoughts away. She didn't know why they came. In reality, she was on the trail of something huge, something monumental.

Natasha had gotten the tip from another hacker on the secret darknet DEF CON bulletin board, http:// defconbb4z3xu7z0199.onion. The poster's pseudonym was "OxyMoron," obviously a reference to "OxyMonster", the notorious darknet market moderator, Gal Vallerius, who had been caught by the FBI coming to America to show off his beard in a beard contest, of all things.

Natasha had laughed at OxyMoron's name when she first saw it, but it had turned out he was well respected on the bulletin board. He'd created a trojan that had given him a back door into CIA computers, NSA, FBI, even some private companies, anyone really, enabling him to view the screen and see what they were downloading, to see everything the user saw on their computer, everything they did.

Of course, most of what he'd videoed from the government employees' computer screens was just CIA agents looking at porn, tax officers goofing off on their Facebook pages while at work, or workers emailing innocuous emails, like an NSA guy asking his wife to get some lamb chops on the way home from work.

Big deal.

Nothing top secret so far, but still, it was an achievement just to get that far, after all, it was usually the government who was using their back door software to spy on citizens.

Now the boot was on the other foot.

They had all congratulated him - and he had shared the code, which showed what a great guy he was.

The hack was effective for a short while but Natasha suspected that it was why Windows had just released another patch in the last few days, and OxyMoron had confirmed that the latest Windows patch had broken his trojan. But he had quickly found a way around it and was boasting now about something top secret he had actually found.

It wasn't anything on a CIA or FBI or NSA computer, though. It was a document he had observed on the premier search engine company i-ogle's servers - he'd glimpsed it for a moment during some sort of foray into the back door of some i-ogle employee's laptop - but he hadn't been able to download it and had forgotten to take a screen-shot of it.

But he had given them the name of the document. He had seen the name and couldn't make sense of the rest, but the other thing he had seen was the accompanying email, which said to keep it completely private, don't let it get into the media or it would cause a huge scandal.

The document was called the BEL Algorithm Project History.

His final message on the bulletin board after posting his new back door trojan had been, 'Not feeling well. Some kind of food poisoning from a bad pizza. Be back soon.'

But he hadn't come back soon, in fact he'd been off the bulletin board for more than a day and everyone had started discussing what had happened to him.

About thirty six hours after that, someone called TrippyGirl posted a simple message.

'OxyMoron was my friend. And now he is dead. We often worked together in his basement. His only mistake was, he ordered some pizza. I told him not to eat anything he didn't see them prepare. A few hours after the pizza he was in hospital, puking with extreme diarrhoea. Then an hour after that he was in intensive care, and pretty soon he was dead. If you're reading this don't eat anything you buy if you haven't chosen it yourself from a selection, like pies in the window at a pie shop! If I'd had a slice of that pizza I'd be dead too. It wasn't food poisoning, symptoms match radiation exposure. Hospital won't tell me, his mother not talking. Whatever you do, don't touch this hack, keep your hands off the BEL Algorithm if you want to live. I'm torching everything, you won't hear from me again.'

To Natasha that sort of warning was like a red rag to a bull. How dare these corporates behave as if they could do whatever they wished? Hiding their secrets and scandals by killing people and destroying the evidence.

Natasha knew there was a way in, though. A way to get that document, to find out what it said.

Microsoft, Apple, Samsung, they all thought they had plugged the Spectre bug, but Natasha knew better. Without replacing every microprocessor on the planet with a completely new design no one could beat Spectre, the problem was inherent in the design. And building on OxyMoron's code and a flaw in the i-ogle search window Natasha knew that she could write the perfect code to put her own Spectre worm onto every server in i-ogle's server farm.

She took three puffs on her asthma puffer. So what, a bit of stress might be making her asthma worse. But so long as she had Ventolin handy, she was fine.

Natasha wasn't going to let asthma or anything else stop her getting that document.

ON THE TRAIN TO BUDAPEST, HUNGARY

Peter had tried to keep Meth away from prying eyes, people's mobile phone cameras, Facebook, social media, but what can you do with a child who looks like a toddler but has the mind and vocabulary of a twelve year old? Any normal person who heard the boy speaking would find the sight intriguing, fascinating, even freaky.

God knows, all it would take for them to be discovered was one Facebook post.

One i-ogle video plus posting.

And Peter had tried to tell Meth not to talk to anyone, he really had tried to explain, but the boy hadn't listened. Peter had wanted to tell him, if you do talk just pretend to be stupid like a regular toddler, but that just didn't seem fair, and he didn't think Meth would have the social skills to do that anyhow after being imprisoned in that little room for the past twelve years with no one but adults to talk to. How would the boy even have any conception of what a toddler's language was like? He had lived a completely insular life.

The train was quietly racing through the countryside. The only sound was an odd whining sound, was it the wind outside, rushing along the train carriages? Or something to do with the electric motors?

Not long now and they would be in Budapest.

They had tried living in Washington, but it just hadn't been working out. Yes, the head had been cut off, but the Adamant corporation lived on, and Peter still suspected the Cabal was still running things, anyway, that Corporate/NSA partnership that had been his employer, even more top secret than top secret.

Eastern Europe seemed the best bet — somewhere where nationalism, not globalism, held sway — to get off the grid. So they were heading back to their former destination.

Budapest. The place they had been getting ready for; Meth had even started learning Hungarian.

He looked at the boy. Poor Meth was upset.

They had managed to swap compartments with a family just outside of Munich but Peter had still been worried that they were being followed. Surely his former employers must have put someone on their tail. It would have been out of character for them not to.

Peter had told him no one outside could hear them when the compartment door was closed, even so, Meth was whispering. "I'm sorry, I know I shouldn't have talked to those people," he wiped away a stressed tear. "It's just they were so interesting. And so interested in me. And it is so exciting being out in the world at last. For the last twelve years, Father, I was imprisoned in that horrid tiny little room. Twelve awful years."

Meth had taken to calling him 'Father', something that Peter found unexpectedly moving.

Peter was not Meth's father in the genetic sense, no, he was the scientist who had created, or rather, recreated him from DNA found in intact cells in the soft tissue in the fossils of paleolithic humans, whom they had discovered had had extremely long lifespans. Thus the boy's name, Meth, from Methuselah, the longest lived of all the Biblical pre-Noahide patriarchs.

Meth knew the risks.

And yet he had talked to those people.

Peter wanted to be angry with the boy about the lapse; he thought it might help reign in the boy's carelessness. He had even considered spanking the child, but honestly, this whole situation was not Meth's fault. How could Peter punish him for it?

The people who were after them had their own agenda and one way or another Peter knew those people would find them eventually.

It was only a matter of time.

Their pursuers had the Government on their side.

And what was intrinsically more valuable than the DNA code for extreme longevity?

More life. Nothing was more valuable.

The one thing everyone wanted.

Peter had made sure all the documentation, the hard drives, the CD-ROMs, the paperwork, all the records were destroyed. It had been his insurance policy.

The only copy of his research now was with him.

The boy himself.

Meth was all that was left of all that information, all that research, all that experimentaion.

The DNA encoded in Meth's cells.

Meth continued whispering, "Seeing other people, talking to them, Father, seeing the trees, the skyscrapers and concert halls and those old churches, the rolling farmland and the wind moving the trees to and fro, and just the vastness of the sky." In his enthusiasm the boy forgot to whisper. "The sky! With all that blue, and when there are clouds and it is rolling with thunder, and the lightning! Wow, thunder and lightning and rumbling winds, Father, they're amazing. I heard the thunder rolling in that horrid room, but I never saw lightning before this. And at night with the stars. I really had no idea how wonderful it would be being out of that horrid little room at last." He laughed, then another tear rolled out of his eye.

Peter laid his hand on the boy's shoulder.

"It's alright, son," he said softly. "It's fine. Look, I imagine someone has posted a video of you doing what you do," he meant, talking like an older boy, but he realised he had caught Meth's habit of assuming someone around them was listening, "Talking. I guess someone has posted a video of you talking on Facebook by now, or youtube, or i-ogle video plus. But don't worry, son, we still have a few tricks up our sleeve. All is not lost."

He grinned and winked at the boy.

"Really?" Meth looked at him with expectant trust.

Peter nodded.

The boy's trust in him just about tore his heart in two. Lord, he didn't have as much confidence as he was pretending to have. The likelihood was that they were going to get captured soon. But until then the child may as well live in hope.

Peter said, "Meth, I actually expected something like this to happen, so I have been putting a plan in place in case it did. Just get a little sleep for the next half an hour, son. Let me organise things, I'll need to be on the laptop undisturbed for a little while. We are almost in Budapest now and when we get there, we may have to get off the train in a bit of a hurry. So get some sleep now, be a good boy."

While Peter had been talking Meth had started drooping and now he was fast asleep with his head leaning on the windowsill. The poor child had been beside himself with stress over the mobile phone video someone had taken, and now he was quite simply worn out.

Peter said, "Good boy," thanking his lucky stars he had fallen asleep so readily, and turned around to open the luggage compartment.

He took out his laptop, put his smart phone on "Personal Hotspot", connected his computer to the hotspot and logged in to TOR.

Natasha had shown Peter TOR and had set up some cryptocurrency accounts quite a while ago, back in England. She had shown him TOR just in case he ran into any trouble.

Peter had been surfing the darknet for quite a while now, finding his way round. With a few judicious trades, or maybe it was just good luck, he had grown the cryptocurrency Natasha had given him at the start into quite a respectable fortune.

And now he was completely ready.

He logged into one of the more useful trading posts

he had discovered in an obscure offshoot of I2P, DEX34Y, logged in to a site called Hackers & Son Anon, http:// hkrnsnanon4qt76tg.onion, and posted a request.

"Need RJ63 direct night train Munich to Budapest to stop before Budapest, at Paty. We are in carriage six, which is the third room on the far left as you're walking to the end of the train, seat numbers 304 and 305. Then we need the train door to open at our end of the carriage. All the other doors on the train including the ones adjoining the cabins together,need to stay closed for two minutes and we need a total surveillance blackout for thirty seconds anywhere in the vicinity inside or outside the train. 20 Ethereum or lowest comparable bid to whoever does this."

A few seconds later a user named BUDAFEST made an offer, but not in Ethereum, which Peter would have preferred. It was 0.7 Bitcoin. Pretty high. Peter sucked in a breath of air. Peter knew he had about .85 Bitcoin left, and Bitcoin had risen lately. It was a very cheeky bid, considering the comparative prices, but whoever this BUDAFEST was, at least he was quick off the mark.

Or she.

Natasha was the only hacker Peter knew, and was a woman.

Peter lodged the 0.7 Bitcoin with the site moderator and pressed "Agree." He saw BUDAFEST's "Agree" button change colour and Peter knew that he would have to hurry now.

He opened the luggage compartment and quickly tossed all the loose items into the suitcase, including the laptop. He zipped up their hand luggage and threw that in as well, closed and locked the suitcase, and slipped his mobile phone and wallet into his body pouch.

He dragged out the suitcase, placed it on the rather efficient wheeled carrier he had been using and strapped the whole lot up.

Meth was still fast asleep, bless him.

He would leave waking up Meth till last.

He watched trees and bushes flagellating in the wind as they rushed past, then the concrete wall of a station, a single monolithic thing only moving in the detail, then more trees and bushes, then the concrete wall of another station, then some sort of grassy park or farmland, then more concrete walls. He stared at his watch.

The train would surely be coming up to Paty station soon.

Finally Peter waked Meth up. "Come on, son, we're nearly there."

Peter got up and lifted the luggage carrier off the spare seat and onto the floor. Meth was still groggy. In intellectual terms the boy was like a twelve year old. God alone knows how clever that child would be when he actually <u>looked</u> twelve.

In so many other ways the boy was still a toddler, for instance in the amount of sleep he needed.

Peter took out a few bottled waters from the suitcase and poured a little over Meth's face, wiped his face with a handkerchief and gave him the rest of the water to drink. "That might help, son. Come on. Let's go." Peter swigged a bottle of water too.

Meth was suddenly a lot more alert. Thank goodness, Peter didn't think he could get through this with the child in a groggy state.

He saw a cross on a distant church and thought about Natasha again. She had talked to him about God. Did Peter believe in God? Maybe a little more than he ever had, after all that had happened. He said a quick prayer, "God, I don't even know if you're there. But if you are and you're anything like Natasha says, then you're listening. Please help us."

He prised open the compartment door gently. He put his head out and looked up and down the corridor to see if anyone was out there.

No one was there.

"This is it," he said and grabbed Meth's hand in his right hand and the luggage with his left, then dragged them both out through the door, with Meth's little legs running almost comically fast.

They reached the end of the carriage. He told the boy, "Brace yourself," and showed him how to hold onto the handrail, but the handrail was too high.

It wasn't going to work.

Peter tied the luggage onto the handrail with one of the luggage straps. Peter picked up the boy and sat down in the corner of the carriage with his feet braced against the opposite corridor, holding Meth in his left hand and pushing against the handrail as well as he could with his right hand.

Just in time.

The train came to a screeching halt, and the moment that it had, the door behind them slid open, causing Peter to fall backwards clumsily for a moment, but somehow he managed to hold onto Meth and right himself.

With a sudden burst of energy Peter jumped up holding the boy. He untied the luggage.

A moment later the door on the outside of the train

slid open as well. Peter went through. There was no station in front of him.

Looking at the distance down to the tracks Peter realised he would cripple his knees jumping at this height, so he sat down gingerly on the edge of the door with his legs hanging over and slid down, with Meth in one hand, dragging the luggage behind him with the other.

The doors slid shut behind him the moment he alighted on the ground.

For some reason Peter felt compelled to look up at the next carriage.

A particularly nondescript man in a black suit was staring at them from the window at the end of the carriage with a very angry expression. Really, really angry. Peter fancied he could hear the man banging on the train door, trying to get it to open, but perhaps the hearing of it was just his imagination. He could see him banging. But then Meth said, "I can hear him banging on the door."

This spurred Peter on again. Barely looking, he crossed the train lines, tripped, stumbled upright again and jumped across to the other side of the second line of tracks holding Meth in one arm and dragging the luggage behind him with the other, just as another train roared past. Something jarred his arm and he realised the luggage carrier must have clipped the train.

Close. Very close. But fortuitous, because the guy in the suit couldn't see them any more, because the train had many carriages and it was still going past.

Peter inspected the luggage and looked at Meth, whose eyes were wide with fear. A horrific thought struck Peter and he looked at his own arm to make sure it hadn't been torn off. One might not notice such a thing if it happened, the pain would come later. The luggage and the carrier and his arm and Meth were all physically fine, nothing missing or damaged or injured or torn off, but Meth was in a bad state of anxiety and stress. Peter wondered if he was hyperventilating, but he didn't have time to check.

Peter kept running until he reached a grey concrete wall. How was going to get out of here?

Peter looked both ways along the line. To the right was little more than the sign, "Paty." To the left there was a street crossing about twenty metres away. He sprinted with the strength of desperation, faster than he would have thought he could run while carrying Meth and the luggage. he reached the railway crossing before the other train had finished going by.

A little black Toyota two door sedan was waiting at the crossing. The driver was a balding man who looked sixty. The lights were flashing and the bells were dinging.

Peter tapped on the driver's side window. The man undid the window, so Peter flipped out two crisp hundred dollar United States bills and said, "Drive back the way you've come, for this two hundred dollars."

Fortunately the man knew English, or he got the idea, anyway. Peter didn't care which. The man grabbed the bills with a fist and quickly threw open the passenger door.

Peter half stumbled around to the other side of the car, still dragging the luggage behind him, stuffed Meth into the back seat and threw the luggage in next to the boy, then lunged in and did up his own seat belt first. The guy threw the car into reverse before Peter had even managed to close the door or check that Meth was secure, but while the car was moving Peter grabbed the passenger door by the little metal tab and slammed it shut just as the guy jammed the brakes on, revved the engine and threw it into second gear and roared off. The man half-clutched it into third then fourth straight away and the car whizzed, rather than revved, up to eighty kilometres per hour.

Peter breathed a sigh of relief and thanked his lucky

stars he had found a little lodge in Munich where he could turn some of the Bitcoin profit back into cash.

They were bouncing along a half deserted Hungarian steppe, mostly low scraggly looking shrub and farmland. A low mist was hanging about three feet above the ground and he could see cattle dung in the thready grass.

They went past an unexpected small car dealership in the middle of nowhere, a few houses and cottages.

But definitely no security cameras.

And nobody around, either, no one out in the open. No one watching the road. No other cars, even. It was pretty deserted.

At that instant the man driving saw in his rear view mirror that Meth had done up his own seatbelt, which threw his concentration and he fumbled the steering wheel. The car almost went off the road but Peter grabbed the steering wheel and kept it steady for the moment it took for the driver to secure his grip again.

He said, "Sorry," in a gruff voice, and Peter wondered again if there was much more he could say in English.

Peter said, "It's alright, the boy's a genius. The US government wants him to do experiments on him and steal his DNA." Well, it was half true, anyway.

The man smiled a gold-toothed grin and the white part of his teeth glinted. "US government, DNA. Big conspiracy," he said and winked at Peter and laughed. "Fringe."

Peter wasn't sure how much the fellow had understood of what he had told him, but he was sure they were safe from the Deep State now, at least while they were in the car, in the countryside.

He took out the folded up map of Hungary from his body pouch, opened it up and said to the driver, "What would be the most deserted area of Hungary?"

The driver shrugged. Peter brought out another $100 bill and handed it to him. He said, "From here? Northeast."

Peter chose five villages more or less randomly. Szilágy. Sajósenye. Jósvafó. Szalonna. Bódvaszilas.

He had to choose one.

"Eenie, Meenie, Minie, Moe, catch a tiger by the toe..."

His finger ended up pointing at a town called Szalonna.

"Please drive me to Szalonna."

"Drive you to pig fat?" The driver laughed as though it was a huge joke. He said, "Szalonna, means pig fat."

Peter pointed to the town on the map.

"Oh! Really? Szalonna is a town? Funny name! No, just joking, I know Szalonna. Szalonna from Szalonna, it's a famous place. What you want to go to there for? Small town. Nothing there but pigs." He laughed again. "Szalonna from Szalonna."

Peter shrugged.

The driver pulled over to the side of the road. "It's a long way. I was going to deliver something for someone. I'll be late."

Peter rolled his eyes and handed over another fifty.

The man beamed with happiness. "Alright. I drive you to Szalonna." As he was about to pull back onto the road the driver's mobile phone buzzed.

"That will be Zoltan." He picked up the mobile but Peter said, "No phones." The man said, "But that is Zoltan. His stuff is in the trunk."

Peter gave him another fifty dollars.

"Alright, no phones. I talk to Zoltan later."

Peter took the battery out of the phone and said, "Don't tell anyone about this, either."

"But what do I say to Zoltan?"

"I don't care. Your phone was out of battery. Make up a story."

The man shrugged and kept driving.

CHAPTER 2 - CHEERS FROM CHERUBIM

"Early morning fog warning for Highway 152 and 156."

Aloquacious Aeolus Bos Junior, or "Leo" to nearly everyone, liked listening to the radio news.

"In other news, Bill Trawlings, former owner of i-ogle, gave a press conference Tuesday talking about the recent sale. 'Yeah, I called it i-ogle as a reference to the fact that 25% of all internet searches are for porn. And I suppose I wanted the name to have something in common with google.'

"'But google actually means a very large number, the name doesn't have anything to do with porn.'

"'Yes, I know what it means. But my name has the same last four letters, see? O, G, L, E. I think that helps make it recognisable for people, it has four letters in common with google. But you know, it's our new search algorithm that has made us successful.'

"'Mister Trawlings, if it was so successful, why did you sell your company?'

"'Because Adamant Corporation made me a very good offer. An extremely good offer. I can retire with a very good income now, just from interest payments alone.'"

Leo was sitting outside on one of the picnic benches,

and he realised he would rather have silence than that whining voice, so he switched off the digital radio.

The fog was lingering and the beauty of the early morning didn't need to be ruined by talking heads.

Past the slow mist rising from his garden, his new mansion was looking romantic as the sun began to light it with flecks of gold.

His mansion was in Montecito, the most exclusive suburb of Santa Barbara County, the most exclusive county in California.

Leo felt an inner glow of satisfaction. Fifteen rooms, several fountains, a spa, a family room, a wine cellar, five bedrooms, eight bathrooms, five fireplaces, a reasonably spacious pool house. And it was right on the coast with clear unobstructed ocean views.

And one of his bathrooms even had three shower heads! That's water pressure for you. Okay, okay, it probably didn't conform to the water use regulations, but so long as the general public never knew, it didn't matter, did it?

A real sweet place.

Yes, he'd keep his latest purchase out of the papers, if he could, especially after the last debacle when some snoopy hacker had published his electricity bill online. Okay, it might have been about thirty times the average electricity bill, around $1800 a month, but he had paid a stiff surcharge of $108.75 on top to get green energy, so really it was irrelevant how high the bill was, wasn't it? He was carrying his carbon load, not like so many people.

Still, there are always going to be critics, whining and whinging all the time. They could talk about all the good he did for the environment, but nobody cared to think about that, did they?

His mobile rang.

The voice on the other end said, "Hi, it's Raymond Adamant here."

Leo said, "Well, what a surprise. Roland's son, Raymond? I was so sorry to hear about your father's demise. Thanks for the tip you emailed, by the way, I bought i-ogle shares. And I bought this place, too. You tipped me about this mansion being on sale too, didn't you? Nice location."

Raymond said, "Right on the sea shore. Too bad it'll be over-run by sea level rise."

Leo Bos erupted into a strange donkey-like snort of derision then said, half seriously, "Yes, but it's insured, Raymond. Anyhow I made enough from selling my weather channel to that oil state to fund a hundred mansions like this one."

Raymond continued, "Heard you've been filming a new movie?"

"Yes, I will be. It's called, 'Global Warming III, CO2, It's Already Too Late.' We're actually starting shooting next week. That is, if the apocalypse hasn't arrived yet." He snorted again but instead of laughing with him Raymond said, "Listen, Leo, you do know Adamant Corp now owns i-ogle, the search engine, don't you? That's why the shares went up."

Leo winced in annoyance. Did Raymond think he never listened to the news? Especially the financial news.

Raymond continued, "Well my i-ogle engineers have been coming up with a few new things and we've come up with a plan. A big plan, actually. And I think you'll like what we've come up with. And I'd very much like to talk to you about it."

"Raymond, I am very busy from next week onwards. I'm not going to manage to do very much apart from the CO2 film. One thing at a time."

"Well, Leo, let me say, you won't have to do anything much, not yet. Most of what we want from you initially can be integrated into your existing filming schedule; and don't ask me how I know that, I just do, friends in high places.

Or hidden places, anyway, you could say. But I don't really want to talk about it over the phone. I want to tell you the whole story in person. You never know when one's political enemies might be listening, too, these days, surveillance is everywhere. Listen, how about I meet you at your new place? I can be on my jet in a few minutes, I'll be there in an hour and a half at the most."

Leo smiled. "Well, Raymond, so long as you don't use too many of your carbon credits getting here."

"Oh, don't worry, Leo. I have plenty of carbon credits. Plenty."

THE ADAMANT BUILDING, NEW YORK

Raymond Adamant put the phone down and started sorting through the papers on his desk.

It actually astounded him that Leo Bos's hypocrisy had not been thoroughly crucified in the media. Suggesting to Leo that he buy that place on the sea shore had been Raymond's subtle way of testing whether Leo still had the magic it took to charm the media. It looked like he still had it, a kind of unconquerable charisma. I mean, the guy was just full of hot air and hypocrisy but the public loved him.

That new place was a huge, wasteful, environment unfriendly mansion, his second environment unfriendly mansion - but that was the amazing thing, only a few random bloggers and right of centre websites seemed to care. The mainstream media still fawned over him, worshipped every word that fell out of his mouth, no matter how vaporous and empty and vapid it was.

Of course Raymond's own frequent use of his Boeing 767-400ER was not exactly carbon friendly either, but i-ogle owned a lot of carbon sinks, bought carbon credits, wind farms, solar farms, forests in third world countries, and if you counted all of that Raymond was certainly on the right side of the ledger. Well, the far left side, anyhow.

At last, Raymond found the revised contract he had just signed with the NSA's Corporate Arm. It had been hiding under the electricity bill for the Adamant building.

He leafed through the pages. He didn't like the punitive clause, damages of four hundred million dollars, just because his company had lost that experimental subject. The subject had been imprisoned in England, but somehow Peter Lazarus-Fox, the scientist who had created the aberrantly long-lived child, had stolen him away.

Yes, that clause irked Raymond, but really 400 million bucks was chicken-feed compared with the potential value of Meth's long-lived genes. And the fact is, Adamant

Corporation couldn't get the subject back without the NSA's help.

Since his father Roland had founded the project to take the long-lived paleolithic DNA (Early European Modern Humans, specifically, in popular writing often called Cro-Magnons) and splice it into a modern foetus, Raymond had often fantasised about what he himself might accomplish with a five hundred year life-span. Why, the greatest geniuses of history would be mere children by comparison with a Methuselah.

You could become a world expert in five or six, maybe seven or eight different fields. You could become an artist, a virtuoso, a genius mathematician, a scientist. And you'd still have time for having many partners and leaving your genetic legacy behind with many children.

He sighed. Sometimes you have to settle for less. Apparently, even if they managed to duplicate Meth's genes, the DNA could only be spliced into a foetus still in the womb, so Raymond was too old to get the benefits of the technology. At least, as far as present scientific knowledge went.

If he could get Meth back, perhaps they could find a way to splice the genes into an older person.

He ran his fingers over the pages. Despite that

compensation clause, the rest of the contract was fine. He had access to the NSA's resources on demand and in return they had a back door to the i-ogle search engine, the i-ogle video feed, and all the i-ogle social media platforms.

It wouldn't sound too good if the general public found out about their agreement.

Anyhow, their aims and values were all the same. It was not as if the NSA would use their power for evil or corrupt purposes.

The NSA, i-ogle, Raymond Adamant, we are the good guys, we share the same aims and ideology.

Not like the present incumbent in the White House.

He's a rare one, that one. A piece of work.

The phone buzzed again. He picked it up.

The voice on the other end said in Liverpudlian tones, "We know who the third hacker is, sir. From Pheonix, Arizona, a woman named Natasha Chase. What do you want us to do about it?"

"Nothing."

"Really? Nothing? You serious? Nothing?"

Raymond Adamant paused.

He said finally, "That's what I want left after you've finished with her."

PHEONIX, ARIZONA

Natasha pulled out her laptop and placed it on the restaurant table. She was too close to the kitchen here and puffs of steam were periodically blowing over her laptop; what that would do to the circuitry she had no idea but she suspected it wasn't good, and it was not the most private place either but it would have to do. She opened Tor Messenger and selected Nathanael as the recipient.

"Nathanael. I'm in trouble. I need your help again. I've stumbled across something huge, something potentially devastating. I'm still in Pheonix but not at home right now - staying at the Joshua's Underlings Motor Lodge, 23.7 South Montezuma Street Prescott units x10. Please come and meet me, if you can, as soon as you get this message. Mist U, BTW."

She pressed send.

And wondered if she had chosen the right person to confide in.

Alright, Nathanael <u>was</u> unusual, that was undeniable – in some ways she suspected he might be autistic, or some kind of savant, anyway; and he was Australian, even more unusual – but he had acquitted himself well in the debacle last year.

Of course, she was assuming Nathanael even read his TOR messages. Dreading that he might not gave her a familiar constriction in the throat. She took out her Ventolin and administered three puffs, then waited a little and had three more.

She had been completely free of asthma since her teenaged hacking days, but after all that trouble last year the debilitating condition had returned.

Since she had begun hacking again.

But that Nathanael Wayfarer - he was notoriously tardy even at replying to emails. She wouldn't be surprised if it was a week or two before she heard from him.

AT LEAST THREE WEEKS AFTER THAT, LAS VEGAS, NEVADA.

Cherubim Security Agency.

Nathanael Wayfarer had heard of them.

The premiere security agency in Las Vegas, at least in so far as card counters at casinos were concerned.

They were the guys watching him.

He could pick them out. They were pretty conspicuous in a Blackjack room where everyone else was playing, standing there with other people's cigarette smoke entwining and swirling around them.

Five or maybe six of them, wearing different clothes, all of them watching him now.

It's very distracting, actually, when you're playing

Blackjack, to have people watching you.

Especially when you're counting cards.

And Nathanael Wayfarer was the king of card counting, if not the ace. Most card counters just kept a running total in their heads as the cards were dealt, +1 for low cards, -1 for high cards, divided by the number of decks in play, with a running total of the number of cards dealt so far going on alongside, perhaps, although many just estimated that from the size of the deck that was left.

But Nathanael knew how many Aces had been dealt, how many Queens, Kings, Jacks and Tens. When it came down to the last few cards in the pack he knew exactly what was available. If you asked him how he did it, he couldn't have told you. But if gambling was a game of chance in which the odds are stacked against you, what Nathanael was doing wasn't gambling.

It was far too statistically precise for that.

Mind you, it was still chance, organised chaos, if you will, the kind of nothingness that all life was made of, if you didn't believe in God. It could all still go wrong. Yeah, it was all like trying to grab the mist. Trying to grasp an exhaled breath.

He looked at the people smoking. Alright, if you

didn't smoke you might still catch lung cancer, statistically speaking, it was still possible.

Just like he could still lose.

But today, he wasn't losing.

You couldn't card count in most casinos in Australia. Most of the casinos had eight decks on the go with an automatic shuffling machine, and they simply replenished the cards as they were dealt. You never got below six and a half decks in play so card counting was pointless.

Thankfully the continuing thirst for two deck Blackjack in Vegas meant there were still plenty of tables playing a finite number of cards, a small enough number that one could have a fair degree of certainty as to what cards were coming up as the end of the second deck approached.

Of course, just because card counting was legal in Vegas didn't make it moral, Nathanael realised that. Some legal things were morally repugnant.

But he had thought it all out.

Statistically speaking, all gamblers except card counters and casinos lose money, if their efforts are averaged out. Odds of 6.25% in the casino's favour basically meant that out of every $100 the gambler laid down over his lifetime, he or she would lose $6.25.

The casinos rig the games in their favour, it's how they make money.

But card counters simply redressed the imbalance. They made sure the statistics were skewed in the customer's favour. The casino had a 1% advantage at Blackjack. But when Nathanael counted cards, it gave him an extra 2.75% advantage in his favour, which gave him a 1.75% advantage over the casino.

Nathanael figured if it was alright for casinos to rig the odds in their favour, then it had to be alright for the card-counters to rig the odds in their own favour against the casino.

These were his thoughts as he tried to continue playing with the six security guards closing in on him slowly.

He shook everything else out of his head. He had to concentrate on the game, the deck was almost finished and he was way ahead. He knew what was coming - there was a plethora of tens and Kings left - it was his game now - he had only laid down five grand on this one - but he could win big. He knew he should throw the game while they were watching but the temptation was too strong. He was onto something here. He was so far ahead.

He took all his chips, ten grand worth, and stuffed

them in the middle, upped his bet.

The dealer dealt him a ten and a King.

He laid down his cards. Twenty one.

The dealer paid out.

The men were getting closer.

Nathanael took all his chips, gathered them up quickly and went to cash them in. But before he could reach the cashier the six men had surrounded him. They clumsily shoved him into a room at the side.

They forced him to sit at a table. He had nowhere else to put his chips so he splurged them out onto the table in front of him.

One of the men, a weaselly little chap, swept the chips into a bag. Nathanael got up in the seat and protested, "Hey, there's-" he worked it out in his head "-thirty seven thousand there." A rather obnoxious looking thug with a nose that had clearly been broken more than once and a scar on his hand pushed Nathanael back into the chair. "Listen, bud. You're cheating. No one could count cards that good."

Nathanael said, "Card counting is not illegal."

"You've been using computer aids," said the thug. "No one could do as well as you've been doing. It's like you can count all the cards, not just plus one, minus one like everybody else. Either you're using a computer or you are one."

Nathanael said, "So, I'm good at that sort of thing. So sue me. No, I haven't been using computers. In fact, I haven't even touched a computer for the last six weeks. Nor do I plan to use a computer in the near future, not till I'm finished with Vegas." Nathanael knew that the laws in Vegas favoured card counters so he knew they wouldn't be able to sue him or call the police if he could prove he could do it.

The thug pressed his hand into Nathanael's shirt and breathed unpleasantly close to his face, "Well if you're using computer aids which seems far more likely than that you're some sort of genius then we can get you. And I am assuming that you are not a genius. It's all statistics, isn't it? Chance. And statistically speaking, the idea that you can get the results you're getting by the mere exercise of your human brain is extremely unlikely."

The weaselly guy pulled Nathanael's chips closer to his chest. Nathanael realised he was about to lose them - thirty seven thousand dollars worth of chips - ironic, really, because that was exactly how much he had started with.

The remainder of his money from the divorce settlement, after the lawyers had been paid and Deb had received her payout.

Thirty seven thousand dollars. Everything he had received from the abortive marriage.

Well it was an amount worth fighting for, Nathanael figured. In the divorce battle he had fought for precisely that amount, as it turned out.

Nathanael didn't think he'd have much of a chance against six men in a fight in close quarters, although the thug didn't seem to be too careful about getting close and he could drop two of the others; they were wide open. Their ankles were close enough to his boots, he could thwok their adam's apples in an instant. But then he'd be on the receiving end of an assault charge.

But he thought the casino would be reluctant to face up to him in court if he could prove that he could count cards as well as he actually could.

The weaselly guy breathed on his face too and rasped, "We just think you're a bag of wind."

Nathanael sighed. "I'm not. I'll prove it to you. Get a deck of cards. Shuffle them, deal say thirty cards, I'll tell you what's been dealt and what's left. If I'm wrong - even in one card mind you - I'll let you keep the thirty seven thousand. If I get it right you give it back to me."

The weaselly guy said snarkily, "No!" but the guy who looked like a thug (obviously he was a little more intelligent than he looked, Nathanael realised) had a more curious expression on his face.

Air expelled from his nostrils. "Well... You know, maybe we do have the Rain Man here, despite the fact that he looks like a regular guy." He smiled, showing a gold tooth. "Yeh let's do it." He waved his hand at one of the other fellows. "Get a pack."

The guy walked back in with a pack of cards and the thug started whipping them out. Nathanael could see each one as it was being dealt, then the next one would cover it.

About three quarters through the pack, the thug swept up the cards that had already been dealt and put them aside and said, "Alright. If you can tell me what's left, I'll give you back your chips. No sweat, it'll be a breeze."

Nathanael said, "Two tens, three Kings, four Queens, one, three, four, three sevens, a nine, an Ace, two Jacks."

The weaselly guy took out an iPhone and took note of what Nathanael had said. Meanwhile, the thug was dealing the cards out into piles, each pile for the value of the card. When he was finished he looked across expectantly.

The weaselly guy read out, "Two tens, three Kings,

four Queens," and as he read the thug checked the piles, nodding as Nathanael's counting checked out, "One, three, four, three sevens, a nine, an Ace, two Jacks."

The thug looked up at Nathanael, scowling, and swore casually; there was no malice in it. "Your head is a computer. I'm not sure that's fair, really." But then he looked over at the weaselly guy. "Give his chips back to him."

"But we were told to..." The weaselly guy's words trailed away into an empty vocalisation.

"Well, I don't want to jeopardise our license. I don't care what you've been told."

The weaselly guy sneered and made a creepy wheezing sound as he handed over the bag containing Nathanael's chips.

Then the thug stared Nathanael in the eye. Nathanael didn't flinch - if you gave an inch to these people they'd take a mile. The thug looked away after a few moments, then breathed heavily, "Don't come back here. We'll find some excuse to make a scene - I'm sure the cameras would show you throwing punches, behaving badly, we can engineer these situations, get it? And before you know it we'd be calling the Las Vegas police and you'll be in the slammer for resisting arrest, assault and battery, grievous bodily harm, and the rest of it."

Nathanael nodded.

The thug repeated. "Don't come back here. Wherever you are in Vegas, we'll know, we've got eyes everywhere. And don't mention this to nobody, neither. Nobody. Don't say nothing."

Nathanael said, "Alright, I won't mention it to nobody." and nodded. He didn't mind agreeing to a double negative, not in English anyhow, where it meant the opposite. If they were talking in Italian it might be a different matter.

Well at least he still had the thirty seven thousand, even if his privacy was now compromised.

After taking him to the cashier so he could cash in his chips they escorted him to a small exit that no one normally used, out of sight of the general public, and shoved him out into a deserted street on the wrong side of the casino, where steam was coming out of some sort of vent in the building.

Nathanael hurriedly stuffed the bag containing the thirty seven thousand into his money belt. He caught his breath and looked around.

Another rush of steam came out from the vent. This was out of the way, not a safe place.

He walked along for a while aimlessly, feeling vulnerable.

Once he found a street sign he called up an Uber on his mobile and in a few minutes he was walking through the door of his hotel room with some relief.

He went to the small wall safe, opened it, and put the thirty seven thousand in, one bill at a time, counting it.

He didn't bother counting what was already in the safe because he knew exactly how much was there. He sighed. Five months work. And now it was time to leave.

All because of Cherubim Security Agency.

One more night in the hotel. He ordered a pizza, a salad, some fizzy mineral water and a $200 bottle of wine. May as well have a little of luxury, it was his last chance to savour the good things of Vegas.

He sighed. If only he'd had time to just make a little more money...

The food and drinks arrived promptly. Nathanael gulped down the mineral water, savouring the sensation of the CO_2 bubbles on his throat, then sipped his wine glass.

It was still early - if he paced himself on the bottle he could make it last three or four hours.

Particularly if he ate something.

He stared at the pizza, still steaming from the oven. Maybe he wasn't that hungry after all. He set the alarm on his watch and left the wine bottle where it was, half finished, sitting on the coffee table, and flopped onto the enormous, soft-as-a-cloud bed with the mineral water in his hand.

He drank a bit more, thankfully the water was still cold, the sensation was painfully pleasant as the bubbles bit into his throat.

Tomorrow morning he would wake up at about eight o'clock in the morning, pack his things and have a steaming hot shower after a quick cooked breakfast of smoked bacon and eggs. Nathanael would be on the road by nine, driving along with the wind blowing in his hair and the top down on the Red 1993 Ford Capri Convertible he had bought for a few thousand when he had first arrived in Vegas. By half past one he would be in Phoenix, and twenty minutes later he would be standing at Natasha's door, listening to the wind-chimes and pressing the door-bell.

CHAPTER 3 - ICHTHUS, THUS.

Orsolya, Meth's teacher, said to Peter at the lunch-break, "I would like to talk to you after Meth's lessons, if that is alright."

Peter said, "Why?"

"I'd... rather not say in front of Meth."

Peter hoped she wasn't quitting. That would be unfortunate. He wasn't sure they could find another decent teacher here in Szalonna, and she was good. Meth liked her too.

And she seemed to be discrete.

Well, Peter could probably tutor the boy himself if the worst came to the worst. The only thing is, he couldn't teach Meth Hungarian, and it looked as though they were going to be in this little village for a while.

He looked over at the boy and the teacher, working hard in the kitchen of the farmhouse. Orsolya was standing behind Meth, leaning over him, he was sitting on a stool, with his book resting on the table. He was working hard writing something or other and she was correcting his work.

Of course, he had assumed it was something about Meth, or her employment. But what if it was something else? What if someone had been asking questions, or she had noticed someone watching them? Peter didn't want to think about that possibility.

He only hoped they didn't have to leave.

Meth liked Szalonna. It was a small village surrounded by farmland. Peter had managed to rent rooms in a comfortable farmhouse, in an old community farm that had murals on all the buildings. Apparently they used to farm a particular variety of fur-covered pig, Mangalica pigs, but there were none there now. Indeed, the community farm was once a successful business selling bacon under the label, "Szalonna from Szalonna". But at some point the mayor had wanted rent for the council land, or some sort of disagreement had happened, Peter didn't know the details. Ultimately the farm had folded and the attached school as well.

But Orsolya used to teach at the farm. She lived down the road and Peter had been very glad when she agreed to tutor Meth.

Peter didn't think they had been betrayed by social media this time. He had found someone with a mobile internet USB stick and he had borrowed it from time to time to go online using proxies and TOR browser to check that there were no more videos of Meth going up and that no one online was talking about them.

Perhaps it was more than that. Perhaps someone was actively looking for them. Would the Deep State be doing that? Sending people from town to town to find Meth? Peter felt the boy's genes were that valuable, but perhaps that was just fatherly pride. Or professional scientific pride, perhaps.

Orsolya told Meth to put away his things and came over to Peter, who was standing at the front door.

Orsolya said, "Someone was here, looking for you both. A man in a suit. I told him I didn't see anyone."

She looked out at the town, silent for a moment. "But who knows who else talked to that man?"

Peter groaned.

PHOENIX, ARIZONA

Michelle answered the door.

She looked worried.

"Come in," she said to Nathanael, her voice breathy, he thought it was as though she had been recently crying. "Come in and have a cup of coffee. I've just made myself one."

"Is Natasha here?" Nathanael said.

"No, she's not." Michelle shook her head and frowned even more than she had been. "We were kind of hoping that she was with you on some hare-brained adventure." She waved him into the house so vigorously he could feel the wind from her hand then gave him a hug which he was too shocked to return. He squeezed her finally and she let go.

Nathanael said, "What do you mean? Some hare-brained adventure?" But Michelle was already in the kitchen operating the coffee machine, which was breathing out steam and froth.

Her laptop was sitting, open, next to the machine, with the screen-saver on, showing some sort of Greek wind-god, Aeolus or Zephyros, blowing the clouds around.

Michelle handed him his cappuccino, picked up her own half-empty coffee cup from the kitchen bench and sat opposite. "She's not here, no one knows where she is, Nathanael. I was really hoping you had heard from her."

"I haven't heard anything." A feeling of guilt pierced the pit of his stomach and he realised he was holding his breath. He expired loudly. "But Michelle, I've been away from my computer for five months. I haven't even surfed the net, much less checked my emails or facebook. Do you really think she might have tried contacting me?"

Michelle looked at him non-comprehendingly. That anyone could go for more than a few hours without checking to see if anyone had acknowledged his existence was beyond her ability to process.

To fill the uncomfortable pause, Nathanael finally said, "You don't think she messaged me or emailed me do you?"

"She's been missing for five weeks, Nathanael. Yes, maybe she has! I just don't believe it." She shook her head so vigorously he could feel the breeze from her hair. "Completely incompetent." Somehow Nathanael knew she wasn't talking about Natasha.

Michelle grabbed the laptop and typed in her password and the desktop appeared. She opened Tor Messenger and passed the machine over to Nathanael, who was puzzled for a moment as to what he should do.

"For God's sake, check your Tor message account." She sighed and Michelle's voice took on the twist of sarcasm. "You don't think maybe she would send you something if she was in trouble?"

Then she looked at him as though he was some sort of caveman and said, "Five months without a computer?"

"I was busy," said Nathanael.

"Busy doing what?"

"Playing Blackjack in Vegas."

* * *

As he left Michelle's place, he checked his rear view mirror.

No cars for a little while at all.

Then nothing but a white SUV behind him with a fairly old lady driving wearing an Arizona Diamondbacks wind-cheater. Her number plate was 153-ICH, an interesting numberplate, really. Nathanael knew the pattern meant it was a pre-2008 vehicle in Arizona.

Hardly the sort of car someone would drive if they were tailing him.

Twenty five minutes later Nathanael was cruising along South Montezuma Street looking for the Joshua's Underlings Motor Lodge. Surely it shouldn't be too hard to find with such a strange name.

The only problem was, 23 Montezuma Street was a park, green with bushes and trees reminding him of sea-weed blowing to and fro underwater.

There was nothing here remotely resembling a Motor Lodge.

He went around the block a few times, trying to think what it could mean. Natasha was definitely not in the park and Nathanael could not imagine her staying in a park, anyway.

It was a bit weird anyway, lot number 23.7 rather than 23 or 24.

Wait a minute, Natasha's message said, 'units x10.'.

Usually a block of units might say, "Unit 10" or "Unit x" but "Units x10?"

Why the x? Then he realised, it could have meant, 'units multiplied by ten.'

23.7 times 10 equals 237. Simple.

He drove to 237 South Montezuma Street. And found himself parking outside the Salvation Army.

But where was "Joshua's Underlings?"

Of course. Joshua was actually the same name as Jesus, whose name meant, "Yahweh Saves."

Salvation.

And Joshua was also an army commander in the Old Testament. His underlings were his army. Salvation Army. Typical Natasha sort of code. Centred on the Bible, with a touch of mathematics.

Luckily, Nathanael had been reading his Bible lately, one Natasha had given him a while back. Something he never thought he would do.

Huh. Natasha must have known, somehow, that he would read it. How did she know?

He parked outside and went in the main entrance.

There was a man in a Salvation Army uniform huffing as he carried several huge boxes through the front office.

Nathanael said, "You wouldn't have someone named Natasha staying here, would you?"

"Natasha? No, nothing like anyone called Natasha," said the man, seeming a bit awkward. "Not at all. No Natasha here. Can I help you find a missing person? Do you mind if I see some identification? Can't have just anyone, you know, asking questions."

It seemed a bit strange to Nathanael but he took out his Australian driver's license and passport.

The man read it. He nodded and looked Nathanael in the eye for a moment. "Nathanael Wayfarer. Australian passport. Alright. She's out in the back, staying in one of the offices."

Nathanael breathed a sigh of relief and followed him through, past a main hall, a kitchen and a booth with "Uniform Shop" written above it. Natasha was sitting at the desk in a small office at the rear of the building, with a view of the car park and children's playground in the backyard, typing on her laptop. In the corner of the room was a small bar fridge next to a rolled up sleeping bag, a suitcase, a pillow with clouds on it, and a blanket.

Obviously she was living here.

"Here she is," said the man, showing Nathanael into

the room.

Nathanael couldn't resist needling him. "Tell me," he said, "Initially you told me she wasn't here. I thought Salvation Army officers were supposed to hold to the highest standards of honesty?"

His reply was rather pointed. "Wouldn't you lie, under the circumstances? She's in trouble, she won't tell us what it is, but she needs help and privacy so we're giving her what we can, and she told us not to tell anybody she was here, unless it was you. We look after people who've been in bikie gangs, or people fleeing drug dealers. Can't always go about telling the truth in those circumstances, can you? Natasha here hasn't told us what her trouble is. Only that if you came along she could trust you."

"What took you so long?" Natasha grumbled as he came in.

"I've been off the grid in Las Vegas for the last five months, getting back on my feet after the divorce. Playing Blackjack."

The man quietly excused himself and left.

"Gambling?" Natasha sounded less than impressed.

"Well, no, not really," protested Nathanael. "Well I suppose so. But the odds were in my favour, so..."

Natasha opened the small bar fridge and got out a can of coke for him and one for herself. They flicked the tabs and the cans gave the satisfying gaseous hiss. Natasha still seemed annoyed at him, but as usual that fact didn't really register with Nathanael until afterwards.

Nathanael continued, "In gambling a person has less than unity chance of making back the money they bet. I had odds that were one and a half percent in my favour against the house. That means that on average, for every one hundred dollars I bet, I would get one dollar fifty extra from the house."

"It's still gambling," said Natasha. "A game of chance. Nathanael, did you think about what I said last year? About following Jesus?"

"Natasha - it was the things our friend Bruce told me over the years that made me think that the New Testament might be historical, historically true - but I think you might be giving yourself too much credit if you think you're responsible for me... even considering these issues, even thinking of the idea of the existence God as anything more than a vapourous thought, a human fancy. But you mustn't worry about me. I wasn't doing anything illegal or immoral in Vegas. In fact, the Casinos rip people off - I was just balancing the ledger a bit, Natasha."

"Oh, come on now, Nathanael, so you're Robin Hood?"

Nathanael grinned. Time for a bit of persiflage, he thought, then remembered he wasn't entirely sure what persiflage meant. Something like ribbing, kidding. "Well he was a good Christian, wasn't he? I mean, Friar Tuck was part of his merry band? Wasn't Friar Tuck a Christian? A monk. How much more Christian than that can you get?"

"I don't see you bestowing your proceeds on the poor." She was smiling, getting in on the joke.

"I <u>was</u> the poor, at least, in comparison to where I started before my divorce. The fifty grand I got wouldn't have lasted me one year, what with rents being what they are at the moment in Australia. Negative gearing, you know, what it's done to the housing market over there... I've made a little bit now, but who knows how long that will last. Easy come, easy go; but it has been hard work, it's not a holiday. Counting cards is a very intense mental work, even for me."

"You know," said Natasha, "If it walks like a duck and swims like a duck and quacks like a duck and farts like a duck, it is a duck. Gambling is gambling, Nathanael. Chance is chance. It's good to see you, though." She reached forward and embraced him, and breathed in his ear, "I missed you." He embraced her back for a moment, then they let go.

He was still being carried along by the subject of gambling like a leaf in a gale, hadn't really absorbed what the embrace meant. "But Natasha, I really don't understand what you have against my activities! After all, it's really no different is it, than people who invest in shares? Or... Bitcoin? Except, perhaps, that with my card counting I have a better idea of how much I stand to gain over the long haul, in fact, in my case, it's more like... insider trading! Whereas the value of Bitcoin, in which I assume you have invested a lot of money, is inherently unstable and might drop tomorrow! Like tulips."

Natasha snorted. "Tulips? What do tulips have to do with it? You've been watching too many episodes of Fringe." She was opening some files on her computer now, with her back to him.

"What's Fringe? I was talking about Holland - it was called Tulpenmanie - Dutch for Tulip mania - the first recorded investment bubble in history. Tulip prices kept escalating until they reached a height in early February of 1637, at which time a single bulb could be bought for as much as 300 guilder. One person is reported to have exchanged 12 acres of land for a single Semper Augustus bulb. In February of 1637, the bubble burst, prices suddenly crashed and many people ended up with their fortunes evaporating, their whole life savings blowing away with the breeze. How do you know this won't happen with Bitcoin?"

She sneered at him as if she thought he was an unpleasant used tissue blowing around on a footpath, but all she said was, "I don't care."

Nathanael breathed in his most rational, paternalistic tone, "Well Bitcoin might crash, mightn't it?"

Natasha shrugged and waved his comment away. "Anyway, I thought your ex-wife cleaned you right out? Where did you get the money for your flight to Vegas?"

"You're nosy aren't you? I came out of the divorce with thirty seven thousand in your currency. Close to fifty thousand Australian dollars."

"And how much have you lost? You've got nothing left, do you?" Her tone of voice was condescending now. Or maybe it was disappointed, or worried? He wasn't sure.

"How much have you lost, Nathanael?"

Nathanael cringed, looked down, embarrassed.

"See, you're embarrassed by how much you've lost. Gambling does not pay, Nathanael, no matter how good your supposed system is. It's all chance, it's like trying to grasp the wind." Then in a softer voice, almost to herself, "It's a shame, my funds are almost gone, I was kind of hoping you might have a bit."

He cringed even more. "Well, actually, I came out of my casino venture with a slight little teensy weensy bit more than I started with. It wasn't completely unproductive." He was reluctant to tell her how much.

She was smiling now. "Come on, tell me how much? What, one and a half percent? About five thousand? Thirty Seven Thousand? The amount you began with? That would be okay."

"Since I got to Vegas in February? I really don't want to tell you." He cringed even more.

She turned around and put her hand on his arm in a conciliatory gesture, looking even more smug. "Come on, don't be embarrassed. Even if you lost it all, even if you've got nothing. I'm just curious, that's all. I won't pick on you, I promise you. It's okay, we can find a way through it if we don't have enough money."

"It's not what, oh, geeze. I've got just over five million, Natasha. Yes, I made a little bit more than I started with."

Natasha went very quiet and just stood there

with her mouth open.

Nathanael realised that Natasha just didn't understand. It hadn't been easy. He had spent a lot, initially, just gambling small amounts away, trying to look like your average ignorant punter. That had been very hard. Indeed, every time he went to a new casino he had bet mostly small amounts for the first day or two. He had saved the larger bets for when he knew from counting the cards that a payout was inevitable.

Of course, this was what had gotten him noticed, eventually. Those big bets at counterintuitive times.

And Cherubim Security Agency were the ones who had eventually linked it all together - his disparate wins in many different casinos - the apparently random timing of his 'lucky' large bets - the payouts that seemed to come about simply by chance.

Well, Cherubim had done fairly well to catch him, really, because Nathanael had gone to some lengths to ensure his forays into Blackjack looked random, fit the bell curve, mathematically speaking.

Yes, it had been a lot of toil and effort. Five million dollars doesn't come easy.

Natasha was still standing there with her mouth

hanging open, and he could actually hear her breathing.

And Nathanael couldn't keep it in, he just couldn't keep his mouth shut, he had to let it out. "How's the Bitcoin going, anyway?"

Natasha ignored him and started packing her laptop away.

Then he said, "How's Meth? Have you heard anything?"

She shook her head as she zipped the laptop bag. "Not a thing. All I know is that they got to Budapest. After that, nothing."

She looked at him expectantly. He looked back at her, not really knowing what she wanted. When he didn't say anything she said, "Come on, Nathanael, let's go out for dinner. You can pay."

He didn't object.

Then she flashed a smile at him. Somehow he felt rewarded, as though he had vindicated her trust in him, despite arriving weeks after she had sent her message.

Natasha said, "I know a Thai Smorgasbord Bar that has good reviews. We'll get an Uber. They like cash, anyway, they don't have card payments."

In the Uber on the way Natasha filled him in on her own year. "I've gone back to work," she said, "Back at the hospital. But I took some time off again, recently, to do some study. That's why I'm not living at home."

"What were you studying?"

"Computer security. I went to some seminars, did a couple of units in San Jose. Just catching up on things, you know, current trends, that sort of thing." She frowned, then said in a slightly more vulnerable tone. "It wasn't good for my habit, you know. Knowing the current security flaws makes it all easier."

He whispered, not wanting the Uber driver to hear, "What habit? What do you mean? Are you hacking again?"

She whispered, "I'll tell you when we get there. Mustn't talk anywhere where they can listen."

The restaurant had a large smorgasbord, where you could serve yourself, but unlike some smorgasboards where the food was mostly cold, in this restaurant it was steaming hot.

Nathanael got himself some hors d'oeuvres and was about to order a glass of apple cider to be brought over, but Natasha shook her head. "Just get drinks that are on tap and watch them serve it. Or something we can choose. Like a random bottle of something from the bar fridge. That's why we're at a smorgasbord by the way and not a regular bistro."

He ordered a pint of apple cider on tap and chose a bottle of champagne for Natasha and they ordered their main courses.

"It's the whole reason, though, as I was saying earlier, that I started again," she said after finishing her second glass of champagne.

"What is? Started what? Drinking?"

"No, I always drank! You know... All that stuff we got up to, the whole Adamant business. And then the seminars and study I did this year too. Altogether it got me back into the habit. I had given it up, you know, for years."

"Habit of what?"

"Looking stuff up." She was grimacing, even Nathanael could tell how uncomfortable the subject was for her.

"You've been googling things? Is there anything wrong with that?"

"No. Looking things up is my little euphemism, Nathanael. Guessing passwords, hacking websites, researching things that the big players don't want us to know. Looking at darknet bulletin boards, researching DEF CON stuff. After we broke open the Adamantine empire's illegitimate activities I started wondering what some of the other big players are up to."

Natasha breathed out through her nostrils, like a horse anticipating a battle, Nathanael thought.

She continued, "Funny thing is, Adamant owns quite a few of the other things now. After everything we did, they're stronger. Nathanael, I tried really hard to give up hacking. But do you know, I don't think I can."

"I guess... It's okay so long as you don't get caught. Although the FBI wouldn't see it that way. But it is just your hobby, that's all." He realised he was making excuses for her.

Natasha sighed. "It's a bit more like an obsession, Nathanael. It worries me." He knew that despite his wins or maybe because of them, counting cards at Blackjack had become something of an obsession for him as well; in fact Cherubim Security's little escapade had broken his stride, luckily, or else he might still be blowing around in Vegas like a tumbleweed, aimlessly, to and fro.

Making millions.

Ironic, that she should judge <u>him</u> so harshly. Then Natasha read his thoughts, "It's a bit like your Blackjack, isn't it? I mean, five months without contact with your family and friends? My hacking disturbs me too, as I assume you have been disturbed by your obsession. It's not as if I can control my curiosity. I sit down at the computer and before

I know what I'm doing I'm trying to hack some company's website or pinging a server to see if it's vulnerable, or reading something someone's posted about a new back door. I don't feel like I'm not in control. And it's dangerous."

He whispered, "But the real question is, did you find out anything interesting?"

Clearly afraid someone might be listening, she looked around warily and whispered, "I'll tell you later." Nathanael shook his head. She was clearly suffering from paranoia as well as obsession. Not a good sign.

She saw his look and whispered in his ear, "It's not paranoia. One person has already died. Maybe two. I shouldn't even be out in the open." Nathanael looked at her with concern. She seemed almost haggard, really, really stressed, he had been so pleased to see her he hadn't noticed at first.

But then Natasha swigged the rest of her third glass of champagne and seemed to sparkle a little, her mood got a bit more bubbly.

She slurred slightly, "Let's talk about other stuff. Hacking is boring."

As they ate their main course a mischievous look came into her eye.

"Nathanael?" she said.

"Yes?"

"What do you think of Casinos, anyway?"

"Well, they rip people off. You know, they take advantage of the gullibility of stupid people."

A few minutes later Natasha said, "Nathanael, compared to you, are the people running the Casinos stupid?"

"Yes. Yes they are. I've outsmarted them all. I came here with a few thousand and turned it into millions. The Australian Casinos aren't that stupid. But there's this huge vulnerability in the Las Vegas Blackjack rules that I can exploit just by counting cards."

"Then you are doing to them exactly the same thing as they are doing to their customers. Essentially you're just as bad as the Casinos are. You're just at the big end of the food chain. The biggest shark of all." She paused, looked into her drink glass then looked up at him over it in a rather engaging way and said, "Well anyway I kind of can't help admiring you for it too. I've missed you, Nathanael, over the past - what was it? - seven or eight months?"

Nathanael had noticed Natasha's look and was a bit shocked by it, so he found himself blathering. "Well, no one gets hurt by what I do, Natasha. The Casinos can afford to absorb a few losses, and they - at least - understand the probabilities. Your average punter is a complete dupe. Anyway, I'm not doing it for the money."

She arched her eyebrows, tipping her glass rather precariously so that the bubbles were going sideways and said, "Really?"

Nathanael sucked air in through his teeth."Well... Partly for the money. I mean, the trouble and strife cleaned me out. Didn't even have a house any more. Well, I will be able to buy one now. I've replenished my reserves without hurting anyone."

"But they have to replenish their funds, don't they? I mean, surely you've hurt their bottom line? Won't that mean they exploit the customers even more to make back what you've taken from them?" Natasha was running her finger over the edge of the glass, which was empty now.

Nathanael snorted. "Hardly! In 2016 the Nevada casinos brought in more than 25 billion dollars. My escapade represents less than 0.0003% of their total revenue." He paused and whispered rather clumsily through a mouthful of the green curry while he replenished her glass with more bubbly. "Don't forget, you were going to tell me what you discovered when you were hacking."

Natasha sighed, "Alright. You told me your secrets, I suppose I have to bare mine. But not here. It's too public. And we have our phones with us. You understand they can hack phones, don't you, listen to everything we're talking about?"

So she didn't say anything more until they were back at the Salvation Army.

She had a set of keys and let herself in.

"Where am I sleeping?" he asked her, hoping in a distant dream that it was with her.

"I got you the office next to mine, at least for a couple of days."

He went out to the car and got his suitcase and his other things and brought them in. As he was unpacking a few things from his suitcase Natasha came in and handed him a sleeping bag. "Almost new. Comes from the Salvation Army store," she said. "Got it for five dollars." A few minutes later as he was unrolling the sleeping bag and organising the room Natasha walked in with two glasses of Baileys Irish Cream, one in each hand, with her laptop under her arm.

She handed a glass of Baileys to Nathanael, sat down at the desk in front of his open suitcase and started sipping her own glass.

As he drank it he realised it wasn't just Baileys.

He couldn't identify what else was in it, just that it was carbonated.

"It's good to see you again, Nathanael," she said, and tipped her glass at his.

"Good to see you too," Nathanael said as he slowly absorbed the precious liqueur. "This Irish Cream or whatever it is. Nice stuff. But the question is, do the Salvos know you have booze in the joint?"

"The Salvos? I don't have a gun here. The joint? This isn't a prison, Nathanael. Honestly, sometimes you Aussies speak in incomprehensible gibberish."

He rolled his eyes. "Salvos is what Australians call the Salvation Army, I'm not talking about munitions, Natasha. They're teetotallers, the Salvos, you know. Don't touch alcohol at all. And a joint is any place, not just a prison."

"No a joint is just a prison, Nathanael. You're in America now. You have to speak American. The Salvation Army officers don't know that I drink, or they haven't asked. But then again, they don't much bother me here at night, or much during the day either - they've only got a few full time staff in this place these days. These offices are not occupied at all. They offered me a place in a home with a family but I asked for something a little more private. Nathanael," she said in a more serious tone of voice, "Can you give me your phone?"

He handed it to her and she turned it off and took out the battery. She put the phone and the battery on the floor between the sleeping bag and the wall then began closing his suitcase and putting it on the floor next to his sleeping bag. "You don't have any more phones or computers or tablets or iPads with you do you?"

"No."

She said, "Well that means all the computers and the smart phones are off, except for my laptop, which is completely secure, as it runs on Linux." She lifted her laptop onto the table. "Alright I can tell you now."

Nathanael sat down next to her and sipped his glass. "So who did you hack, Natasha? What did you do?"

"The search engine company, i-ogle. I got into their password protected company site."

"Are they part of Google or something?"

Natasha shook her head. "No. They're next in line to Google - Bing and Yahoo are now way down the list of search engines people use now. Dave Trawlings, the owner and founder of i-ogle, managed to do something many people would have said was impossible: he created a search algorithm that is faster, more accurate and more in tune with user wishes than google. In the news they said it has something to do with some sort of AI program that his engineers have written."

"So you found out something scandalous about them?"

"A few things not really related to their search engine. You see, this hacker whose bulletin board I read had stumbled across something. He's dead now, Nathanael, they killed him. He went by the handle OxyMoron, I don't even know what his real name was. The only person who knew him was someone who went by the handle TrippyGirl. He was searching for their AI program and came upon these documents. The whole project is called the BEL Project - stands for BEL Engineered Linked Project."

"Really? The B in BEL stands for BEL?"

"Nerdy thing. Like 'GNU's not Unix' and 'Curl URL Request Library' and 'LAME aint an mp3 encoder'."

Nathanael nodded. "It's a recursive acronym." He remembered the term from a book he had read once, Godel, Escher Bach the Eternal Golden Braid. "A meaningless, empty gesture, really, meant to suggest infinity, but all it suggests to me is an empty gesture."

Natasha shrugged, "It doesn't matter what you think. What matters is that I didn't have long in their servers before they shut me down, but I don't think they got my IP Address." She puffed out her chest a little and said proudly,

"I was using a system of proxy servers that feeds through the dark net before it arrives back at my computer. Ha! I'm good. It's a rather clever invention of mine actually - it feeds packets of random sizes simultaneously back through the same TOR node from many different locations, making it very hard to identify the exit node, but the fact is, while they could not trace me, I was able to trace them and I know for certain that it was i-ogle who was trying to trace me."

"I have only a slight idea of what you're talking about Natasha."

"Anyway," she said, waving her hand dismissively, "They didn't catch me, that's what it means. At least I don't think they did. I can't be completely sure. Using some sort of back door combined with a text search, maybe they could identify me. But I doubt it."

Nathanael cried out in frustration, "But for God's sake tell me, what did you find?"

"I'll show you the document I found. I think it's some sort of conspiracy, Nathanael."

She opened her laptop up and opened up a folder, and clicked on a file. "It's incomplete."

"Why?"

"To cut a long story short, I exploited a vulnerability

in the i-ogle security protocols when documents are being encrypted, it's to do with Spectre, a bug in all microprocessors, you see, they run on ahead when they're performing instructions, past the end address."

Nathanael wanted to interrupt to tell her he didn't have a clue what she was talking about, but the fact is, she was so proud of herself he didn't want to break her flow.

It was all empty air to him, but he pretended to listen. She continued, "I managed to upload a self-replicating worm that infected the i-ogle servers through the search window by writing itself onto the RAM after the end address of the machine code instructions. It was designed to find documents in the process of being encrypted and upload them in their partially encrypted state to my darknet server. I managed to get the beginning of the document. For some reason the middle is garbled, but there is a large chunk at the end that's readable too. But before I got the whole thing their anti-virus software must have discovered my worm and shut it down."

BEL Algorithm Project History

PROJECT DESCRIPTION:

The BEL Algorithm is designed to deal with the most pervasive modern problem in politics - the 24 hour news cycle. Politicians as never before are confronted with an unfair microscopic moment-by-moment examination of every single thing they say or do, the kind of analysis no human being could possibly endure without slipping up. In most normal social circles, 'faux-pas' may cause problems for a week or two (unless it has been filmed and shared publicly on facebook, effectively a rarity). In politics, a faux-pas can ruin a whole career.

In other words, there seems to be no way back in the public perception when a politician says or does something inappropriate or embarrassing.

And the fact is, that every human being acts in a socially inappropriate way on occasion. Today we have virtually perfect news coverage of public events. Technology has made it possible to capture nearly every moment of a public person's public life. And as St Augustine said, it is the function of perfection to make one know one's imperfection. Too many promising Presidential candidates have had their hopes ruined by the momentary lapse in good judgement, the type of lapse we all commit from time to time. Thus the 24 hour news cycle works against inculcating excellence in our political leaders. The present President could only get elected by being so abysmal in his behaviour that the public's expectations have been lowered all the way to the gutter. What our political analysts have called the Camelot

Effect, referring to the popularity of the

presidential reign of John F Kennedy, may

no longer be possible without some sort

of intervention to control the negative

effect of the 24 hour news cycle on public

perception.

The type of intervention that the BEL

Algorithm may be able to provide.

Considering that i-ogle controls at

least 60% of legitimate internet media, and

the fact that i-ogle has the most extensive

compÜ|²CN/cÚPÉ@@Î±ÙÇ-Rð¨'<ÕΔI-Çæ$Rðt'ÓEX¥d

&<²Ôì6ŽL&X÷[$vÖtxÜÙ÷ôv¡<&Ùœ6÷(Ž6h*'ô†êâÙ#5¼

ÿò%±Ö65Î'vi¾ú®x/,wÎdìÇŽ-/¼¥f

There were several more pages with apparently
random characters in the same manner, then it turned into
normal text again.

ÇæEÓx²o<ÎÈÑ[¼²Û°t6Ž#Û6I$8%¨ 6ÆÎ2&Δ÷}
Øc¿<˜$Ž-Çc¿<&xìÆh½9cýJš} '<,x/ãœtÔŒâ2*Coc'
ØÚc{²»|ðæd=",Á¾ýÑ@2ê'°ðÛÎtq²÷(6more likely
to have a positive response or effect on the
populace. IV) MANAGING DISSENTING VOICES

1) Content can also be removed. Remove
content as soon as it goes up.

2) The original content on mobile
phone apps could be edited or managed,
to avoid dissenting images being
disseminated.

3) Prevent people from talking about
this on Facebook etc. Apps or viruses on
mobile phones important in this regard.

4) iPhones in particular will need
added effort as they are harder to hack.
V) OTHER USEFUL TECHNIQUES

1) Remote Magnetic Neurostimulation?
Unlikely to work.

5) More efficient perhaps to insert
neurostimulators into campaign hats
(Sell both the pro and anti hats) using

```
magnets. Have flashing lights on the hats
to justify the electrical components.
    6) Creating awe using low frequency
vibration (already used in motion
pictures)~~~
```

Natasha said, "I really can't definitively say what they're planning. But if removing dissenting content is part of it and even inserting neurostimulators in campaign hats... It looks to me as if they're trying to manipulate democracy. It's definitely some sort of pretty weighty conspiracy. The guy who got killed mentioned just before he died that the i-ogle staff were told in the email not to let the document out or it would cause a huge scandal."

"You're right," said Nathanael. "That would cause a scandal. Manipulating elections. And the fact that they are talking about solving the problem of the 24 hour news cycle fits with that theory. And it's strangely inconsistent, too, since i-ogle is a large part of delivering instantaneous news. They benefit from the 24 hour news cycle. They don't like the present incumbent much, do they?"

Natasha said, "Nathanael, whatever it is they're planning to do, it'll be a lot worse than simply removing people's videos. The casual way that that is mentioned, it sounds like just an additional measure, an add-on; don't you think the rest of the document is about something else, some other more potent means of influencing public opinion? Oh, and did I tell you? Soon after purloining this from i-ogle the server my darknet site is on was hacked, I mean, like, only a few minutes later. A few other documents were deleted, but luckily I had managed to download this to my own computer a few minutes before. Nathanael, they were very quick. Must have been i-ogle, surely. Then Michelle and I started getting very strange phone calls, people hanging up, multiple calls from India and Nigeria, strange mistaken deliveries to our doorstep, and Michelle's computer was infected with some sort of rather obvious trojan. That's when I messaged you and came and found this hiding place."

Nathanael rubbed the stubble on his cheek. "I wonder what it's all about?"

Natasha said, "I don't know. It's got to be more than just editing..." She folded her arms and pursed her lips thoughtfully. "Do you know, despite having this document in my possession, I have no clue what the BEL algorithm actually is? The part that is missing is the most important part of the whole thing."

At that moment Nathanael heard a car pulling up, glimpsed the glow of headlamps through a gap in the curtains. He leaped up and whispered, "Close your laptop. Someone's out there. I'm going to turn off the lights. Go into my room, the curtains are closed in there."

Nathanael flicked the lights off and repeated, "Stay in my room."

Natasha grabbed her laptop and her drink and moved into his room. Nathanael heard her wheeze and she pulled an asthma puffer out of her computer bag and inhaled several times then breathed easier.

Nathanael whispered, "I didn't know you had asthma."

She said, "When I was a kid. It came back this year. Stress, I think."

He peered out through the gap. A woman was putting a bunch of clothes into the clothes bin in the carpark. He glimpsed a Diamondbacks wind-cheater among them. Could it be the same woman he had seen following him? But there would be plenty of people that have those in Phoenix. She was looking around. Had she seen him?

Then he saw the car number plate.

153-ICH.

He whispered, "It's the same number plate."

"What?" said Natasha.

"I saw the car near your sister's place. A white SUV with the number-plate 153-ICH. She's snooping around."

"Come on, Nathanael. You're just getting paranoid. You can't possibly remember a number plate all day."

"No, it's easy. Vesica Pisces - the number of the fish."

"What do you mean?"

"Archimedes' estimation of one divided by the square root of three, was 153/265. And the number of fish Jesus caught, in John's gospel, believe it or not. 153. It's one less than 154, which is 2 to the power of 5 times 7. And ICH is the first three letters of the Greek word for fish. Ichthus. Easy to remember. That's definitely the same car."

Natasha swallowed. "Well, I don't know. You sure know a lot of useless stuff."

"You know," said Nathanael, watching the woman's movements more carefully, "I'm not even sure she's a woman. I think it's a man dressed up as a woman." He stood up. "I'm going out there."

Natasha said, "Don't, Nathanael! You'll only confirm that we're here, I mean, if they're looking for us. At this stage we don't even know if she saw that the lights were on when she got here. And she - or he - might have a gun."

"She's coming over," said Nathanael. "She's left her car lights on, and the engine is still on, look, I can see the exhaust. Her headlights are illuminating the whole area. How could I...?" He thought for a moment. "The uniform shop."

"What?" said Natasha.

Nathanael leaped up and around the corridor. The uniform shop window was still open. He jumped over the benchtop and got out his phone to use as a torch and started examining the sizes. He found trousers and a jacket that would fit. Luckily he was already wearing a white shirt. There was a cap that fit him as well. In all of about a minute and a half he had dressed himself in a Salvation Army uniform.

He went back around to Natasha.

She laughed.

He said, "You've got keys, haven't you? Let me out the front."

"What are you going to do?"

He rummaged in his luggage. "I just need a torch. I've got one here, somewhere." He found it. "I always keep a torch, a big one like this. If I shine it in her face she won't be able to see me properly."

Natasha let him out of the front.

Nathanael walked around the building. The lady's

car was still parked where she had left it, the engine was still pumping exhaust fumes into the cold night air and the headlights were pointing towards their rooms, showing the odd fragment of mist. The lady was snooping around the windows, looking in, trying to see if anyone was in there.

Nathanael turned off her car headlights and the engine and took the car keys out of the car, then turned his torch on.

The lady turned around and stared at him, just slightly shocked that someone would touch her car.

It was a fairly unfeminine turn.

"It's alright," said Nathanael, putting on his best Arizona drawl, which probably wouldn't fool a native but it was the best he could do. Maybe she'd just think it was a strange accent, some kind of hybrid. "I was a bit worried. You get guys coming down to take stuff out of the clothes bin from time to time - not the most savoury sorts - likely to purloin your vehicle, Ma'am, if you're not watching." He cringed. His accent had slipped north all the way to Seattle. He was walking towards her rapidly and threw the keys to keep her off balance.

She caught the keys easily in a way that didn't look even slightly feminine to Nathanael. It was the way she bowed her legs, making the skirt whip up into the wind, showing suspiciously hairy legs.

Nathanael continued, "Anyhow, though, this is church property. I guess we don't mind you giving your old clothes to the poor, if that's what you were doing, in fact we encourage it. But we draw the line at you looking in the windows to see what you can pinch - ah - filch. Stick around and I might have to call the police. We're charitable but we're not stupid, Ma'am, we're not airheads." (He cringed at his use of the word 'airheads', what had made him say that?)

The woman, if she was a woman which Nathanael was certain she wasn't, glanced at him sideways as she or he hurried back to the car without saying a word, hopped in and gunned the engine. The car left a cloud of dirt and exhaust fumes behind as it roared off down the road.

Natasha opened the back door and let him back in.

Nathanael said, "Do you think we might need to find somewhere else to stay?"

Natasha nodded. "Yes, I saw. It was the way she caught those keys. Looked like a man, didn't it?" She swallowed. "Well, she might be transgender I guess. But I think you're right. Oh, no, now I'm worried about Michelle as well. I've really tried to keep her out of it."

"I'm sure she didn't follow me all the way from your place... She latched on a bit afterwards. Maybe we'd better check my car for trackers or bugs though."

While Natasha packed up her things, Nathanael brought the car around and quickly checked in the engine bay and around the edge of the chassis and found nothing.

As she bundled everything into the car, Natasha commented, "Ultimately we'll need some place with decent internet."

Nathanael nodded. "But for now, let's just drive until we're sure no one's following us. Then just take the first place that looks likely. We only need to stay for a day or two, initially. The more random we are, you know, the harder it is for them to pin us down."

Natasha sighed. "Like tumbleweed, just blowing in the wind. Well it looks like we really are on the run again. You know, I wouldn't have expected this of i-ogle. They're the good guys. But Adamant Corp owns them now, so I guess everything's different."

CHAPTER 4 - DREAMY DRAW

Nathanael was a lot more careful this time. He took a freeway and made some audacious lane changes, ones that he knew anyone tailing them would have a hard time emulating without being completely obvious. He kept an eye on the different cars, memorising their plates. 777-BEZ, LUB-212, 276-ERE, 934-CER, and so on.

Natasha directed him. She pointed at a freeway exit. "Get onto that one. Piestewa Freeway." After a few minutes on the Piestewa Freeway she said, "Pull off at the next exit. North Dreamy Draw Drive." He pulled in to the centre lane and at the last moment roared across several lanes and pulled off, almost cutting off a truck that was changing lanes.

It was unfortunate that Nathanael didn't notice LUB-212 following nine or ten cars behind. A white Toyota, LUB-212 calmly drifted over to the exit, pulled over to the side of the off-ramp and waited until they had already turned the corner and couldn't possibly see him before turning onto the road and parking underneath the freeway bridge.

Suddenly they were away from buildings and other cars and there was nothing but low shrubs blowing in a calm desert breeze and desert grass around. Nathanael had put the top down at their last stop, so the warm wind was blowing their hair.

It was a pleasant drive.

Natasha said, "We're in the Phoenix Mountains Preserve. It's relatively deserted at this time of night."

Nathanael pulled over at a parking loop and they waited with all the lights off and the windows open, but he got out and put the top back on. They were in a desert park and the wind blew softly through the car. It was silent apart from a distant rumble of traffic and the swishing of the shrubs in the breeze. The moon was up now, it hadn't been before, and some clouds were blowing gently past.

No other cars passed them for at least fifteen or twenty minutes.

Breathing his words almost silently, Nathanael spoke. "Well I guess we're fine. Unless of course they're using government surveillance like last time."

In hushed tones Natasha noted, "The problem being we won't know, will we, whether this is about this i-ogle hack of mine or some kind of continuation of the Roland Adamant business?"

Nathanael turned to her. "Well we could try reversing tactics. Go completely public on it all. Find out who's after us that way?" In his head it had seemed sensible but when he spoke it aloud it sounded like a stupid idea.

Natasha shook her head. "I'm not ready, Nathanael. I need more time. I need to find out more. I don't even know what the BEL Algorithm is. I know it's not right, I know it's some sort of conspiracy, but it's not a smoking gun, either. We just need to find a place where I can set myself up for a week or two. Do some more hacking." She sighed. "I thought it was all over, once we'd uncovered the whole Adamantine mess. Now we're in the middle of something else. Or maybe a variation on the same thing." She swore coldly.

Nathanael scratched his chin absently. "Do you really think Roland Adamant's empire has something to do with this as well?"

"I don't know. But you know there's been a share arrangement between Adamant and i-ogle since Adamant's shares slumped when we revealed what they were doing. Roland's son Raymond is running the company now. But when Adamant's shares rose again, very dramatically actually, he bought i-ogle outright." She groaned. "This has been a struggle, Nathanael. Not knowing who to trust. I've been feeling very alone. I know I wasn't alone, though, God's Spirit was with me."

A desert owl hooted a desolate song, a sort of 'whoop whoop whoop' that echoed through the deserted park.

"Sounds lonely," said Nathanael. "Everything struggles, you know Natasha? Even that desert owl. I don't think it's happy, do you? It sounds like a complaint, that sound, a desperate cry. It's the whole struggle to survive. All of nature is in the same boat as we are. We're just like... A breeze. A breath, that blows away in the wind."

"What you're saying, Nathanael. It reminds of a psalm I once had to memorize for Sunday School. God knows why they made me memorize it, it's one of the depressing ones."

"What?"

"Oh, some of the psalms are depressing. It went something like, 'Behold, you have made my days a few handbreadths, and my lifetime is as nothing before you. Surely all mankind stands as a mere breath! Man heaps up wealth and does not know who will gather! And now, O Lord, for what do I wait? My hope is in you.'"

"It is beautiful language, I have to admit, in those biblical passages. I could almost think I'm beginning to believe... something. God might be real. But at other times... Life, Natasha, is so brief and futile. We are like a breeze that just blows away and is gone. Is that how a good God designed it?"

"Yes. For the creation was subjected to futility, not of its own will, but because of the One who subjected it..."

The owl hooted again as though it agreed, and the moon went dim for a moment behind a cloud. The air was moving almost motionlessly in the gentlest of gentle breezes.

Natasha reached out and squeezed his hand and held it for a little while. "I'm glad you're with me. I really did miss you."

Nathanael felt his face heating up. It was shame, he realised, for leaving her in the lurch. "I'm sorry I didn't get your message for so long. I should've thought that you might try to..."

She released his hand and patted it, like a small rebuke. "Well, just keep an eye on your messages, alright? I actually needed you with me on this. I really couldn't have done it on my own. I've been really struggling..."

Nathanael nodded. "I won't be going to Vegas again for a while, Natasha. It started to become an obsession for me. That's the only reason I didn't check my messages for so long. But I am... sorry that I didn't get your message."

She reached forwards and breathed for a sweet

moment, right next to his face, then suddenly kissed him and then pulled back again. He was surprised, almost shocked.

Her eyes were engaging in the dim moonlight, vivid, he thought, unforgettable, like black dots, the brown irises around her pupils so dark they were almost black. Her breath was so close to him.

No matter what happened in the future, he knew he would never forget this moment. He brushed a stray black strand of hair away from her face and the cool breeze blew it back.

She said, "I don't know if this is a good idea," and he thought it was over but then she reached forwards and breathed and kissed again. He returned the kiss this time, and they stayed like that for a while.

She said, "I really missed you."

Until now, he hadn't realised quite how much.

* * *

Dawn was noisier than Nathanael might have expected because the birds made a racket, as though inordinately pleased at the sun's decision to begin rising at last. Natasha was asleep with her head on his chest and a pleasant, cool breeze was blowing in his face.

Their seats were both positioned right back and

Nathanael started to wake and realised that he was rather uncomfortably sprawled across both seats with the handbrake digging into his left kidney. Natasha was mostly on top of him and he could not believe he could possibly have slept even a wink in such an uncomfortable position. Her arm was draped over into the space between the seat and the door, almost as though she was reaching for something, but she was still completely asleep.

He did not want to move in case he woke her up.

He resigned himself to his predicament with a sigh and looked at her. She looked so peaceful, breathing so softly, beautifully brown.

A computer hacker, yet highly principled. A very intelligent person, fully acquainted with science and history and biology, yet a dedicated Christian.

And he had thought he was the last person who would have a chance with her.

Strange.

But what had Natasha stumbled into? This whole thing was very disconcerting.

He felt like it was time for action. He wanted to take the bull by the horns. But first they'd have to find them a den, a place to hide away in while Natasha worked out what was going on.

The birds screeched even more loudly and Natasha finally stirred.

"I'm thirsty," was the first thing she said.

Then she gave a small cough.

Nathanael reached across her as she blurrily rubbed her eyes, opened the glove compartment and pulled out a couple of water bottles and gave one to her and started to open his.

"Thanks," she said, and proceeded to prop herself up on his chest and drank it.

Nathanael starting laughing.

Natasha said, "What's so funny?"

He coughed out the words, "Well, your elbow is really painful in my chest. Like, it was painful before, but that's…"

"Oh, sorry." She opened the passenger door and they extricated themselves.

Nathanael stretched and sucked in the early morning air. Natasha took out her phone and looked at the time. "It's six o'clock in the morning, Nathanael."

He nodded. "Let's go and find ourselves a place to stay."

She said, "I'm sorry about last night. I didn't mean things to go so far."

Nathanael really wanted to say, "I'm not," but he didn't. He just looked at her, thinking, 'Don't say it, don't say it.'

Then Natasha put her hand out and said it. "Friends?"

He shook her hand and said, "Of course. Always." But he felt sick at heart, as though everything he had thought was happening was just some sort of mirage in the desert, or a bit of mist that disappears when the wind blows.

But then, as they were driving, Natasha reached over and held his hand. This distracted him, especially as he started to ask himself what it meant. Was it a friendship hand hold or an "I love you" hand hold? He felt completely the futility of his own opinions on the matter.

Natasha said, "We need a public library. I need a place where I can go on the net."

If he wasn't so distracted by her holding his hand he certainly would have noticed the man parked just behind the freeway bridge on North Dreamy Draw Drive, standing with the wind blowing his untucked shirt around, watching the cars come and go. His car had the number plate LUB-212, one that Nathanael had seen momentarily on the freeway the day before (easy to remember because it was sort of palindromic. B was the second letter of the alphabet, U was the 21st letter, and L was the 12th letter, thus 212).

But he didn't even notice the car.

Whatever it meant, her hand felt so comfortable in his that he really didn't care what it meant. He became annoyed at himself. Why did he even have to work it out?

But it was lucky the car was an automatic, though.

As Nathanael turned onto the Freeway, LUB-212 pulled out unobtrusively and followed him once again, nine or ten cars behind, just as before.

And Natasha said, "We need to find some food as well, and a chemist. I need some more Ventolin, I'm on my final two puffers."

CHAPTER 5 - HOUSE SITTER, SCOUSE HITTER

"How long will I need to do this?" Leo Bos was standing completely still in the middle of a 3D scanner and all his joints were starting to play up.

He had never had to do this in the first film.

The annoying little poop said, "Keep still! Just a little while longer, Mister Bos. You know it used to take all day to do this, it's so much shorter now, just a few minutes. We'll still need to get your phonemes, though." The annoying little poop hadn't even bothered to wear decent clothes to Leo's mansion, he was dressed in jeans and a pair of old sneakers and some sort of rock band T-Shirt with a dishevelled set of rat-tails for hair and a three day shadow, precisely the sort of useless petard that really annoyed Leo.

Leo complained, "I don't even know how this ended up on the schedule for shooting."

"I was just told to come here. Don't blame me, we've already rung them and asked, Mister Bos, it's all there on the online schedule and the director confirmed it. I suppose they must need some 3D CGI shots of you, swimming through the middle of NY when the sea level rises, I guess, or perhaps a shot of your skin sizzling in the summer sun when the temperatures rise twenty degrees because of global warming. Or a miniature you, flying through the wind-storm destroying CO2 molecules." He sounded sarcastic and Leo didn't like it. Probably a climate denier.

A few minutes later the annoying little poop brought over a stool for Leo to sit on and put up a prompt screen in front of him. "Look at the prompt screen, Mister Bos, and just say everything that comes up."

A sentence began to appear,

```
That quick beige fox jumped in the air
over each thin dog. Look out, I shout, for
he's foiled you again, creating chaos.
```

Leo read through it silently. "This is addled nonsense. It's just empty wind. Why should I say this?"

The annoying little poop pressed rewind to get it back to the start and said, "Ah. Well, Mister Bos, these sentences contain every phoneme in the English language. It means we can recreate the vicissitudes of your accent if... something untowards happens to you. Or if we need to for the film. You know?"

"Can't I just say, 'the quick brown fox jumps over the lazy dog? This is pediculous."

"No, Mister Bos," the annoying little poop said in a

patient, condescending tone which irritated Leo even more. "You see, sir, 'the quick brown fox jumps over the lazy dog' only contains all the letters in the English language. What we need is all the phonemes. Every single sound in the language, every breathed and unbreathed consonant and vowel, not just every letter."

"That's ridiculous. The letters are the same as the sounds. What are you talking about, you annoying little poop?"

"No they aren't."

"Of course they are. 26 letters. 26 sounds. ABCD etcetera. I can make every word in English from those 26 letters, or are you calling me a liar? God, what a windbag you are. You know what nincom means? Annoying little."

"What about the letter E?"

"What do you mean the letter E? The hell? Hey?"

"Exactly. E can be spoken as ee as in, say, teepee, or eh, as in hell, or ei as in hey, or abseil, etcetera etcetera etcetera. The same letter has at least four or five sounds, Leo, and that's just the letter E."

"Oh. Okay." He read the sentences aloud, feeling as though it was all some stupid air-head's joke at his expense.

That quick beige fox jumped in the air

over each thin dog. Look out, I shout, for
he's foiled you again, creating chaos. Are
those shy Eurasian footwear, cowboy chaps,
or jolly earthmoving headgear? The hungry
purple dinosaur ate the kind, zingy fox,
the jabbering crab, and the mad whale and
started vending and quacking. With tenure,
Suzie'd have all the more leisure for
yachting, but her publications are no good.
Shaw, those twelve beige hooks are joined
if I patch a young, gooey mouth. The beige
hue on the waters of the loch impressed all,
including the French queen, before she heard
that symphony again, just as young Arthur
wanted.

As soon as he finished Leo grumbled, "What a load of empty noises. Couldn't they at least make these make sense? I mean, for instance, 'the quick brown fox jumps over the lazy dog' - now that makes sense. The fox is quick and brown and the dog is lazy."

There was a long pause while the poop was doing something technical, Leo had no clue what it was.

"Well, that's it, Mister Bos. Thank you very much for

making this easy for me. You know, some of the actors I scan for CGI complain the whole time."

For a moment Leo was puzzled - he thought he had complained a lot, but obviously he hadn't been as bad as he thought. Well of course, he was a way better person than any pathetic actor. Look at that Leonardo Di Caprio, always pretending to care about real issues, when it was all just a bold-faced publicity stunt. Leonardo was a wind-bag, too. Leo smiled charismatically at the annoying little poop and shook his hand.

The annoying little poop looked over at his minions and they were so quick to pack all the equipment back into their truck that he could feel the wind coming off them as they rushed past.

Thankfully they finished in fifteen minutes and Leo had a short break to go get some lunch and a bottle of sparkling mineral water. Man, what a frustrating day.

Then he remembered Raymond Adamant saying at that meeting before shooting started that something would be added to the movie schedule.

He looked at the CGI guy's truck in the distance, bouncing out through the mansion gates onto the road, and wondered if that had been it.

Then the truck was gone, leaving nothing but a cloud of dust hanging in the air.

And Leo wondered, perhaps that guy knew Raymond Adamant?

Perhaps he should have been nicer to him?

PHOENIX, ARIZONA

They found a Chemist fairly quickly. The lady at the counter brought out several asthma puffers when Natasha requested them, but Nathanael insisted they bring out all of their stock so that Natasha could choose some at random. She refused at first, but Nathanael asked to see the pharmacist and he agreed to let them do it this way after muttering something about feeding paranoid fancies.

There were fifteen puffers and Natasha bought five of them.

Nathanael purchased a permanent black marker pen as well. As she drove away, Natasha said, "Why the rigmarole?"

Nathanael said, "The same people who poisoned your friend might be following us. They might want to hurt you. And we need to make sure that if you buy medication it can't have been tampered with, just like the food."

She said, "You're right."

As she drove, Nathanael took the marker pen and put a big dot on the back of all her asthma puffers, including the two that still had some medication remaining in them so that she could easily identify her own puffers.

They quickly found some lunch and followed the same protocol, choosing items from the open display cabinet and watching them being prepared.

Then they went to the nearest library, which turned out to be the Mesquite Public Library.

Nathanael browsed through the library while Natasha worked on her laptop, trying to hack the i-ogle servers again. From time to time he glanced through the shelves, to check on her.

Nathanael asked her, "How long will you be?"

She said, "All day."

In the corner of his eye, Nathanael noticed a guy sitting at a desk behind them. The guy was sitting too still, he was definitely watching Natasha. And he was watching him too.

Nathanael looked around the library, for someone approximately his own height, someone the same build and hair colour as he was.

Perfect - there was a man probably in his thirties

wearing a baseball cap and a jacket browsing through the 100s, Philosophy and Theology. Nathanael went over to him and made an offer.

The man accepted the two hundred dollar bills gratefully and sat at the corral behind Natasha. Nathanael had his mobile charger in his pocket. He tossed it a few times, making sure the guy who was watching Natasha could see him doing it. Then he bent down as if to plug it in.

While he was bending, the guy with the baseball cap bent his head down into the corral, took off the baseball cap and the jacket and gave them to Nathanael.

Nathanael, still bending down to the floor, put on the baseball cap and the jacket and stood up, facing away from the man who was watching Natasha. Then the guy with the baseball cap lifted his head enough so that the man watching Natasha could just see the top of his head.

Keeping his face averted from the man who was watching them, Nathanael quickly walked out into the garden around the library. There was a pleasant breeze blowing outside but he didn't stop to enjoy it. He jogged along the concrete path that led round the library, through a sparse garden into the carpark and started looking at the number-plates, seeing if there were any he recognised, and memorising all the others.

LUB-212. A little white Toyota. An easy number-plate, as B was the second letter in the alphabet, U the 21st, L the 12th, simple. Then there was QED-931, more complicated, but of course 9 was the Pythagorean number of the universe, truly philosophical if anything was, and QED meant 'Quod erat demonstrandum'.

Wait a second. He backtracked to LUB-212.

He had seen it before. This white Toyota, nondescript, but such an identifiable number-plate! But where?

He couldn't place it. He closed his eyes and tried to imagine himself seeing it the first time, but it was no good. Dammit, if only Nathanael's extraordinary memory could tell him when he actually first saw that number plate.

It was the guy tailing them, though, it had to be. The fact was Nathanael had never been to the Mesquite Public Library before, so any number plate he remembered had to have been following them.

He had to find out what this car was doing here.

Nathanael looked for security cameras on the library and the surrounding buildings. It seemed to be good luck - or perhaps design on the part of whoever owned LUB-212 - Nathanael judged that the car was parked in a blind spot on the cameras. What were the chances of that?

Then he suddenly remembered when he had seen the car - it had been the day before when they were on that freeway with the funny name. Dreamy Draw Drive. The car had been behind them, at least four or five cars behind them.

A vague memory surfaced of seeing it after that, too, maybe when they were leaving the park.

Definitely following them.

After surreptitiously looking round to make sure no one was watching he peered in through the driver's side window. There was nothing in there to identify the driver at all.

He pulled out his wallet. He had a little tool in there for picking locks and this was not an old vehicle, only four or five years. It would have an alarm.

With his other hand he got out his handkerchief from his pocket.

He moved around quickly and unlocked the passenger door carefully using the lock pick and the handkerchief and the alarm began screaming, but Nathanael reached in and as efficiently as he could opened the glove compartment using the handkerchief to make sure he didn't leave any prints. He found a handgun and some money. He took both, put the handgun in his pocket and the money in his wallet, and, trying not to make a big deal of it, closed the glove compartment and locked the car door again.

The alarm continued to sound.

Thankfully no one had come out to look.

Nathanael walked back unhurriedly to the library garden path, for the sake of the security cameras. Just as he reached it the man who had been watching Natasha rushed out the back door of the library and ran over to the car. He must have recognised the alarm on his own car.

Fairly professional, not everyone does that.

Wearing a neat suit, well groomed, the guy was about thirty five years old with a distinctive pug nose, a sly smile, small pig-like eyes and thin eyebrows that looked plucked. He had a mobile phone in his top pocket and a bulge on his chest where Nathanael assumed another gun was holstered, a rather large gun.

The man's response was quick and professional and he established fairly quickly that the handgun was gone. Nathanael was now around the corner, watching the man from a veiled position behind some bushes.

When the man reached in to the glove compartment a bit further and saw that the money was gone too he started banging the car with his fists and swearing vociferously in some sort of Liverpool accent, like one of the Beatles in a rage.

Nathanael laughed softly to himself and walked back into the library. He went to the fellow in the corral behind Natasha and gave him back his jacket and his cap.

Natasha was working intently on her laptop.

He didn't want to disturb her, but if this bloke was looking to harm them he had to do something. The quicker they were out the better.

The other alternative was to wait the guy out. Nathanael looked at the opening hours. Open till eight o'clock at night. At some point he would need to make a ruckus, make sure the police turned up, that would be the best way to get rid of the guy.

It was ten o'clock in the morning now. Well, he had ten hours to work something out. But he had to know what this guy was up to. He must have stuffed up the guy's plans by stealing the money. That was probably getaway money, money for hiring a car or buying a train ticket or something.

Natasha continued typing, completely oblivious to it all. Well, that's okay, at least this situation is not distracting her. He walked out again around the little pathway and watched the guy.

He was on his mobile phone.

THE ADAMANT BUILDING, NEW YORK

Raymond Adamant's phone buzzed.

He breathed into the phone, "Yes?"

It was the guy with the Liverpool accent. "Someone twocked me bleeding money. Got into me car, took me spare gun and the cash. I'm skint. Completely broke, mate, if you can, you know, like, give me a bit more."

"Did they make you? I told you, Nathanael Wayfarer is clever. He made you didn't he?"

"No, of course not. He was in the library the whole time, sitting at the desk, I saw him. Look it's alright, they have no idea, I'm watching them. And she's going to be in the library the whole day. But it won't work unless I've got my money."

"What do you want? That's not my problem, buddy."

"More cash. Can't do nothing without it. It's my getaway plan."

Raymond rolled his eyes. He really thought this guy was a professional, at least that's what George had told him.

George must be doing a favour for someone by recommending him. That's the problem with this business, everybody's just too pleased to recommend some useless fart just because he's done something for his brother-in-law or something.

Raymond said, "Look, open up a new Paypal account to put it in or something. If I do a bank transfer and then you withdraw it, it ties you to me." He swore coldly. "You have really stuffed this up. Just SMS me where to send it. But don't use the banks. Do it some other way."

The Liverpool accent swore as well. But then he seemed to realise. He swore again. "They've got the chair here, don't they? I'm going to bail."

Raymond said, "Look, just, drive to another town or something to get the money out. Plausible deniability. Don't bail out on me. Come back and do them once you've got the money. I don't know. You're the expert, you sort it out." Raymond sighed. You just can't get good help these days. "God, you know, we're talking about this on the phone. I can't believe it, don't you realise the NSA record everything? You're only lucky I've got them in my pocket. If you ever do a job like this you need to grow up and keep off the phone like one of the big boys, you twerp."

"Look. I'm doing your job. I just have to stick to the plan. But if I'm going to stick to the plan and sack off this car, I'm going to need money to get out of here. No use doing this hit if I can't get away, right? I've got to think of myself, too, here."

Raymond snapped, "Look. I'll put the money in your bank if that's what you want. I've got shelf companies that can do that, without it being connected to me. But you've got to sort yourself out, buddy. I'm paying you good money to do a job here, and you're stuffing it up."

"Alright, alright. Look, I'll send you a Paypal account. I can do it all on my smartphone. You just put it in there, I'll transfer it to one or other of my other accounts and take it out of there in another town. Plausible deniability."

"Make sure you don't lose them."

"I told you, I heard her say, 'I'm going to be here all day.' And Nathanael was inside sitting at the corral behind hers the whole time some kid probably was thieving from my car."

The phone clicked off and a few minutes later a text message came through with the Paypal account details. Raymond rang one of his men and had him organise it.

Last time he'd be using this idiot Liverpudlian for anything.

MONTECITO, CALIFORNIA

It was Bretta who had been nagging Leo for ages to get another place in which they could carry out their trysts in private.

She never liked that other mansion, too many reminders of family everywhere, paintings, photos, the Queen-sized bed he and Misty had slept in since their marriage. Of course, now that he'd left his wife it didn't matter that much, did it? But now, what with his situation of impending poverty after the outrageous divorce settlement, Bretta had insisted he make another climate film. Well, hardly impending poverty. Just a few hundred million less in his assets, that's all.

God, he was sixty seven. Didn't she understand? He wasn't young any more. He had arthritis and after a few hours of doing anything he was bone weary and gasping for breath.

Oh, he longed for Misty now. What had made him turn on to this piece of vacillating whiffle, Bretta, when Misty had stood by him all those years? What a fool he had been.

Bretta, society girl, heiress, had grown up with silk sheets and velvet cushions, with a silver spoon in every orifice, drinking only bottled water and breathing only bottled air. She was spoilt, that was the only way to describe it. And now she expected him to do this stupid movie, just to support her epicurean taste for luxury, when the amount of money they had would have more than enough to support a whole town full of normal women anywhere in the United States unless they were from Bethesda, Maryland.

"Leo," Bretta had said, "We can't live on my income. You know that. Why, we wouldn't even be able to afford to go to Paris on the weekends, and that Australian wine - what's it called? - Grange Hermitage - would be out of the question for lunch. Good Lord, we'd have to start drinking clean-skins or even Italian wine."

Misty had never needed Grange Hermitage for lunch every day. By God, Misty would have been happy just making some lemonade with her own sweet hands, she wouldn't have even needed a servant to do it for her, and they'd be drinking it on the porch, sitting next to each other in their old, comfortable swinging seat, letting the afternoon breeze blow the pleasant fragrances of their country estate over the way.

He really missed Misty's company.

She had been like an old pair of sneakers, you don't notice how comfortable they are till you throw them out and get a new pair.

But there was nothing he could do about it now.

That part of his life had just wafted away. He was stuck with Bretta. He couldn't survive another divorce, and if leaving Misty had caused a storm, Bretta would be a tornado.

The director's voice went husky, "Leo, Leo, you'll have to do that scene again, Leo. Not enough oomph. It's not grabbing me by the guts. It's insipid, lifeless, Leo, you're like a spineless shift of foam blown across the seas, a jellyfish tossed around in the under-ocean currents, a whiff of something unpleasant someone smells on the breeze. I can't even believe C-O-two means anything to you. You're just going through the motions, Leo, you're like an unproductive vapour, a mist, a freaking cloud of putrid methane breaking loose from a horse's rear end like the foul effervescence of a sewerage farm. In other words, you're not convincing me, Leo, not one bit."

Leo groaned deeply. It was not a good day. He was getting used to the director's insults now and they weren't motivating him any more. "Alright, alright. I'll try to put more passion into it."

One of the girls brought him another coffee. "Here you go, Leo."

He sipped it gratefully and read through his lines again, and looked up, wondering if they were really doing it again because he had forgotten a few words or something.

He swore. He wouldn't be surprised. His memory these days was as unreliable as a windvane, blowing this way and that way and he didn't even know where it would blow next. Everything just blowed out of his god-forgotten head.

Maybe there was just not that much in there to begin with. Of course, he knew that was why he courted fame in this manner, in an intellectual issue, because that was precisely what he was afraid of. He knew that.

He studied the words some more.

"Alright," he said finally and stepped onto the chalk footprints they had drawn on the ground to show him where to stand.

The director said in a flat voice, "Okay. Scene Three Take Eighty Seven. Silent on the set. Don't even breathe! Not you, Leo. Cameras Rolling."

MESQUITE LIBRARY, PHOENIX, ARIZONA

Liverpool rolled back into the carpark at about one thirty. He'd organised the cash at a bank at a little place called Mesa about thirty five minutes drive away. As far as he knew he hadn't gone past any freeway cameras, but cameras are so ubiquitous these days. Thank goodness for google maps, though, he'd never have found that bank otherwise.

When he got into the car park he saw the red

convertible still sitting in the same parking spot. Thank goodness for that, too, he thought. His targets were still here.

Oh, no, not quite the same parking spot. They'd taken his, the one in the blind spot of the camera. They must've gone out for lunch or something, then come back and parked there.

Thank goodness.

Then he laughed silently to himself. He was thanking goodness, but actually, what he was going to do didn't qualify to be listed under the 'good' column. No, he was a bad man. But within a few hours he would be a rich bad man, and what does it matter what you do when you're going to end up in the ground anyhow? The same end happens to the good and the bad, so you may as well make the most out of your brief time on this earth.

Hell, our lives are as temporary and useless as a fart. Here one moment, disappeared the next.

He stayed there for a long time waiting for them to come out of the library.

Them being parked in the blind spot, it was perfect, a stroke of luck really.

When he shot them it wouldn't be on the cameras.

After several hours' sitting there with his gun ready

he walked into the library, looking for the two targets. For a moment he thought he saw the tall one, sitting at one of the corrals.

He walked around until he could see the guy's face. The guy actually looked up at him and then he realised it wasn't the same guy. It wasn't Nathanael.

Then he looked at the corral where Natasha, the Indian lady, had been sitting at her computer when he left.

She was gone, too.

He looked around frantically.

Neither of them was anywhere to be seen.

He went up to the library desk and asked, "That Indian lady who was sitting there, she was a friend of mine. I haven't missed her, have I?"

The librarian, a tall, thin lady greying at the temples, looked over her spectacles at him and said, "Yes I'm afraid so. She left about half an hour ago with that tall fellow she was with."

"Oh, darn," said Liverpool, though he certainly felt like saying something a bit stronger than that, but he didn't want to make a scene, not in front of the security cameras.

MESQUITE PUBLIC LIBRARY, PHOENIX, ARIZONA..............

<u>*ABOUT ONE HOUR EARLIER*</u>

Nathanael stood behind Natasha. He was waiting until she had stopped typing before butting in.

She turned around. "I know you're standing there, Nathanael."

"Sorry," he said. "I was just waiting till you'd finished."

"I've made absolutely no progress, Nathanael. None."

"Well I don't know what to say."

"Nathanael, I need help." She turned a pair of beseeching eyes on him. "I really need help."

He tried to be helpful. "Well, I'm sure there are some groups, you know, that would help you. Something like Alcoholics Anonymous, but for Hackers, surely. Hackers Anonymous? But Natasha, you have to finish this job first."

"Oh, you stupid," she said, and hit him gently with her fist. "I meant, I can't do this on my own. The i-ogle security protocols are too strict and I can't break through. I need help. I need other hackers, more equipment. Maybe a decent sized server farm, big enough to crack the encryption."

"Oh," he said. "Still there's something else, more important, Natasha we must-"

On her screen at that moment something flashed up with a small bell sound. "Message available on TOR Messenger".

Ignoring completely the fact that Nathanael was still suspended in mid-sentence, she quickly navigated to TOR Messenger and read the message.

Time to leave the library!
You are in danger. TG.

She looked around at Nathanael. "What's this? Do you know who 'TG' is?"

Nathanael shook his head. "No. Don't you?" She shook her head, no. Nathanael grabbed the opportunity to speak, "But the fact is, whoever 'TG' is, they're right, Natasha. It is definitely time to leave. We are in imminent danger. There's a gunman outside somewhere who has some bullets with our names written on them. I've mucked up his plan a bit by stealing his spare gun and wad of cash and he's gone to get more cash, but he'll be back, and he'll be pissed off too."

"Why didn't you tell me?"

"I didn't want to break your flow."

She gathered her things together.

And he added, "And we really need to find another vehicle. More's the pity, I liked that convertible."

Nathanael made his way to the car very quickly and got out their sleeping bags, pillows and luggage, and told Natasha, "I did a quick search on the library computers for car shops. Bell Toyota is only about nine minutes away. I've got the cash on me for whatever we need, so we'll buy a car, bring the convertible back here and dump it in the carpark. That will give us some time, because this guy may think we're still here. Then we go and find some other hackers so you can get the assistance you need."

BELL TOYOTA, PHOENIX, ARIZONA

They arrived at the car sale-yard in minutes and looked over the cars. They quickly agreed on a second hand Ford four wheel drive Super Crew truck, for which Nathanael offered twenty two thousand in cash if the manager would keep the paper-work off the books for a month. Since they were offering more than the asking price and there didn't seem to be any down-side for him, the manager was happy to oblige.

He asked them if they wanted to trade in the convertible, but Nathanael said no. The manager shook his head as though they were idiots, but he didn't comment.

Natasha drove the truck and Nathanael took the convertible back to the library. The whole round trip had taken no more than thirty five minutes.

Nathanael quickly parked the convertible in the blind spot where LUB-212 had been, then leaped into the passenger door of the Ford truck.

"Drive," he said.

Natasha said, "Where to?"

"You tell me," said Nathanael. "Surely you know some of the people you hacked with still, from when you were a teenager?"

Natasha nodded. "I don't keep in touch with them much, especially since I gave up hacking. Heh. But they occasionally send me things, you know, on TOR. I think Squid 555 is still living at his parents' place, actually, and that is not far from here. His real name was Aaron." She turned the huge powered steering wheel and directed the truck out onto the road.

THE ADAMANT BUILDING, NEW YORK

The phone rang. Raymond Adamant saw who it was and groaned.

Liverpool. Not again.

Hopefully he was telling him he'd done the job.

He excused himself from the meeting he was in and went out into the corridor.

Raymond said, "Hello? You're going to tell me you've finished."

"They got away. I need you to use your... contacts at the NSA to find them again."

"They're still in the same car?"

Liverpool was silent for a moment, then he said, "They had made me. You were right. They got a different car now. They had already made me at the library. I'm pretty sure it was them that stole the stuff from my car. I don't know how. I swear he was sitting there the whole time. It's like blinkin' magic."

Raymond sighed. "You didn't listen to me, did you? I told you that guy is clever. They used misdirection."

Liverpool said in a strained voice, "I'm sorry-" Raymond cut in. "There is no sorry. After I do this for you you've got no more chances left, right? I'll talk to my friends at the NSA, I'll get them to go on high alert for these two, that means every security camera, every internet cam, every mobile phone camera and computer camera in the country that's on the internet will be looking for them. But if I find them for you and then you stuff this up, I'll have to get someone else in to do the job for me. And I'll add you to the target list. You'll be the one they hit first."

Liverpool said haughtily, "I thought we wasn't supposed to use words like 'target' and 'hit' on the phone."

Raymond Adamant said emphatically, like an adult talking to a child, "I have to, with you. Talking to you, Liverpool, is like talking to a brick wall. Listen. Bad way to die, radiation poisoning. Do you understand?"

Liverpool swallowed audibly and breathed out in a suddenly hoarse tone of voice, "I understand."

WEST BUSONI PLACE, PHOENIX, ARIZONA

Natasha parked in the driveway of a relatively recently built cottage in the Egyptian style. It was one of those places Nathanael was familiar with from new building estates in Australia, squeezed into a small block with increasingly tiny rooms. "Are you sure this is the right one?" said Nathanael. "It looks like it was built yesterday."

"They moved here about ten years ago," said Natasha. "His parents had a bigger place with a basement, actually a very old place, but when Squid got caught hacking his parents had to sell it to pay the legal fees for his defence. He was only seventeen then."

She knocked on the door.

A pleasant, cultivated lady answered the door. She had grey hair and smile lines at the sides of her eyes, like Johnny Appleseed's grandmother, but she looked tired somehow as though her life had worn her out. She spoke in what Nathanael thought might be a New Hampshire accent. It was definitely an educated accent, Harvard, or somesuch. "Oh, is that you, Natasha? Aaron hasn't seen any of his friends for a while."

Natasha said, "Yes, it's me."

She welcomed them in. "Well, my son hasn't touched a computer now since the incident and that's well over ten years. His father and I are very proud of how he's changed. Mind you, these days it does limit his employment prospects, but luckily he has some friends he can do manual jobs for, and they give him somewhat more than a subsistence income, which he passes on to us, in toto, to pay us back and pay for his expenses now."

As she led them through the kitchen, Natasha introduced Nathanael. "This is a friend of mine. His name's Nathanael."

"Hello, Nathanael. Were you one of Aaron's online friends as well in the old days?"

"No, I'm just a friend of Natasha's. Nothing to do with computers."

"I don't think he even knew what half of his friends on that message board looked like. Most of them were about twelve or thirteen at the time, I think. Who knows. Anyway, Natasha was really the only one who ever came over during the trial or visited him while he was in prison, after that terrible debacle. He was very grateful for your support, you know, dear, very grateful indeed."

"Well, Mrs Kershowitz, I felt as though I was partly responsible for what happened to Aaron."

She didn't comment on that, just led them up stairs to a little room on the second floor. She knocked on the door and Aaron said after a moment, "Come in."

They went in and Aaron closed the door behind them, shutting his mother out.

Natasha said, "Your Mum says you don't use computers?"

"It's just easier that way," said Aaron, moving his desk chair and indicating for them to sit on the bed. He was overweight but had a tan and appeared not to be as unhealthy as his size suggested, for he was quick on his feet and not at all lethargic. A large white cat was laying on the bed, and

Aaron pushed it off. "Go on, Brisa, you can find somewhere else to sit." Nathanael and Natasha sat down, while Brisa came and sat on Aaron's lap, and he started stroking her white fur gently.

After whispering something to the cat, Aaron continued, "Actually you must know I have a laptop here, cause I've messaged you often enough on it. But you probably don't know I hired several racks in a server downtown. I've got some pretty high end equipment with Bitcoin and Ethereum mining running, twenty four seven. Those profits is what has been paying my bills. Mind you, I divested myself of most of my Bitcoin at the last fork, turned it into Ethereum. Ha. Good timing. Anyone could see it was going to drop - the code has been getting so unwieldy. The Ethereum at the moment is paying Mum's and Dad's bills right now, though they don't know. And I'm paying them back for the lawyers bit by bit, pun unintentional. I like to pay my way, my own food, pay the power and water bills, I really don't want to impinge on their retirement income, what's left of it, so I do a bit of fruit picking when the season's right as well. But the crypto is my main income. But you know, the crypto currency boom won't last for ever. It's not real money - it's vapour, it's mist - it's just nothing - it's got no value. But while it's still increasing why not take advantage of it?"

Aaron shifted his weight in the chair uncomfortably as the purring cat stretched up and nudged his chin. He began stroking her again and she quietened down and he continued, "You know I feel bad that Mum and Dad had to sell their house and move here. You understand they could only afford to rent this place because the owner moved overseas for a short while and needed someone to house sit for him? Then he decided to stay overseas and let them have it for less rent. God knows I would undo it all if I could." He sighed and said, "Enough vapid from me. So to what do I owe the pleasure of this visit, Natasha? And who's this guy?"

"I'm Nathanael."

Aaron reached forward and shook Nathanael's hand, and the cat jumped off his lap and went and sat in the corner. Aaron got up to shake Natasha's hand, but Natasha embraced him quickly, then stepped back. Aaron seemed a little embarrassed or uncomfortable with the physical touch and he sat down again on his chair, trying not to look at anyone. Nathanael immediately liked him.

Natasha said, "Aaron, we're in a bit of trouble."

He actually looked at Natasha now. "You haven't gotten caught by the FBI have you? They're not after you, too, now, are they?"

She rolled her eyes. "Aaron, you know this is the last place I would come if that had happened. I wouldn't bring them here. No it's more of a corporate thing."

"Well, who are you in trouble with, Natasha, if it's not the FBI?"

She sucked in her breath for a few seconds, then breathed out quickly, "i-ogle."

Aaron shook his head as though his ears weren't working. "Sorry, for a moment there I thought you said i-ogle."

Natasha pressed her lips together. "Mm. I did."

Aaron's eyes boggled. He was speechless.

Natasha said, "Actually, I suspect it's not so much i-ogle or Dave Trawlings, as much as their new owners."

"Adamant Corporation? Raymond Adamant? There are rumours they're in bed with the NSA."

"Really? That would explain a few things," said Natasha, visibly wincing.

Aaron said, "Well, I'm saying, I hope you didn't bring the NSA here."

Natasha said, "So do I. But Aaron, if you're not doing anything wrong you don't have to worry."

Aaron said, "Well, what was it you found? What do you need help with."

Natasha evaded the question. "A guy on a bulletin board put something up about a document and I did a little bit of extra research. It was nothing really."

"You weren't hacking again were you? You were, weren't you?"

"Kind of," admitted Natasha.

"I thought you gave that up when you became a Christian. I'm really disappointed in you."

"It's not like that, Aaron."

"Well what is it like? Hacking is not only risky it's immoral, Natasha, you yourself gave me that speech when I was in jail. But you also said God forgives our sins. It helped me a lot to believe that. You brought me back to my faith. But I just can't believe you've gone back to hacking. I can't believe you're backsliding."

"Aaron, I was forced into it. Nathanael was fleeing for his life and we were the ones who exposed the whole Methuselah conspiracy."

Aaron's whole demeanour changed. "Really? The leak from Adamant Corp that everybody was talking about on the net and in the news? That was you? Far out. That's extreme. That's awesome. You are by far the most famous hacker in the world, Natasha, and nobody even knows who you are. But now I know."

"The FBI kept my identity secret, and Nathanael and Michelle's as well, for our own safety. That whole affair brought down a lot of big players."

"Far out. That's completely extreme. So you're a white hat now. But it didn't do as much as anybody thought, did it, cause Adamant Corp is still out there? And now they own i-ogle." After a short silence he said, "What did you find?"

"I found some documents. Aaron, somebody has already died for them, OxyMoron, a guy on a bulletin board, they killed him. I haven't been back on that bulletin board in case they traced me. Actually, I'm pretty sure someone traced me, cause they sent someone to where I was staying last. At the moment we're free from tails, though, I'm sure of that."

She took her laptop out and handed him printouts of the Bel Algorithm documents she had made at the library. "There's a lot missing, it was in the process of being encrypted. But we think it's some sort of conspiracy to get control of the elections."

He flipped through the documents. "A state election?"

"Or a presidential election, even. Could be."

"Far out. This is deep stuff." He was silent for a while, reading through the document more carefully. "This is some sort of deep encryption, Natasha, I don't think we could hack it without a state of the art server farm, faster than mine. You were just lucky to get these out of the RAM while they were still being encoded. How did you do it? Was it the Spectre vulnerability?"

Natasha nodded.

"Smart work. No one can protect against it, really, but it's just good luck if you can get anything interesting, though. And you did." He looked at Nathanael. "I don't do hacking any more but I feel a sort of professional interest in the whole field, you know? So how can I help you both?"

"Well your Mum kind of curbed my enthusiasm in that respect when she told me I'm the only one who took the trouble to keep in touch after you got charged. I was hoping you might point me to someone who is still in the game, someone with enough chops to take on i-ogle with me."

"Far out. I don't even know if anyone in our message board would have had those kind of chops even in those days. You can't use me, the NSA is continuously monitoring my server farm, so if they're in cahoots with Adamant you're already stuffed. Sandeep456 is out of the picture. I haven't heard anything from Yeti11. But now... You know, what about Beowulf33? I get messages from him from time to time. Mum doesn't know about that. He's got a darknet site, but I don't know how much hacking he does."

"I don't know. He's not into selling drugs or child porn or something is he?"

"Of course not. He's a white-hat like you these days. He works for big companies, probing their vulnerabilities and helping them improve their security. His darknet site is more just a way of keeping in touch with us guys, a kind of proxy message board, nothing uncool goes on it, he wouldn't even let anyone post illegal stuff. It's called Beowulf's Bulletin Board. You know, I'm surprised he doesn't include you on the mailing list."

Natasha shook her head. "Well, when I gave up hacking he wasn't impressed. He said it was a waste of everything he'd taught me and that I was betraying the Linux philosophy."

Nathanael said, "What on earth is the Linux philosophy?"

Natasha said, "I looked it up, and there's this funny Linus Torvalds quote. This is what Linus said." She framed it with quotes:

"'The Linux philosophy is, "Laugh in the face of danger." Oops, wrong one. "Do it yourself." Yes that's it.'"

They laughed.

Natasha continued. "So I don't know, I think Beowulf33 might have been saying in a roundabout way that I should laugh in the face of danger."

Aaron said, "It's all a long time ago, Natasha, he has a family now you know. Or so he says. He talks about them without mentioning their names or where he lives. I've never seen him in person, though. Who knows what he even looks like? Beowulf33 could be a girl or a big black guy or a fat transgender individual wearing leathers and chains and smoking crack. Hell, he might even be Linus Torvalds himself, for all I know. You should contact him, though. He's your best bet. He's still got the edge, he keeps up with the code, he knows everything there is to know about security. And he's got a hugely fast server farm."

Aaron turned to Nathanael and breathed in hushed, reverent tones, "He was our Sensei." Nathanael hardly knew whether to take this comment seriously, but Aaron certainly seemed serious enough.

Then Aaron turned to his desk and wrote down a darknet address for Natasha, http://beowulfbb4y79pq1.onion, and a password, 'BeowulF127', folded the piece of paper and gave it to her. "His site's on TOR, here's the onion address and the login. You know, I'm glad you came. Now you better get out of here. I don't want Mum and Dad guessing what you're up to. And I definitely don't want you involving me in this mess you've gotten yourself into. You weren't followed were you?"

Nathanael said, "No, we weren't."

Aaron got off his chair and Natasha embraced Aaron again and Nathanael shook his hand. As they were walking out the cat jumped back up onto Aaron's bed.

Seeing them out, Aaron's mother said, "You will come around again, won't you, darling? He doesn't see his friends very often these days."

"Yes, I will," said Natasha, nodding. "I've got a busy period coming up with work, Missus Kershowitz, but after I've got through that I will come over again and say hello."

"Bless you. He's a good boy, really. And you must not blame yourself for, you know, what happened. It's not your fault. Aaron has taken responsibility for his own actions.

You were just lucky not to get caught as well." She looked at Natasha for a long moment. "Do you know, it helped him a lot, you going to see him when he was in prison, the fact that you stood by him and prayed for him meant a lot to him."

Natasha didn't know what to say.

The whole time Aaron had been in prison she had felt that she ought to go to the authorities and confess her role in the hacking. She had actually gone to see a lawyer about it, but he had said, "They will only prosecute you as well. Just because you helped doesn't mean he will get less jail time."

She still felt awkward about it all and she certainly did not see herself as the loyal friend. She wanted to confess it to Missus Kershowitz, but maybe that would just be to justify herself. She knew how these sorts of things went - they usually just made things worse.

But Missus Kershowitz repeated, "Thank you, Natasha. Don't leave it too long till you come to see Aaron again."

Natasha nodded. "I'll come soon."

And Missus Kershowitz said, "God bless you."

CHAPTER 6 - A DEEP DATE WITH THE DEEP STATE

SZALONNA, HUNGARY

Orsolya wore an uncharacteristic frown that morning. When Peter greeted her, she mumbled an unintelligible reply and seemed very distracted but then she said, "Come, twinkle csillagom, little starbug, you must get to work." She quickly guided Meth into the backyard, and sat him down with some problem or other, it looked like work to keep him busy.

Peter was concerned. He said, "Orsolya, are you alright?"

She said, "No, not very good. We must talk while Meth is working."

They went into the kitchen, where Orsolya could keep an eye on him but Meth couldn't hear them talking.

Orsolya sat down at the kitchen table heavily and sighed. Staring at the table, she said, "I thought you were safe here. For weeks the American man was looking for you and no one said anything. But then it turned out that someone was talking. I don't know who; really could be anyone. Perhaps even the visitor to the town, maybe he doesn't belong to the locals, but some say the new Mayor. I do not think so. But now your enemies, I think, believe that Meth is here and bring other people to Szalonna to find him." She looked up directly at Peter and grasped his hand. "You must leave now. It is no point in Szalonna. You're not safe here. Listen, Meth has learned our language very well. He really knows the languages very well, really, with all his school-work. He can speak Hungarian almost like one born here. I've never seen anything like this in one so young. Peter, you must go to Lipovnik, Slovakia, there are many Hungarians living there. Go right there. Do not waste more time."

Peter went and found his road map and came back and unfolded it on the kitchen table. He said, "Show me on this map."

She traced the route with her finger. "Ady út, Kossuth út, I mean street, then this highway, then sixteen. Turns here to the left and to the left. It takes about forty-five minutes. There is a relative living here, Páldeák István, István Páldeák in English. He's a good man. I will give you a letter to give it to her, I mean, him. He helps you hide there."

"We won't be driving," said Peter. "They will be watching the roads and especially the borders. No, I'm afraid we'll be walking."

Orsolya said, "Most of the day it will take you to walk. It's a comfortable walk, I guess, I do not think you're going up to five or six hundred metres up or down. You look fit, Peter, but if you're carrying Meth I think it can take longer than the usual six or seven hours."

Peter said, "We will leave our car here; you stay here all day, in fact, keep coming back every day as if we're still here. That ought to keep them busy. As far as the car goes, I'll sign the ownership papers over to you. Do with it what you wish."

Orsolya took a piece of paper and wrote the letter and gave it to Peter. "Give this letter to Istvan when you get there."

Peter unfolded another map onto the table showing the terrain as well as the roads and highways. He said, "Now, Orsolya, please show me which way we should go if we walk."

* * *

Immediately Peter began packing what he could of their possessions into a Kelty Pathfinder, a particular type of backpack that he had managed to buy from a hiker who was passing through a few weeks earlier in case of this eventuality. The thing about this backpack was that Meth could travel in it as well.

The other good thing about the backpack was that Peter had painted it green and had chosen clothes or dyed them as well to match the green of the Hungarian countryside. Even his hat was green.

Orsolya said, "I know someone who could take you out of town, to get you started. He is called Bela."

Then they had to tell Meth. He cried at first and protested, "But I will have to leave Orsolya. And I like living here. I don't want to leave."

Peter said, "Yes, but it is better to be free, Meth. And these people want to take you and put you in another room like the one you grew up in. You must be brave."

As soon as Peter said this, Meth stopped crying.

Peter said, "Meth, you need to work out what you're bringing with you. We only have room in the backpack for essentials."

With that, Meth started working out what he could take with him and what he had to leave behind.

Bela arrived about forty five minutes later and they were ready to leave.

Peter and Meth hopped into the car.

Bela drove them out of the town, and in minutes they were passing through sparsely populated farmland, where early morning mist was still rising from the ground. They crossed a small bridge over a river where the mist was concentrated and stopped just outside a farmhouse. Peter looked for cars or anyone following them. There were no cars or people to be seen in any direction.

Bela pointed to the mist-laden river passing through the green, fertile summer pastures, and said, "Follow that river. Go on the northern bank. To the south there are four or five tributaries. You will see when the road crosses the river, after the fifth or sixth tributary, I forget which one. You have a map? Yes. Then follow the highway, but stay off the road if you don't want to be seen. God bless you."

Peter thanked him and packed Meth into his seat in the backpack.

Meth said, "It's really comfortable," and promptly fell asleep while Peter began the walk.

It soon became muddy and it was hard work. He stayed close to the river while the mist was still hiding them but after that he found a wilder area of forest that ran parallel the river. Peter was aware that their pursuers might have drones, so he had been wearing a hat, as though that might be protection, but now he walked beneath trees when he could.

He eventually realised the river was bending further west than he needed to go. He checked his compass and walked up one of the hills.

Meth was still asleep.

When he reached the top of the hill, Peter stopped for a moment to have a drink of water from his canteen and took out the map. Following the river wasn't as quick as walking over the hills, so he took out his compass and calculated a quicker way to get to the nearest bridge.

It was then that he looked to the south and saw the men following them.

They had just arrived and were getting out of their car. There were five of them and Peter reckoned from their body language that they were armed. They were about two miles south of where he was. He didn't know if they'd seen him yet.

A van pulled up behind the car. Another man came out of the van and let loose something from the side of the van, apparently a white cloud, that rose up into the sky then separated into individual units.

Drones.

Good news. If they were sending up the drones, it meant they hadn't seen them yet. They didn't know where they were.

Peter got up slowly, trying not to catch their attention.

He was on the summit of the hill, but they were not looking towards it, they were heading west, following the river on the southern side, and the drones were still a long way away.

It was only a few steps onto the other side of the hill. Once he was there, he thought he might be moderately safe.

He looked at the map again as he came over the hill. Orsolya had told him what to do if he was pursued. There was not much tree cover here.

He began to jog. He knew it was a three and a half hour walk to where he needed to be. If he ran, maybe he could get there in an hour and half.

The bouncing of Peter's jog waked up Meth. He yawned and cried out, "What's going on?"

Peter said, "It's alright, Meth. We've just got to get to that hill Orsolya told us about."

Meth said, "Why?"

Peter said, "Oh, it's just a better plan. A better place to hide out for a bit." He didn't want to tell Meth about the drones, somehow. It just seemed too scary for the boy.

He made much better progress over the hills than he had along the muddy ground. As they went further north, the landscape had scars, signs of past mining.

Pete's side had a stitch in it and his back was aching,

but he didn't stop running. So far he hadn't heard the drones. They were too far away still. Perhaps they would be flying too high for him to see anyhow? In that case they could still see him. He kept drinking from his canteen, but after about half an hour his own water ran out.

Meth said, "Here, Dad, have mine."

Peter gratefully accepted the offer.

To Peter it seemed a very long run. But he had not yet seen the flat topped hill he was looking for.

Finally, as Peter came over another boring hill, he saw it.

A flat topped hill in the distance with a small village to the West.

The hill had been gouged out a long time ago, for mining, but that wasn't what Peter was looking for.

He redoubled his speed and Meth said, "I didn't know you could run this fast, Dad."

Peter panted the words out, "Neither did I, son."

He was now not worrying if they were under tree cover or not, he was simply going as fast as he could. But he did try to keep to the lower edges of the valleys between each hill.

Finally he came down over a hill, into the village. He

leapt a few fences, thanking his lucky stars that his knees did not buckle, and finally found himself walking up a shallow slope.

Orsolya had described this area well. He came to the crater, where the mining had been, and looked up to see a drone flip up over the brow of a hill.

Peter backtracked a little to a copse of willow trees. The drone went past, without turning around so Peter reasoned they hadn't been seen. Peter was perturbed by how silent it was, it merely made a quiet whirring sound that was almost inaudible even though Peter was less then twenty feet away from it.

Peter waited until the drone had left then ran into the rocky remains of the mines. Small bushes grew up everywhere and a slight mist was still hovering above the ground, though Peter judged that it wasn't a very high elevation.

Orsolya's description had been good. He could see everything as she had described it.

In bounding steps he leapt over the rocky ground and past a copse of chaotic rocks and bushes he found what he was looking for.

The cave entrance. It was a large, gaping hole in the side of the mine. Inside, the cave walls glinted and glistened.

Peter ran into the cave. His footsteps began to echo strangely, as though the cave was saying, "Hush, Hush, Hush" with every footstep he took.

He kept jogging until they were far enough in that it was getting dark and then slowed to a very slow walk, feeling his way along quietly. Even his softest footsteps the cave breathed back loudly and even the drops of water that fell from the ceiling echoed with a "huff" as though the cave was expiring a slight breath.

Peter found himself bending low, to get through, then they were in another cavern.

Peter felt they were far enough into the network, so he found a smooth patch of ground and took off the backpack. The sound here was more muffled. There were pools of water around and Peter wondered if they were dampening the sound, or perhaps it was the more sandy ground in this part of the cave.

Meth crawled out.

In the absence of Peter's footsteps, the natural sounds of the cave became louder, a regular drip, huff, drip, huff, drip, huff. Peter stopped moving completely and listened.

"Father," Meth said, "It's very quiet in here, isn't it? All I can hear is the dripping of the water and the funny echo the cave makes. And it's very dark, isn't it?"

Peter nodded, then remembered that Meth couldn't see him. "Yes it is quiet, son, and dark. That is precisely why we should be safe here for a little while."

Peter took out his mobile phone and started the flashlight function.

He looked around a bit. There was a convenient alcove in the wall.

"Son," he said, pointing to the alcove. "Go in there if anyone, or anything, comes into the cave. Right there. We'll hide behind the stalactite."

"Alright," said Meth. "What sort of anything might it be?"

Peter said, "A drone."

"Oh," said Meth. "I know what those are. Little flying things with cameras."

"Yes, that's right," said Peter. "How did you know?"

"I had a computer, remember? I used to get on the internet and read things."

"Oh, yes," said Peter. "I had no clue at the time that your computer could actually go on the internet."

"It couldn't. I fixed it so it could," said Meth, and Peter again had a strange feeling of being confronted with the otherness of Meth. This boy was something different from the rest of us.

Yes, he was human, but he was somehow a better, more efficient sort of human than the rest of us. He was not only longer lived but smarter, more capable. How could everything in the human genome have deteriorated so quickly? I mean, at the most Meth's DNA was a hundred thousand years old; of course, a bit younger if you took the carbon dating of the fossils Peter had plundered for Meth's DNA at face value, but Peter didn't, of course, that would have been career suicide at the time. One doesn't question dating.

Not that it mattered now.

His thoughts were interrupted by the slightest of whirring sounds.

A drone, entering the cave.

Meth and Peter both rushed into the small alcove, behind the stalactite. Peter quickly rummaged through his pack and found a large sheet of black plastic, folded up. He had found it on an old building site in Szalonna and had kept it, for he had read somewhere that black plastic could fool infra-red vision.

He opened the plastic up and covered the alcove where they were hiding as well as he could then took out some gaffer tape and taped it onto the crystalline stone.

The plastic was covered in drops of paint and might fool a cursory glance at least, slightly resembling the intricate crystalline patterns of the cave wall.

The drone whirred in, shining a cone of light whichever way it was facing. It looked here and there and then turned around, but just as they thought it was about to leave it turned again and explored further on in the cave.

It came back past them again, shining its light, then hovered not five feet from where they were, shining its light in a slow circle, getting closer and closer. Silently Peter prayed, "God, help us."

Suddenly Meth picked up a stone from the cave floor and Peter was about to cry out, "No!" when he remembered he shouldn't make any sound. Peter tried to grab Meth's arm to stop him, but Meth had already jumped out from behind the plastic and Peter had no clue where he was.

Meth's hands were not very large but he and Peter had been practising playing catch as part of Orsolya's prescribed education (she would say, 'the gymnasium was as important in Plato's ideal Republic as studying dialectic and philosophy. And the boy has to learn the catch. When he looks twelve, who's he going to play with?') Because of their regular practice Meth had developed a deceptively strong throwing arm, if a rather stumpy one.

Meth tossed the stone at the drone while the cone of light was facing the other way. The stone thumped, it must have hit the drone, to Peter's surprise. Peter looked out from behind the plastic. The drone whizzed strangely, and then seemed to regain its balance, but it was no longer navigating so quickly. Meth must have damaged one of the rotors.

Peter got out from behind the plastic and picked up another, bigger rock himself and tossed it at the drone. He missed and the rock clattered against the far wall.

The drone's light swivelled away from them towards the sound of the clattering rock. Peter picked up another rock to throw and this time he hit the drone. It whizzed and whirred and down it tumbled, out of mid-air, in a strange looping dive into a pool of water some distance away from them, and gave a splash.

It didn't come back out.

Meth gave a 'hmph' of vindication. But Peter said, "Wait. They will come in here looking for it. Those things are expensive. We'll have to stay behind the plastic, completely silent, for another half hour, Meth. Please tell me you can manage that."

Meth said, "I can." He had already learned the cost of speaking when told not to.

Meth climbed back into the alcove as Peter held the plastic up. They huddled together in the tiny space.

A little while later, just as Peter had thought, three of the men came into the cave, clambering along the rock face. Peter could hear them but he couldn't see them, but he assumed they had guns and night-vision, probably infra-red.

One of the men stopped near their alcove and said in English, "It was around about here when it stopped transmitting."

The were silent for a while.

Peter thought they might have gone.

He peeked out through a gap between the cave wall and the plastic.

The three men were shining their torches around in an ever-widening circle and for a moment one of the torches shone directly at Peter's eyes.

Peter was sure he had been seen but the torch whirled away just as quickly. Nothing happened, perhaps the man hadn't been looking.

Peter was holding his breath and he realised Meth was as well. The boy was gripping Peter's hand more tightly than

Peter thought he could grasp it, his chubby fingers actually causing him pain.

Then one of the men shone his torch in the pool of water and said, "Look, here it is." He pulled the fallen drone out of the water by one of its four rotors, gingerly, like someone picking up a dead fish by the tail.

It was completely broken.

The second man pointed his torch at the ceiling, revealing a beautiful, complex pattern of crystalline stalactites. "What are those things called?" the man said, "Stalagmites or stalactites? What do you reckon - Archie got too close to the roof and the rotor flicked one of those and he bounced off into the water."

The third man shrugged and said, "Search me. Nothing else in here that could've done it, is there?"

They left the cave, taking the drone with them.

Meth was still gripping Peter's hand so tightly that Peter could feel the boy's fingernails biting into his skin. Peter whispered, "It's alright, son, you can breathe again now." Meth relaxed.

"I think we'll stay in here for a day or two," said Peter. "We've got enough tins of food and there's plenty of water here. Let's do that."

Meth said, "Alright, Dad, if you think it's for the best. It's very dark, but if you're with me I know I'll be alright."

Peter nodded, then remembered again that the boy couldn't see him nodding. "Yes, I think it is for the best."

MONTECITO, CALIFORNIA

Leo Bos was on the last day of shooting.

The director wasn't really talking to him any more, which Leo could kind of understand. He had become a bit temperamental in the past few days, thrown one or two temper tantrums (or maybe fifteen, the director said, apparently he was counting) and it was possible Leo had alienated everyone on the set with his childish antics. In fact the whole mood of the place had changed and it was now a mood of collective desperation, waiting and wishing for the end to come. The girls were certainly cooler towards him, handing him his coffees without speaking, and no one was really saying anything much to him.

But you know, that's the price of genius. I mean, when Wagner slept with his patron's wife, his patron boasted of what an honour it was. Leo Bos was creating a masterpiece among climate films. Surely people should be willing to put up with a few eccentricities, in the service of art.

Or truth, anyhow.

"Rolling," said the director.

Leo placed his feet firmly on the chalk footprints and delivered his last speech. "This cause stands in the tradition of every other righteous political movement in history and just like them, it suffers resistance from those who would try to deny justice for purely self-centred reasons. The terrible bane of carbon dioxide, spreading its poisonous fumes through the atmosphere like the dread filaments of a deadly fungus, infecting the lungs of our planet, must be stopped lest we irreversibly damage the climate of the earth and make it unliveable for future generations. Let us oppose the deniers and move forwards into the future with the confidence that we can make a difference. Let us continue the battle to rid the world of evil fossil fuels and replace them all with renewable technology, morality demands this of us, we must change, humanity must change, or die. And maybe, just maybe the earth would be better off without us. But if we can change, then, and only then, can we expect Gaia the goddess of the earth to bless our nation with fruitfulness and the gift of life."

Thank God for speech writers, Leo thought, there was no way he could have thought of this rubbish on his own.

He liked the Gaia thing, though. He might use that

again.

The director got up, folded his deck-chair and said, "Well, that's it, people. Go home." He began tidying his notes and Leo said, "Um," but the director wasn't listening. Leo tapped him on the shoulder and he still ignored him, so Leo grabbed his arm and pulled him up.

He wrenched his arm out of Leo's grip and snapped, "What?"

Leo said, "When will I get to see the final cut?"

"I don't know. I won't have much to do with it. Talk to the editors."

Leo scowled. "What do you mean, talk to the editors? Aren't you supposed to supervise the editing?"

"The assistant director can do that. I've had a gutful of you, Leo, and I don't want to look at your ugly face for one microsecond more than I absolutely have to."

Leo said, "But that's your reputation on the line, buddy! Don't you want to make sure its done properly?"

The director responded with a variegated range of expletives.

Leo shook his head and left him to his packing up. If it wasn't any good he would sue the pants off him. He could afford to do that.

Leo's phone chose that moment to ring. He nearly threw it away but then he saw the name on the touch-screen.

Raymond Adamant.

Leo answered it, "Hello?"

"Hi, Leo. I understand you were finishing shooting today."

"I was. I have. What do you want?" And Leo winced. He hadn't meant to come across so short-tempered.

"I wanted to see you, Leo. To talk to you about my proposal."

"Listen, next Wednesday would be fine."

"I was thinking a little sooner than that. What if I flew over tomorrow and took you out to lunch?"

Lunch sounded rather more agreeable to Leo than just a meeting. "Alright, I don't mind. What time will you be here?"

"About eleven in the morning."

Leo said, "Okay, I'll see you then."

"See you then, Leo."

THE FÖLDVÁRI ALADÁR CAVE, HUNGARY

Peter was listening to Meth's breathing as he slept. It was a calming sound and the strange echoes in the cave now seemed familiar and homely. They were safe here, that was all that was important. And luckily he had packed these warm waterproof sleeping bags. Despite the dampness and the cold, they were fine.

Peter couldn't sleep, but that wasn't a new problem. But being in here, he had started to think differently about things.

All they had in here was time, time to think.

Peter had begun thinking about his life. Meth seemed more important to him than now than just another member of his family. In a way he was proof, proof that this life might not be all there was.

Peter's heritage was Jewish and Meth was proof of the historicity of the early part of the book of Genesis. A strange thought.

If that part of the Bible possessed historical validity, what about the rest? Could there really have been a Moses? A Joshua? A King Solomon?

And what about Jesus? Now there was a conundrum. He had to talk to Natasha sometime about that. Peter wasn't sure what he thought about the New Testament.

So, say there was a Noah, an Abraham, a Methuselah. What about God?

He looked around at the crystalline cave, inanimate

matter, yet somehow needlessly beautiful.

Someone made all this, made the universe so that beauty and tenderness was a part of it.

And didn't he have a responsibility now? To pass something more on to Meth than mere facts?

Values. Morality. Faith.

But Peter had always worshipped at the altar of science. He had always believed in rationality.

Sitting in the darkness, a thought hit him. If he just assumed his thoughts were random firings of neurons, how did he know that his thoughts were rational? What was the measure of rationality? He had always simply assumed that he knew what was rational. But if his thoughts were just the product of electrons moving in a piece of grey matter that had arisen by chance, the random movement of electrical impulses in a random collection of atoms, why would he assume they had any logical correspondence with the world outside?

Somehow the existence of God seemed necessary to explain the fact that science worked. If there was a God then there was an order to the universe. And if there was an order to the human mind that corresponded to the order in the outside world, then it was because the mind was designed by the same God.

CHAPTER 7 - LURCH IN CHURCH

Nathanael was driving. They just took local roads for a little while, kept off the main roads where there might be security cameras in the shops or traffic cams.

Natasha said, "What now, Nathanael?"

He said, "Well, we've got to find a place to stay tonight. Unless we do the park thing again."

Natasha said, "Not tonight. I need a real bed."

Nathanael said, "Motel, then? Nah. Not a motel."

Natasha shook her head. "Maybe something more informal. A guest house, perhaps? A bedsitter?"

"Or a bed and breakfast?"

"Yeah. Something like that. Some place where they don't have cameras continuously pouring images onto the internet and they don't put their guest lists into some piece of software the NSA has got a back door to."

"Okay," said Nathanael. "Best thing we could do is buy a newspaper. Anyone who is advertising in there is probably a traditional type, probably not online."

"Look," said Natasha, pointing at a small group of local shops on the corner ahead. "There's a newsagent in there."

Natasha got the paper, and when she told the newsagent she was looking for a place he gave her several older papers and a real estate guide as well.

Nathanael went and purchased some other supplies.

They stayed in the car for a while, searching through the advertisements in various newspapers. There was a small ad in one of the older papers, "B&B short term furnished 2 br $90/night reduced desert views."

"Looks nice," said Nathanael. "We even get reduced desert views."

"Two bedrooms. Well, that's good."

It was clear she meant, it's good, we don't have to share a bed. Nathanael felt stricken, and thought it must have shown on his face, but Natasha didn't even seem to have noticed.

MESQUITE LIBRARY CARPARK, PHOENIX, ARIZONA

Liverpool was sitting in his car waiting for the call.

Finally it came.

Raymond Adamant voice said, "They went into a newsagent yesterday and bought a newspaper, a bunch of newspapers. They were looking through it for something. Possibly a place to stay."

Liverpool said, "What do I do?"

Raymond's voice sounded strained. "Buy some newspapers. See if there are any places to stay listed in there. Check them out."

Liverpool said, "So you can't even tell me which newspaper? What if I can't find them?"

Raymond said, "The NSA is still surveilling everything in Arizona looking for them. They can't have gone far yet."

PHOENIX, ARIZONA

It took about half an hour to get to the place, because Nathanael was taking the back roads and they were relying on the street directory rather than i-ogle maps. But when they got there it turned out to be a reasonably attractive place, with two rooms, sharing a single balcony.

They sat at the balcony and Nathanael brought out a glass of white wine, a Greek salad and some curry puffs.

He said proudly, "I got it at those shops."

Natasha frowned a little. "It's a motley meal."

Nathanael shrugged. "I'd prefer to think of it as multicultural." He started to lift one of the curry puffs to his mouth.

Natasha said, "Wait."

He put the curry puff back on the plate but still held it in his right hand. "What for?"

"Grace."

Natasha grabbed his left hand and closed her eyes.

Nathanael rolled his eyes.

She said, "I know you're rolling your eyes Nathanael. Don't. Our Father in heaven, thank you for your bountiful gifts. Please bless this food in Jesus' name. And bless Nathanael, Amen."

Natasha squeezed his hand, and despite himself he heard himself saying, "Amen."

As they ate, Natasha said, "So what do we really know, Nathanael?"

He said, "Well, not a lot really. It looks as if i-ogle is planning on fixing the election, or at least manipulating the electorate. But beyond that, apart from the dodgy campaign hats (and will that really work?) and them taking i-ogle videos offline, we don't really know what else they're doing. We just know that it's not good." He chomped on a curry puff and added as an afterthought, "Oh, and someone's trying to kill us."

Natasha said gloomily, "Well, it's not the first time, is it?"

She was eating her curry puff with her right hand. He took her left hand in his and looked into her dark brown eyes and said, "Well, you'll just have to stop hacking, won't you? If you want a peaceful life."

"Yeah," she said, leaving her hand where it was. Nathanael wanted to kiss it, but he didn't want to push things too far.

Instead, he just put her hand down on the table and patted it, and immediately regretted the ineffectual gesture. Natasha laughed and snorted curry out over the table. Nathanael started laughing as well and they both laughed for a long while until Natasha had tears coming out of her eyes. Then she gave a gasp, almost like a sob, as though the tears had suddenly become sad instead of happy and Nathanael wanted to comfort her but she said, "It's alright." And he wanted to ask her what was alright but when he opened his mouth to speak she said, "Not now, let's not ruin this night." And she added, "It's too much fun," but she said it affectionately, as though hidden in those words was something precious that she was giving him, so that Nathanael was completely puzzled and had no clue where he stood in relation to her at all or what their relationship meant.

There was a couch on the balcony and the night was so peaceful and calm that they sat on the couch and Natasha fell asleep on Nathanael's shoulder. He wasn't sure if he wanted her there, because he was finding it hard to sleep and her elbow was uncomfortable in his side, but he didn't want to move because he liked being so close to her, so he sighed and stayed there like that, watching the celestial canopy slowly turn above them.

* * *

He woke up in the morning with someone shaking him. "Nathanael, get up!" Natasha was shaking his shoulders. "Wake up! We have to get going. I just got a message from Beowulf33. He wants to meet up!"

* * *

Twenty minutes later they were sitting in a small café in downtown, waiting for Beowulf33 to arrive.

The café owner, a large bosomed grey haired woman who looked somewhere between fifty and sixty years old came over and asked for their orders. Natasha ordered a soy milk café latte and Nathanael ordered a black coffee with cream.

She brought the orders over a few minutes later, and put down the soy milk latte and the black coffee and the cream, and a cappuccino.

Natasha shook her head at the cappuccino. "We didn't order that."

The café owner said, "That's alright, that one's for

me." She sat down at the table with them. They were both staring at her. Was she NSA?

She said, "It's okay, my assistant, Roman, is perfectly able to keep the café running."

Natasha said, "Sorry, um, we're waiting for someone and I don't think he'll want to have anyone, you know, listening in."

She slumped into the seat as though she was going to stay there. "Who are you waiting for?"

Natasha said, "None of your business." She got up and said, "You're very rude," only with a few extra words.

The café owner said, "Wouldn't be Beowulf thirty three, would it? Natasha?"

Natasha stared at her.

She said, "That's me. Sit down, Natasha. I'm Beowulf thirty three."

Natasha's eyes narrow suspiciously, "If you're Beowulf thirty three, then what was my handle on the message board?"

"Catwoman fourteen. Cool handle."

"Are you really that old? Is it really you? You didn't seem old online. And what's your name?"

"Come on," she said. "I'm not that old. We're talking

what? Twelve? Fourteen years ago? Or was it sixteen years ago? I'm not even sure. I was thirty nine, maybe forty one, when we were doing that. I'm fifty three now. Mind you, I've got grandkids now. Got married early, had my first kid at eighteen. Never regretted it though. When I reached thirty eight, both of mine had left home. Half my friends, who had said what a mistake it was me not having an abortion, were going through IVF and trying for children and considering adoption. What a nightmare. I got sick of listening to their tales of woe so I went to university and studied computer programming, which is how I ended up on that message board, back when they still gave message boards in i-ogle searches."

"It's weird seeing you," Natasha admitted. "I really thought you were a man. Honestly." Then Natasha noticed the name of the café. "The Baying Wolf Café. Beowulf. Of course."

"Yeh, that's right. Thing is, I considered putting my real gender online, but back then it was fun, you could pretend to be someone you weren't. Bit harder these days."

"But you told Aaron you had just had kids?"

"Grandkids, actually, and it has impinged on my spare time a bit. You've got no idea, my daughter is always wanting me to babysit for her."

Nathanael put his hand forward and said, "I'm Nathanael."

She said, "I know, Nathanael Wayfarer," and shook his hand. She looked at him quizzically, "Well, what do you want to ask me, Nathanael Wayfarer?"

He lowered his voice to a whisper. "Are you really up to hacking i-ogle with Natasha?"

She rolled her eyes and lowered her voice as well. "What, is it because I'm old or because I'm a woman? Look, son, my whole job is trying to hack websites to find their flaws. I'm a white hat hacker, and I'd warrant you could find someone better than me. But I don't know if you could find someone who you could rely on. But you can rely on me. You know you can, Natasha."

Natasha nodded. "She didn't dob me in when she could've, back when Aaron got caught. I was just as culpable in the hack that got him arrested."

"That was bad luck for the boy," she said. "Yeh, I still think about that. I think those two years aged me about ten years. Very stressful when you've got the feds looking over everything you did. Look, since I know your names, I guess I may as well demonstrate my goodwill by telling you my name. My real name is Lisa Heppert."

Natasha said, "Wow. Pleased to meet you, Lisa."

Lisa shook both their hands then reached into a pocket in her apron, and took out her purse, and her driver's license. She showed the picture to them.

"See? Lisa Heppert. Fifty three years old. Now, I've got my computer setup out the back there, with a couple of servers and so on. Come out back." And she led them through the employee entrance of the café into another room behind the kitchen; it was well hidden from the front and Nathanael would not have even guessed it was there.

It was not just a couple of servers. It was a room about fifteen feet by twenty feet full of servers stacked on racks. There were six rows of server racks, each set of racks with at least a hundred small black computers on them. The innards of the computers were showing and each one had a large heat sink sticking out on top of it. Still, Natasha fancied that she could actually see the air shimmering above some of the computers, as though the heat sinks were barely enough for the amount of processing that was going on. At the very rear of the room there was a fifty one inch screen showing a screen saver, with a keyboard and a mouse next to it. Against the wall, behind the other server racks were a few other screens, but none of them were turned on.

"Are these home-brews?" asked Natasha. "Looks impressive. How fast does this run?"

Lisa nodded. "Put them all together myself. That was the good thing when I did my computer degree - I managed to get a few units in the practical side of actually putting together your own machine out of parts - not sure they would still be running those units today at the tech, it's all gotten much more esoteric. This building costs a fortune in electricity to run, though. Luckily I bought Apple shares before the iPhone came out." She patted the desk chair in front of the screen. "Take her for a spin, Catwoman. You'll be surprised what she can do."

Natasha sat down in front of the screen. "It's Linux, but I've never seen this GUI before."

Nathanael said, "What's a GUI?"

Lisa said, "Graphical User Interface. Like Windows, but on Linux. Nah, this is my own. I wrote it. It doesn't have all the bells and whistles but at least I know how it works and have complete control over the vulnerabilities. If someone hacks me I've only got myself to blame." Lisa took the mouse and clicked on something. "Here, this one is the web browser."

Natasha typed in the web address for the i-ogle servers but Lisa said, "Wait, Catwoman, use my software." She opened up another application and a bunch of code began to scroll down on the screen.

"What's that?" said Nathanael.

"It's the source code for the webpage, but with my tool you can see a few things you can't normally see, it's like an x-ray machine for website coding. There's a few flaws, you see, cracks you might say in the security layers between HTML and PHP, which means I can get a lot more information with a few judicious code inserts. But it's all automatic."

Lisa's system prompted her for possible entry points, so Natasha typed in a few addresses.

Natasha said, "How will we get around the i-ogle Captcha mechanisms?"

Lisa said, "What do you think these servers are for? I've got about a quarter as much computer power here as Tianhe-2. Each of these units has a Xeon Phi 7290F processor in it. That's a hell of a lot of computing power for decoding any sort of encryption, and I mean any. Dammit, I bet if I used this server farm to calculate the weather I could do a hell of lot better than the Hadley Climate Supercomputer, which is old and outdated now. Do you know I've been in this game a while now, Natasha, and so far, nobody's caught me doing anything illegal, touch wood?" She tapped the table. "Well, most of my stuff these days is legal anyhow. Just probing company websites for vulnerabilities. Oh, wait, something's coming up."

She took the mouse again and tapped on an "OK" button on the screen.

"My software is trying multiple access points, multiple user names, multiple passwords. You'd be surprised at how many passwords and usernames have been hacked and are sitting on Russian servers. And it's number crunching, working out some big prime numbers, you can bet, cause that's the other way in. Now, we wait. Anyone for coffee? I'll get Roman to bring us some. We could have some eats too, maybe. It's getting close to lunch time, and this could take hours."

MESQUITE LIBRARY CARPARK, PHOENIX, ARIZONA

Liverpool was getting sick of sitting in his car.

His butt was getting sore and it wasn't the best place to sleep in.

His phone buzzed.

Raymond Adamant's voice said, "Did you get them? Did you find out where they're staying?"

"No, the landlady wouldn't give me the address. Said

it wasn't for rent any more and she liked the tenants."

Raymond said, "Give me the landlady's phone number."

He recited it.

Raymond paused, presumably writing it down, then said, "Alright. I'll get the NSA to follow that up. They drove into the Phoenix city centre. They're still there now. I'll send you the address and their new car license plate number if I can get it, on your disposable mobile." He paused again. "You realise you have not impressed me with your professionalism so far. You'd better not stuff it up this time."

Liverpool swallowed. He still remembered Raymond's threat, radiation poisoning didn't sound good. "No, I won't stuff it up, sir."

THE FÖLDVÁRI ALADÁR CAVE, HUNGARY

Meth stared around the cave. His eyes had adjusted to the darkness now and he could see the details of the crystalline walls, the stalactites, the stalagmites, the pools of water reflecting everything. It was like a home now, a place he felt comfortable in. He whispered, "Dad, how long have we been hiding in here?"

Peter said, "Nearly forty hours, Meth. About a day and a half. I think." He couldn't be sure. The phone had run out of battery and so had the torch. He was trying to gauge the time by the light in the cave, but even that was difficult; what if it was cloudy outside?

"How much longer do we wait? I'm hungry." Peter had been filling their canteens from whatever flowing water he could find in the cave, they still had water. But the food situation meant they had to leave soon.

No, the longer they could stay here the less likely it was that the Americans would still be looking for them.

He had to distract Meth from thinking about food.

Meth repeated, "How long?"

"I don't know, Meth. But I've been thinking."

"What about, Dad?"

"A lot of things. You know, how your lifespan is much longer. Your genetics. It indicates that some of the ancient texts were right about people living a lot longer."

"Yeah?"

"Yeah. And do you know, of all of them, the one that matches, well, how long you will live, only one book really does. The rest are ridiculous ages, thousands or millions of years. But the one that seems to actually match the facts. Is the Bible, Meth. The book we got your name from. Methuselah. In the early part of the Bible they all lived, you know, anywhere from five hundred to a thousand years. That's how old you should live for, son."

"And?"

"And I've always doubted that book. It's part of my heritage, I'm Jewish, but it never seemed plausible. I mean, miracles and all. Especially that early part, people who live for hundreds of years. But if one part can be true... But you know, sitting here in the dark gets you thinking, son. And all through this, I've felt like Someone was looking after us. Protecting you. Looking after us both. Not just an impersonal force, you understand. Some sort of Presence, a Person."

"Me too," said Meth. "I can feel Him when you talk about Him."

"When I was a kid I went to Shabbat."

"What's Shabbat?"

"It's where children used to go to learn about Adonai. God, that's another name for God. And the Torah. I believed it all then. And now, with everything that's happened, I think I'm starting to doubt my agnosticism. I'm really starting to believe there's a God, son. And - it's crazy, I never thought I'd hear myself saying this - I think He's the God of the Jewish people. I'm even thinking about praying. Maybe He can help us to know when to leave this cave."

"What's 'praying?'"

"It's talking to God, son. Talking to God. Asking Him for His help. Thanking Him for things. Praising Him."

"I've read about God. Did He make everything? Like you made me?"

"No. I made you from parts of other people. God made everything out of nothing. He sustains the universe. God is everywhere. You can't see Him, because the whole universe is in Him, and only continues to exist because of Him. He saved the people of Israel by using his servant Moses."

"Who was Moses?"

"Well... I suppose I had better tell you the whole story, then. Now Pharaoh was the king of Egypt..."

At that moment, someone shouted at the mouth of the cave.

"Hello! Hello! Peter, I know you're in here with Meth. Come out now!"

Peter didn't recognise the voice.

THE BAYING WOLF CAFÉ SERVER FARM, DOWNTOWN PHOENIX, ARIZONA

They were sipping their coffees and eating sandwiches when an alarm sounded, "pip, pip, pip, pip". Lisa jumped up from her seat and turned on one of the other screens behind another server rack. She pressed a red button and a metal door slid shut with a clang.

"Someone just walked into the café packing heat."

Natasha said, "What?"

"Packing heat. Carrying a gun. Someone just came into the café with a gun and he's walked straight through, out into the back corridor. I've locked us in here. There's four inches of steel all around the room except for where the power cable and the optic fibres come in and out. He can't shoot us in here and the door to this room just looks like a blank wall out there."

Nathanael said, "How are you prepared for this?"

Lisa said, "I anticipated this kind of thing might happen, a long time ago. Actually, when Aaron got caught. I suppose I was more worried about the FBI then. But the fact is the FBI would have come in with two officers who would have shown their badges when they come into the café. No, this guy thinks he snuck past Roman, didn't even show a warrant or anything. Whoever this is he ain't FBI and he ain't any other legitimate law enforcement. Look, he's walking past now."

They looked at the screen. He was walking along the

corridor. He stopped and took out his phone.

Nathanael realised it was the same guy he had seen in the carpark. He said, "Lisa, does this thing have any sound?"

She turned up the sound.

Liverpool was on his phone. "They're not here. Just an empty corridor."

"Bzzt Bzzt Bzzt."

There was a buzzing sound and Lisa fiddled with some controls on a device in one of the server racks, that wasn't the same as the other computers. "I can't compress the sound feed enough to get the voice of the person he's talking to."

Liverpool continued. "So it's somewhere in this block? A big drain on power and some sort of darknet connection you reckon? Well, look, mate, all I can see is a café and some toilets."

"Bzzt Bzzt Bzzt."

"Come on."

"Bzzt Bzzt."

"Yeh, well I've been right round the building. What? Measure it? What with? I don't have a tape measure on me. You honestly think there's a hidden room in there? Sounds like bollocks to me. You're sure."

Frowning, Natasha banged her fist against her head.

She was kind of smiling as well, which Nathanael put down to stress. Under her breath he could hear her praying, "Jesus, help, Jesus, help."

"Bzzt Bzzt Bzzt."

"Alright then, send your guys in, get them to measure it, work out where it is. Alright, I'll sit tight in the café and have a latté till they get here. It's break time anyway. You really reckon they're hidden somewhere in that building? Well couldn't they be using proxies or something, couldn't the server be elsewhere? The proxies all meet here? How do they know that? Geez, there ain't no privacy any more is there?" His voice changed tone then, more humbled, scared maybe. "Yeh alright. I will. I'll remember that."

He turned his phone off.

Lisa got her mobile out and rang a number. "Roman, did you see that guy who snuck out the back?"

It was on speaker phone so they could hear Roman saying, "Yes."

"Well he's coming back in to get a coffee."

"Alright. What do you want me to do?"

"I reckon he'll be right ready for an afternoon nap, don't you?"

Lisa turned her phone off and said to them, "I don't

really want to get involved in a siege. Once he's asleep we'll deal with this. I'm going to leave the computers running. There's a few things I have to do first."

She went to a box on the wall and pulled a lever. A generator started chugging. She watched a dial next to the lever. About a minute later the dial had turned around about 180 degrees, and she pulled another lever. "Right, the whole room is on its own power now, and there's I don't know how many days worth of diesel in the tank. It will take them days, by the way, to even find the fibre optics, much less turn them off. It's a shame, I liked this one." She looked around the room fondly. "But that's it. Life is what it is. We're going to have to leave."

She went back to the fifty one inch screen and typed a few things in. Numbers and words were still scrolling down. She checked a few other windows then finally said, "No, my password breaker hasn't broke through to i-ogle yet."

"Does that mean you can't help us, then? Sorry about this, Lisa."

"No it's all fine. You don't realise, I can access all this remotely. And I have three other server farms, too. Hire them out for various things, you know, film companies, universities, climate organisations, government agencies. This is the smallest of the lot. But it's kinda handy cause there's no paper trail and nobody knows I own it."

Her phone rang.

Roman's voice said, "Rock-a-bye baby."

"Good job Roman. Come on, peeps, lets get going."

Lisa went to a cupboard at the very back of the room and pulled out two white coats. There was a gurney folded up in there as well, which she unfolded. "Unfortunately our friend is not very well. Most likely the effects of some... unprescribed sleeping medication. You're paramedics now, did you know that?" She gave out the two coats to Natasha and Nathanael.

Lisa opened the door, letting Natasha and Nathanael leave first, then pushed out the gurney. They took the gurney.

Lisa said, "Wait. Give me your car keys. I'll get Roman to drive your car back to my place in South Mountain Business Park, which is where we're going."

Nathanael passed the keys over.

Lisa opened an app on her phone. She clicked a button on the app and the door to the server farm slid closed. "Run," she said. "Paramedics are always in a hurry."

As they ran along the corridor pushing the gurney, she ran behind them saying, "The minute that room is compromised, it all goes up in smoke. Every processor, every piece of RAM, every Solid State, every 3D Xpoint drive in there will be fried. They won't get a single bit of information out of it."

When they reached the café, Roman was standing next to Liverpool, slapping the gunman's face. He wasn't responding.

Lisa handed him the car keys. "Roman. After you close up, drive ahem - my - ahem - car, to the server farm in South Mountain Business Park."

He took the keys and nodded.

Natasha and Nathanael lifted the gunman onto the gurney and pushed the gurney back out through the rear of the café. Lisa followed them. Once they were out of earshot of the guests in the café, Lisa put on a pair of latex gloves and reached into the gunman's jacket pocket and gingerly took out his gun, wallet and mobile phone. Lisa told Nathanael, "Check him for any other weapons."

Nathanael checked him thoroughly. He said, "Nothing. What are we doing now?"

Lisa said, "You don't seem to get it - I planned for this a long time ago. I've got a van out there. We'll slip him into the back."

They exited through a door past the café toilets. A white van was parked there. Lisa opened the rear doors of the van and they rolled the gurney in.

She offered some latex gloves to Nathanael. "Put these on."

Then she gave him the gun. "Know how to use one of these?"

He nodded.

She said, "You better sit in there, case he wakes up."

Nathanael climbed in the back of the van next to the gurney and Natasha got in the front with Lisa.

Lisa pressed a button on the dashboard and Natasha heard something flip at the front of the van. "What's that?"

"Flips the number plate. It's a rectangular prism. Four possible number plates. Makes it more difficult for the van to be tracked. I've just reset it to the usual one."

She drove out of the carpark, onto the road.

After a few minutes, she turned into a carpark and parked for a few minutes. She gave Natasha a hat and a wig and put one on herself.

Then she slipped into another bay and flipped the number plate, then exited back onto the road and flipped it again as they went under a bridge.

"That should confuse anyone from the NSA who's watching us, at least for a bit. Hold on." She operated her hands free and a number rang.

Roman's voice said: "Baying Wolf Café. Roman speaking."

Lisa said, "Close up shop, Roman. Get the customers out. Tell them there's been a death in the family."

Roman said, "What about tomorrow?"

"Look, there might be some legal problems to sort out. I'll pay you four weeks' pay in advance. If I haven't sorted the problems by then, you go and get another job. But as far as the café goes, don't go back there unless I say! I can't accentuate that enough."

"Can I look for another job in the meantime?"

"Of course you can. You can keep the four weeks' too if you find one."

"Thanks, Lisa. You're a generous lady."

The call ended and Lisa said, "Well, that's that I guess. Unless we can get all this sorted."

Natasha said, "Where to now?"

"One of the other server farms. I can control the café server farm remotely from there, until they either break in or give up." She was silent for a moment as she turned a corner.

"You know, this is what I always feared would happen, ever since Aaron was arrested. Thank God I prepared for it. And now that it's happening it doesn't seem as bad as all that."

Nathanael was watching the gunman sleep on the gurney.

Suddenly the gunman moved, just slightly, flicked a few fingers, then his eyes blinked. Then his mouth opened just slightly. Nathanael thought he heard him groan.

Was it just his imagination?

Or was the gunman waking up?

STONEHOUSE RESTAURANT, SAN YSIDRO RANCH, MONTECITO, CALIFORNIA

Leo was sitting in the Stonehouse Restaurant at San Ysidro Ranch at his private table waiting for Raymond to arrive, sipping his favourite wine.

This had better be good.

Raymond was going to tell him what it was all about today. Leo had been through a lot and didn't have any patience for stupid ideas. Making the film had not been easy and Leo had a lot of expenses. Maintaining Bretta was not cheap and he couldn't afford another divorce. Hopefully Raymond was coming to him with a good business opportunity.

He looked around at the place. The trees, with those silly little lights. Why did they do that? Leo thought it looked stupid, but then again, it was the place to be seen, which was the only reason he ate here. He didn't like the food much.

It wasn't bad.

He sipped his glass.

Ah, 1997 Screaming Eagle Cabernet Sauvignon. Leo's favourite wine. He swirled it around in the glass, such a rich red lustre. A truly exceptional wine. Robert Parker had given it a mark of 100. Leo had only two more bottles left at the house. This was the third last one.

He wasn't sure he wanted to waste it on Raymond, after all, the man could afford his own wines. He was a multi-billionaire. Still, Leo wanted to impress him and make him feel welcome.

Raymond walked in, right on time.

Leo stood and pulled his chair out for him. "There you are, Raymond."

"Thanks Leo."

"1997 Screaming Eagle. You want a glass?"

"No thanks, don't drink."

Leo rolled his eyes and thought, well, so much the more for me.

Raymond said, "And if you ask me, you probably should cut down a little yourself."

"Why?" said Leo, not really wanting to hear the answer.

"Because you're about to make a big announcement."

"I beg your pardon?" said Leo, looking at the glass. Was there something in this stuff affecting his hearing? "I thought you said, I'm about to make a big announcement. What kind of announcement would I be making?"

"That's what I said."

Leo poured himself another glass and drank it in one gulp.

"How would you know?"

Raymond said, "Because."

Leo was completely puzzled. "What sort of announcement?"

THE FÖLDVÁRI ALADÁR CAVE, HUNGARY

The voice shouted again, it was a man, Peter realised, speaking in what sounded like an educated English accent, "Peter! Meth! Don't worry, it's alright." Peter was certain he didn't know who it was.

Meth shrank back into the alcove they had been hiding in.

Peter said, "I'll go and see who it is. No, maybe I shouldn't."

Then the voice shouted again, "Hello! My name is Martinus. Orsolya sent me. She told me to tell you - this phrase - twinkle little csillagom, little starbug."

Meth's eyes lit up. "Orsolya used to say that. I don't think anyone else would have known that. She told me she made it up for me."

Peter sighed a sigh of relief. He said, "We're coming." He started packing everything away. "Come on, Meth, let's go."

The light of a torch appeared. It shone in their eyes and dazzled them so that they covered their eyes with their hands, so he averted the beam. "Sorry," he said, and immediately became visible. He was about forty five years old with a friendly, mustachioed demeanour. He smiled. "My name is Martinus. I am Istvan's brother. My English is good, yes? I went to school in England for two years, when I was young. Orsolya sent a message to me to come here and see if you're here, when you didn't arrive at Istvan's yesterday."

Meth said, "It could only be Martinus. Orsolya described him to me. She said he went to school in England."

"Come on out. I have my car. Quickly, who knows

whether they have drones watching this area?" He looked up. "They might be high up in the sky, too high to see them. We must be quick."

Both Meth and Peter found it hard to walk and Martinus had to help them. Peter held the plastic above them as they walked, in case a satellite or drone was watching.

They came out into a dazzling light and it was not until Peter had walked all the way to Martinus' car that he realised it was moonlight. It was not even day time.

Martinus helped them to get in and put their luggage in the boot.

"Thank you," said Peter. "How long were we in there for?"

"Four days," said Martinus, hopping in the car. He said, "We sit in the car for a little while. Fifteen minutes, or wait until another car goes past, confuse them. I believe their satellites can see the car exhaust. By the way, Orsolya told me everything that was going on. I wouldn't have believed if it wasn't her telling me."

Peter said, "It's hard to know who to trust, but she seems trustworthy." Saying this, he suddenly doubted and wondered why he had trusted anybody.

"Very trustworthy," said Martinus.

Peter sighed. Of course Orsolya was trustworthy, and if so, then so was Martinus and his brother.

Martinus handed them water, a thermos filled with warm coffee, and some sort of dumplings wrapped up in a tea-towel. They ate and drank gratefully.

Finally Martinus started up the engine.

It took about forty minutes to drive to Lipovnik.

Martinus turned into the town centre, went past the church and then parked in front of the gate of one of the houses opposite the church with the engine running. The house was covered in white plaster which had broken off in places, revealing the bricks beneath. There was a dirt track leading to an old wooden shed at the back and an old paint-spattered ladder leaning on the house.

Martinus got out of the car, opened up the gate, got back in, drove onto the dirt track a little way, got out again and closed the gate behind him, then drove along the dirt track to the shed. Again he got out, opened the shed door, parked the car inside the shed and then closed the shed door before opening Meth and Peter's car doors.

"I was worried about drones and satellites," he said. "If you are underneath the clear sky they can see where you are, they will know where you are. We don't want anyone to know you are here. These Americans, we once thought they were the friends of freedom, but now they have drones and satellites watching us. Is this how friends behave?"

The shed was lit by a single globe hanging from the ceiling that Martinus must have bumped when he got out of the car, because it was still swinging.

Martinus said, "I'll get your luggage, come through. Oh, put these on." He gave them both hats from a hat rack at the back then led them out of the shed door.

For a moment they were under the clear sky, just for a moment, as they went from the shed to the back door of the house. Peter doubted that it was long enough for drones or satellites to pick up that it was them, even if they had some sort of computer image search or something, since they were wearing their hats.

A gregarious, well-padded man with a full beard and moustache met them at the back door as they were coming in. "Hi! I'm Istvan. Peter, Meth, how are you? Come in. There is a meal on in the oven. We'll eat soon. Come into the kitchen."

He led them through a plastered corridor into an open room with a large table and six chairs. Everything in the house looked old and worn out, but the scent of roasting pork filled the room. The wood stove had a flue above it that led up to the chimney. On top of the stove sat a boiling pot of water. "Sit down. Cup of coffee? Keveredes? I have a kettle on the boil." Peter said, "Yes please, keveredes." Orsolya had made the delicious beverage for him in Szalonna, a mixture of milk, coffee and honey.

Peter said, "Perhaps some hot chocolate, or a glass of hot milk and honey, for Meth? No coffee, though, for the boy."

"Certainly," said Istvan. As he was pouring the steaming keveredes he said, "I don't usually like foreigners, but you two have suffered just like Hungarians suffer. You know I always knew, I always told Martinus, we cannot trust the Americans. Now they are spying on everybody. These foreigners just try to take over our country. First the Mongols, then the Turks, then the Habsburgs, and the Germans, then the Russians. The Americans take over by stealth instead, they come here and spend lots of money and control our economy and now they are spying on us with their drones and satellites and invading our borders. Always the foreigner tries to bend us to their will. But we are Hungarians."

Strangely Peter found this tirade comforting, an assurance of Istvan's trustworthiness.

Meth said, "But I thought we were in Slovakia here?"

Peter frowned but Istvan waved his concerns away. "He is just a child. How should he know? This part of Slovakia, Meth, should be part of Hungary. There are many Hungarians living in Lipovnik. It used to be part of Hungary, the border was once in a different place. This whole town a hundred years ago was a Hungarian town. But this is what happens to our country. If they cannot defeat us all at once they do it in a slow, patient way." Then he added, "They're not too bad, the Slovaks here in Lipovnik, though. We get on well. None of us likes the outsiders. And at least we can get the Hungarian television stations here near the Southern border." He turned to Meth, "You know Frédi és Béni?"

Meth said, "No, who is that?"

"The Flintstones. A cartoon. Our poet József Romhányi translated the English dialogue into poetry. It is very clever. Come, I have it on video. Orsolya told me you understand our language. I am sure you will enjoy it."

And Istvan sat Meth down in front of the television in another room, and soon Meth was absorbed in watching the cartoon. Istvan came back in and sat at the table with Peter. "Dinner will be ready soon," he said. "And Martinus should be back in a moment. He's just gone shopping."

Peter said, "I really want to thank you for all your help. I really do appreciate it."

Istvan nodded.

A few minutes later Martinus came in with a cardboard box full of shopping.

He said, "I saw a drone. Near the Jana store, about twenty feet up." He looked at Peter and nodded. "You and Meth must not go out in the open. You can stay here, as long as you need to."

Peter said, "Look, I have money. We're going to pay our way."

Istvan said, "Don't be ridiculous. You are our guests."

Peter said, "I'm not being ridiculous. I don't want to seem rude but I can see very clearly that people in Hungary - and Slovakia - are not very well off. I would feel terrible if I thought we were freeloading on you. You must accept my payment. I insist on paying you at least the same amount as we were paying in Szalonna for our rent, if not more, and I know full well what our living expenses were as well, so I'm going to make sure you and Martinus are not out of pocket because of us, not even one penny. For goodness' sake, Istvan, you must let us pay our own way." Peter counted out some bills. "Look, here's the first month in advance. Please don't insult me by complaining."

Istvan's expression was somewhere between bemusement and a frown, but he took the bills, saying, "Alright, alright, Peter. You can pay. Thank you. You are right. We are not rich."

SOUTH MOUNTAIN BUSINESS PARK, PHOENIX, ARIZONA

Nathanael was watching the gunman, trying to see if he was waking up or not.

Right now he was motionless on the gurney.

But Lisa was driving rather manically, and the gurney was bumping to and fro as they careened around the corners.

Then the man actually gave a clearly audible groan.

There was a small window into the cab. Nathanael opened it and said, "Drive a bit more carefully, he's waking up."

Lisa said, "Don't worry. He would have had enough flunitrazepam to put a horse to sleep."

The gunman groaned again.

Nathanael said, "He is waking up."

He stirred, tried to turn over, but his arms were tied to the bed.

Nathanael said, "Did you check that he had actually finished his coffee?"

Lisa said, "Well that was Roman's job. I don't know if he checked. I would expect so." Then she paused and said, "I really don't know. Maybe not."

The gunman moved, he definitely moved. Then he groaned again, seemed to be trying to shake himself awake. Or maybe that was just Nathanael's imagination.

Nathanael said, "Of course, it might be a paradoxical reaction."

Lisa said, "What's that?"

The gunman was groaning loudly. He was definitely moving now, his eyes were still closed, but his movements were becoming agitated.

Nathanael said, "Some sleeping tablets - particularly benzodiazepines - can have the opposite effect, causing agitation, sleeplessness, anxiety, aggressiveness, disinhibition, and violent behaviour."

The gunman sighed and went back to sleep.

He began breathing peacefully and regularly.

Nathanael said, "Oh, okay, that's fine. He's asleep now."

Suddenly his eyes opened and he tried to sit up. The restraints on his arms were stopping him. He pulled at them, struggled against them. His eyes were fully open now and the muscles on his neck were contorted with the effort.

It surprised Nathanael so much he stumbled backwards and shouted, "He's awake! He's awake!"

Lisa said wryly, "Well if he wasn't already he is now, what with all the racket you're making."

Nathanael lifted up the gun and said, "Stop struggling."

The gunman swore at him.

At that moment Lisa said, "Nearly there." The van rounded another corner at high speed and Nathanael's elbow bumped against the wall involuntarily and he lost his grip on the gun. The gunman shook the gurney, very hard, and he flipped it over onto its side, giving a huge "oomph" as he hit the van floor.

Liverpool tried to grasp the gun, which was just inches away from his hand, but the restraint kept his hand from reaching it. He shook the gurney again with his whole body and inched closer to the gun, but Nathanael saw what was happening and dived over him, tumbling into the other wall of the car just as they went around another corner. The gurney with the gunman still tied to it and the gun all went careening over to the right hand side of the car.

The gunman exhaled and wriggled towards it.

Nathanael was slipping backwards, but he pushed his feet against the left wall and propelled himself towards the gunman with a sigh of effort. Nathanael grabbed the gunman with both hands by the shirtfront and flipped him right over, crashing him into the left hand side of the car, then kicked him in the stomach and used the impetus to push himself towards the gun which was still resting next to the hump where the right rear wheel hub was.

They went around another corner and the gun slid towards Nathanael, but he had been reaching for it and now it had moved and he had to move his hands to try and get it. The gunman was sitting on the floor of the van, wheezing for a moment.

Nathanael grabbed for the gun - it was so close! - but the gunman and the gurney were suddenly on top of him and the gunman was rolling over, he had grabbed the barrel of the gun with his hand. The gunman exhaled again, a sound like a steam engine puffing out mist. Nathanael saw and reached out, gripped the stock and put his finger through the trigger. The gunman still had the barrel in his hand and tried to twist it away but Nathanael had a strong grip on it and kept hold.

The car stopped and they both slid towards the front.

The gunman said, "You wouldn't shoot."

Nathanael said, "Try me. I think if I shot you now I'd put a hole in your hand. But that wouldn't kill you. Not right away. It would be pretty painful though. Probably cripple your hand."

The gunman thought better of provoking him and moved his hands away in a gesture of submission and said, "What does it all mean anyway? It's all meaningless. You shoot me, I shoot you, we're all going to die one day."

Nathanael nodded at him as if to say, what do you know? But then he stood up, keeping the gun trained on him, and the gunman sat himself up as well as he could on the gurney with his hands slightly raised and said, "Alright, alright, a live dog's better than a dead lion, isn't it?"

OFFICES OF THE WASHINGTON POST, ONE FRANKLIN SQUARE, WASHINGTON D.C.

Leo Bos was standing at a perspex sheet, or maybe it was glass, on the edge of the upper mezzanine looking out over the Washington Post offices, an open plan office full of reporters tapping away at their computers, speaking on mobiles, penning notes and clicking through websites.

He tapped on the transparent sheet and realised it was probably tempered glass.

He was waiting for two reporters, Michael and Jenny, he knew them well, they had interviewed him before.

Still, he had nerves. What if he said something ridiculous? Occasionally Leo's mouth ran away from him. And sometimes, like with those annoyingly pesky climate denialists, he was left with nothing to say, when they bombarded him with data or flummoxed him with facts. Not because he didn't have the answers. I mean, it was obvious, climate change was happening. I mean, look at the terribly cold winters we've been having. That is the climate changing.

They thought he was there to announce the new movie. But he had other plans. Plans that Raymond Adamant had brought to birth.

Adamant not only had the funds and the desire to help, he had the online reach. The i-ogle search engine, i-ogle video and the social media platform Ioglebook were now the most popular on the internet, with Adamant's help they had surpassed google in the last three months, so i-ogle, more than any media organisation or television station or news aggregator, had the power to influence people.

And Leo had the truth on his side. The truth about

global warming. And this was something that most people still believed in, despite the inroads the deniers and the tea party had made at the far right, Leo was convinced that most reasonable, rational people still believed in global warming.

Leo was looking through the crowds downstairs for them. Michael, a grey haired, bearded man of about fifty. He thought he could probably recognise Michael from the top of his head. And Jenny, a petite, neatly dressed woman in her early thirties, if she was there he would see her brown hair, her power suit. But they were nowhere to be seen.

A cadet journalist, or perhaps some sort of aide or office boy, came out from one of the offices. He spoke in a soft, breathy voice. "Mr Bos, they're ready for you now. Please follow me."

He followed him down a corridor and he opened the door to the office. Leo went in.

It was a sparsely-but-pleasantly decorated lounge. Three plush, comfortable seats were arranged around a coffee table. Michael and Jenny were already sitting in their seats, ready to begin taking notes. Jenny had some sort of device as well, a dictaphone or something, or maybe it was a mobile phone with some sort of microphone plugged into it.

Jenny said, "Welcome, Leo. Would you like anything?

A cup of coffee? Water?"

"Just water thanks," said Leo. "A jug of water. Not a plastic bottle." He laughed. "Can't have anyone seeing me drinking from a plastic bottle." Neither Jenny nor Michael laughed, which seemed to be a bad start. Jenny noted something on her pad.

She started the recording device.

Jenny said, "Relax, Leo. We're on your side."

He relaxed a little. Thank Gaia (his little joke to himself, Raymond had told him the voters prefer God), they wouldn't ask him any awkward questions about figures, or where the missing heat was. Leo had never understood how the missing heat could end up hiding in the deep ocean, when at high school he had been taught that heat rises.

"Listen," said Leo, trying to assert his power in the situation, "I've got an announcement to make. It's not on the film topic. It's something else. It is the reason - I wanted you two to be the first to have this news - I wanted you to break it."

Jenny raised her eyebrows.

Michael said, "Well. That certainly is interesting. Go ahead, Leo. We're all ears."

"I'm running for President. Americans need someone

in the White House who believes in climate change and will do something about it. Americans need a champion for those who will be poor and the dispossessed in the future because of climate change. People shouldn't underestimate me. I might not be the greatest Twitter user, I may not be good at disseminating chaos, but at least I am a credible candidate with prior experience as a governor and in the White House."

Jenny said, "Wow. That is big news."

And Michael said, "Wow."

SOUTH MOUNTAIN BUSINESS PARK, PHOENIX, ARIZONA

The back doors of the van swung open. Nathanael backed out and stepped down rather clumsily onto the ashphalt, keeping his eyes on the gunman and his finger on the gun's trigger.

He glanced to the side. Lisa and Natasha were standing there, holding the van doors open for him.

Lisa climbed into the van with a pair of scissors and cut the ties holding the gunman's arms to the gurney. She ordered him, "Turn around." But he didn't immediately obey so Nathanael jiggled the gun and said, "Do what she says."

The gunman turned around, allowing Lisa to put some plastic snap ties on his hands, like handcuffs, but he said, "You do realise this is kidnapping? And I've seen your faces."

Nathanael said, "Well you're not smart are you? Do you really think that is commending the idea that we let you live?"

He scoffed. "You're not a murderer, mate."

Lisa pulled him backwards by the snap ties, suddenly, so that he stumbled backwards and rolled out of the van. "Owww!" he said.

Nathanael saw Natasha wince as the gunman's head bounced on the ground, but the man was tough, he lifted up his head immediately and spat out, "That hurt!"

Lisa kicked him savagely and said, "I'm not your mate. Never say that. You made yourself my enemy."

The gunman lay still for a moment but it was just a ruse, because when he thought no one was looking he immediately gazed over their surroundings, examined the ashphalt floor, the elegant post-modernism of the car-park architecture, and Nathanael thought he had noticed what Nathanael had noticed, that there weren't any other cars in this particular car-park. A private car-park. Only a limited number of buildings have those in Phoenix.

The gunman said, "We in some basement car park of some building or other, are we?"

Lisa said, "You talk too much," and rummaged in her handbag. She took out a stocking filled with sand and said, "This has been sitting in my handbag getting grains of sand in everything. If you don't want me to justify my decision to bring it by thumping it against your left temple, shut up."

He said insolently, "Why my left temple in particular, mate?" But Lisa thumped the makeshift codger against her hand and he shut up then.

They dragged him to the elevator. Lisa used her foot to shove him in and Natasha and Nathanael went in after him.

Lisa pressed the button for the top floor.

As the lift went up, Lisa took out a roll of black gaffer tape and taped up the gunman's mouth.

The lift opened at the top floor and they got out. It was the top mezzanine level and was apparently completely deserted.

There were several offices and conference rooms.

Lisa said, "I got everybody out; sent a text message to my assistant saying I needed the top level to myself for a few hours. Advantage of holding the controlling share in the company. Actually, I hold ninety seven percent of the shares and own the building, they just lease it from me, but that's another story."

Lisa led them to a particular office and Natasha and Nathanael each carried the gunman in by the arms.

It was sparsely and tastefully decorated with a large desk and an enormous window with a view of the tops of trees in the park waving pleasantly in the breeze and the skyscrapers, pale purple in the distance, a bar fridge and a small stereo system that was on standby.

Lisa closed the door behind them and got out a role of masking tape. She began taping his limbs to a chair positioned in front of the desk, facing the office door.

Lisa checked the door was locked, even though she was the one who had locked it, then ripped the masking tape off his mouth.

He coughed out a shocked, pained exhale, then started crying out, "Help! Help! Somebody help me! I've been kidnapped! Help! Help!" excruciatingly loudly. But after about thirty seconds of relentless shouting he stopped to take a breath.

Then he asked in an almost comically quiet voice, "Why isn't anybody coming?"

Lisa gave a funny sort of half-smile. "Because nobody can hear you, buddy."

He said, "My name's not buddy. If I can't call you mate, you can't call me buddy. It's not fair." He was whining now in a fretful, abject tone of voice. "Why can't anyone hear me?"

Lisa didn't look at him as she spoke, "This room is thoroughly sound-proofed, completely insulated, and checked for bugs and listening devices daily, I might add. To protect against corporate espionage, actually, but it certainly comes in handy for other uses. For instance, hiding my hacking from prying company eyes."

She took out a laptop from her desk, opened it up and typed for about thirty seconds.

Natasha took out her mobile phone and opened the camera app and turned it onto video.

Lisa examined the computer screen and said, "The hack is still going. Not a lot to show yet. But now... Let's see what this guy has to say for himself." She opened the drawer of her desk and pulled out a staple gun.

Lisa said, "It's amazing how useful staple guns are." She pointed the staple gun at the guy's testicles, pushing the business end right against the crotch of his pants.

"Fair go," the gunman said, "That's molestation what you're doing now."

Nathanael winced and Natasha said, "Don't do it. Please don't do it. I can't bear to watch."

"What?" said the gunman. "What is that she's got pointing against my nuts? What is it? An electric cable or something? Come on, this is torture."

Natasha grimaced and said, "A staple gun."

He swore. "No, please, don't, I got a wife, she wants to have more kids. If you staple me crown jewels who knows what that will do to my ability to reproduce?"

Lisa said, "I'm not just going to put a staple in them. I'm going to staple your nuts together, as a memento of our meeting today. Then every time you want to bang your testicles together and they're stuck to each other you will remember me. Mate." She held the gun a few inches from his crotch and pressed the button a few times, making staples pop out and bounce off his crotch.

"Oh, no," he cried, "Not me nuts, not me nuts."

"Please don't," said Natasha. "Don't you realise many studies have shown that torture doesn't yield usable intelligence?"

Lisa said, "Yes, but it's fun, Catwoman, real good fun."

Nathanael shook his head. What sort of people did studies like that?

Natasha complained to Nathanael, "I never realised when I communicated online with Beowulf that she was this much of a psycho."

Lisa snickered and the gunman was weeping and snorting with grief. His tone of voice was grovelling, "But I just did this job cause we needed a bit of extra cash for the nursery. My wife's having another child in two months time. And then we're going to try for a third. Please don't injure my bollocks. Please don't." He sobbed, bending over as well as he could in the seat despite the restriction of the gaffer tape surrounding him like a cocoon. "Please, please, don't do it. I'm begging you."

Lisa said, "Alright, alright," then paused, as though wanting him to think she had relented. "You know what would be - ah - fun? Stapling him in the temple. I'd say it would cause bleeding on the brain or something? We could try sticking a pencil in the hole after that, see if it would go all the way through."

Nathanael didn't think Lisa was being serious, but even he wasn't sure. The gunman clearly believed her because he started weeping. "Please don't kill me."

"Who hired you?" said Lisa. "Adamant?"

"Oh, no it wasn't Adamant," the gunman said.

But Lisa popped the staple gun a few times. The staples shot out and reflected from his crotch onto the floor again.

Meanwhile, Natasha pressed "record" on the video app on her phone.

"Alright, alright," he cried out. "It was him. Raymond Adamant. The head of the Adamant Corporation and the owner of i-ogle now. He was the one who hired me to kill you both."

Lisa went to her desk and opened her handbag. She took out the gunman's phone.

She raised her eyebrows at Natasha and said, "Keep recording."

Natasha had turned the recording app off. She turned it back on.

Lisa opened the phone but there was a passcode. She tried "1234" and it worked. "Common passcode," she said, and went to the preferences and put the phone on silent.

Lisa went through the phone numbers in the contacts. Raymond Adamant was not listed. But she looked in the recent call list.

There was a New York landline.

Lisa brought the mobile phone over behind the

gunman. She beckoned to Natasha to bring her mobile closer. Natasha brought it close, so close that the only thing showing in the view-finder was the guy's ear and his mobile phone, held by Lisa just behind his head.

Lisa pressed the last number and it dialed. She nodded at Nathanael and mouthed the word, "Hello."

Nathanael said to the gunman, "Hello?"

The gunman said, "Hello? What?" He looked completely puzzled.

A voice on the mobile phone said, "Hello? Liverpool. Have you done the job yet? Or do you have more excuses? Remember I've got the ones who did in that hacker on my retainer, Plutonium makes a nice Pizza topping, don't you reckon? A little surprise for your evening meal. I'm getting sick of waiting. You need to finish the job or as I said before you'll be on their list of potential customers as well as Natasha and Nathanael."

Lisa raised her eyebrows and did the 'thumbs up' sign. Natasha turned off the video recording and Lisa closed the phone connection.

Lisa said to Natasha, "Did you get that?"

The gunman winced and his whole face scrunched into an expression resembling that famous Edvard Munch painting and he said, "Oh, no. I'm dead meat. I'm a goner. What have you done? I'm going to have to spend the rest of my life on the run. You bitch." He swore coldly.

Natasha said, "Yeh, I got it. And this is a Samsung Note 9, it's got 4K video at 64 frames per second and three microphones that record at thirty two bits eighty eight kilohertz, so we've got stereo with high directionality, in other words, the ability to pinpoint audio sources in three dimensions from the data."

Lisa nodded. "I understand. That's pretty good. Well, what do we do with him now?"

Nathanael said, "Let him go?"

Lisa said, "I think so. He's going to be spending the rest of his life on the run, now. Did you hear how Adamant threatened him?" She swivelled the chair around so he was facing her. "Alright, buddy. This is the facts. We've got this recording now. We'll be uploading it. If anything happens to us it's going public right away. And it will be going public, I can guarantee it, in the next month or so, once we work out what's going on."

The gunman sneered. "I'll just say its a fake recording. They can doctor these things these days you know."

Lisa rolled her eyes. "You obviously are deaf as well

as stupid. That's what Natasha was saying. Yeh, someone could doctor a normal audio recording, but this is three tracks of audio recorded at thirty two bits and a sample rate of eighty eight kilohertz, complete with ambient noise and high directionality. Do you know what that means?"

He shook his head. "No."

Lisa sighed. "It's going to be pretty hard for anyone to say that this was doctored. A forensic audio specialist would be able to determine that this recording is genuine. Particularly with the hum of my bar fridge and the stereo system in the background. Do you realise these days they can analyse the power hum, compare it to the hum of a particular power grid, and use that determine if a recording is genuine?"

He said, "Really?" He clearly didn't understand what Lisa was saying.

Lisa rolled her eyes and said, "You can't reason with these sorts of numbskulls. Physical threats is the only language they understand. I've still got your gun." She put on some latex gloves again and grabbed the gun from Nathanael. "Let's just make sure your prints are on this gun."

The gunman's arms were completely disabled by the gaffer tape, but he could still move his fingers. Realising what she was planning he clenched his fists.

Lisa said, "He was right handed, wasn't he? That was the hand he held his coffee cup in? And the gun?"

Nathanael noticed that his right shirt sleeve had a coffee stain on it. "He spilled coffee on his right shirt sleeve. Probably is right handed."

The gunman said, "No, no, you're wrong, I'm left handed!"

Lisa prised the fingers of his right hand apart one by one and squashed each finger onto the barrel, the handgrip or the trigger of the gun rather carefully, apparently to ensure that the position of the fingerprints would be credible.

Once she had finished, Lisa said, "Right. Now, if you come after us, we will come after you. We will shoot your wife and child with your gun, that still has your fingerprints on it. Then we will leave the gun in a garbage bin in a street nearby for the police to find. Get it?"

He nodded.

Nathanael noticed that Natasha was standing in the corner of the room, looking down at the ground. She didn't look happy. Then he noticed she had the asthma puffer in her hand, with the black dot on the back. She must have had an asthma attack. Oh, that was alright then. He thought for a moment she might have objected to Lisa's rather harsh treatment of their prisoner.

Unless, of course, the stress of that moral contradiction had caused her asthma attack.

Lisa continued, "And if you try anything right now, I'll shoot you in the head at close range. Then after we kill your family we'll dump your body at night at your house with the gun and the police will think you killed yourself, because your fingerprints will be on the gun."

Lisa held the gun on him and directed Nathanael to undo the gaffer tape and the restraints. Nathanael did so. Lisa said, "Put it all in the garbage, quick." Nathanael collected all the rubbish and binned it.

Lisa pressed the intercom button on her desk. A man's voice answered, "Yes, Ma'am?"

Lisa said, "Send security up. I've got an intruder here. I want you to escort him off the premises."

"Yes, Ma'am."

Lisa said, "Unlock the door, Nathanael." Nathanael unlocked it.

Two beefy security guards came into the room about ninety seconds later and escorted Liverpool out of the room, into the lift, and off the premises.

Lisa showed them her laptop screen. The security

cameras followed the guards in the lift, then out through the main entrance of the building and onto the front lawn. The men escorted him to the footpath and pushed him onto the footpath.

He waved his fingers at them, as if to say, untie the luggage straps, but they ignored him and walked back into the building.

Lisa said, "He won't go to the cops. All they have to do is get one fingerprint from him and he's done for."

Then Lisa said, "Oh, yeah, I've just got to delete a few hours of footage." She chose something on the software menus and the security footage began rewinding back to when they had arrived. After a few judicious clicks, the footage showed nothing but blank space for several hours, from when they had arrived to the moment the guards had arrived in her office.

Then she said, "Oh, yeah. And I've got to delete me deleting it."

The screen showed the camera in her room, showing Nathanael looking over her shoulder and Natasha in the corner, still not looking happy. It went blank as well.

Nathanael went over and put his hand on her shoulder.

Natasha turned around and said to them, "I don't know if I like all this. Making threats and promising violence and suicide against people's families."

Nathanael said, "That guy was going to kill us, Natasha. What Lisa did was justified."

"Still," said Natasha, rounding on him with a frown and almost shouting, "We've never behaved like this in the past. We've always kept our integrity."

"Well I'm sorry," said Lisa sarcastically. "I'm sorry I saved your worthless ass and slightly compromised your precious integrity in the process."

Natasha looked at her. "Well, it's just that we haven't compromised before this. You know, kidnapping, threats, extortion, it's a bit different from how Nathanael and I have run things in the past."

Lisa said, "Haven't you heard about the philosophy of the Royal Navy? Haven't you seen Master and Commander? You must always choose the lesser evil. I think threatening a contract killer's family is the lesser evil than killing him or even allowing him to kill one of us."

Natasha said, "It's a bit too close to 'doing evil so that good may come of it' for my taste."

Lisa said, "Well, excuse me, little princess, that you

can have the luxury of moral standards now, considering all this is happening because you hacked i-ogle's servers and stole some private documents, activities that - the last time I heard - did not exactly fall into the domain of either legal or ethical, CatWoman Fourteen."

Natasha nodded and looked at the ground and her voice seemed suddenly small and far away to Nathanael. "I was worried that this would happen. Once you backslide a little you find that you're suddenly falling into a huge pit. Once you cross one line, you end up crossing another, and another, and before you know it you don't know which way is up." She glanced at Nathanael in a way that he found particularly engaging, if you asked him he wouldn't have been able to say why, and said in a determined tone of voice, "I need to go to church this Sunday."

He nodded. "Alright." He reflected that he wasn't sure if this tender morality of hers was a strength or a weakness. Probably a strength, he decided. It was why he loved her.

And Natasha said to Lisa, "I'm sorry I was critical of you, Lisa. You have helped us and saved us and I'm not even sure the police could have done more."

Lisa jutted her chin forwards and said, "And I kept that guy alive, which is what you wanted. Don't forget that."

Natasha pressed her lips together and said, "Thank you."

Lisa bent down at her desk and looked at her laptop, "Look, we've got some work to do. First we've got to back up your phone, get the uncompressed video-and-audio files uploaded onto a few cloud servers somewhere and make some sort of provision for releasing them if anything happens to us. And I think the i-ogle hack might be getting somewhere. Something is coming down the line, a file of some sort, very slowly. At about 240 kilobytes per hour. I'd say it's coming straight out of the RAM, via the machine code. But it's coming through. And I think it's the same as that file you showed me. But with any luck, we've got the complete version."

Natasha nodded.

A notification dinged on Lisa's computer.

Lisa said, "Oh, and look. TG has sent me some big news."

Natasha said, "Who is TG?"

Lisa said, "I wouldn't have a clue. Every now and then TG sends me messages, hints if you like."

She clicked the mouse turned the laptop screen towards them.

It was the i-ogle news site.

The headline said, "Leo Bos First Rally For His Presidential Bid At Roosevelt Island New York Next Tuesday - Wants Supporters There!"

Lisa said, "I think we had better be there, don't you? Looks like we're all joining the -"

Natasha said, "I've never been a member of a political party before."

Lisa said, "Well, you won't be. Your alter ego will be." Then Lisa looked at the laptop. "Have you guys got somewhere to stay?"

"Yes," said Natasha. "We're booked into a B and B."

"Well, go home and get some rest," she said. "This file won't have downloaded till Sunday morning. Roman's brought your car here from the café to the public carpark in the basement. Go back to your B and B. Meet me back here in the early afternoon on Sunday and we'll have the whole file by then. Go and enjoy yourselves for a few days."

They went back to the Bed and Breakfast and stayed in until Sunday, doing very little but eat, drink wine, read books and watch Netflix.

Despite the languorous atmosphere, nothing happened between them, and Nathanael didn't push it. He didn't want to alienate her any further, not after that day with Lisa in her offices dealing with the gunman. No, he had behaved badly enough then.

LIPOVNIK, SLOVAKIA

Martinus was in town again shopping for food. Peter wasn't too much bother, but Meth ate a lot, in particular, but who cares? Peter was paying, so it was fine. Everybody loves American dollars.

He paid the cashier and started picking up his boxes.

A man in the line came beside him and spoke in heavily accented Hungarian. He was probably English, Martinus thought. "Hello. You are Martinus? We know you are buying more food than you usually do. Come outside with me."

"No," said Martinus. "I don't feel like it."

He felt something metal being pressed into his ribcage.

The man said, "This is not a request."

Martinus went out of the shop and the man led him to a nearby bench where people wait for buses and told him to sit down.

The man pulled out a mobile phone.

With one hand still holding the gun he managed somehow to unlock the mobile phone and pulled up several photographs.

Martinus studied them.

It was his sister's children, and his sister, who lived in Budapest.

They were not at home and they did not look happy. The children were crying and his sister had rings under her eyes and looked haggard and tired.

"You need to hand over Peter and Meth to us. Then, we will set these free."

<u>*IGLESIA DE CRISTO, PHOENIX, ARIZONA*</u>

The following Sunday morning was the first time Natasha and Nathanael left the security of the Bed and Breakfast place after their adventure with Lisa (a debatable term that neither of them agreed was appropriate to describe the day). Knowing they would be driving to New York they had packed their bags and thanked the lady at the Bed and Breakfast.

As they left they were very careful that they weren't followed and they were both wearing hats and sunglasses.

* * *

As they walked from the church car park towards the church door, Nathanael said, "I'm going to be like that fellow, Lurch, from the Addams family, sticking out like a sore thumb in a church full of normal people."

Natasha asked, "What do you mean?"

In a voice that sounded shaky to his own ears, Nathanael continued, "It's the first time I've been in a church, Natasha, since I was baptised, I reckon. Oh, except for a wedding or two and maybe a funeral. But I think the place will burn down if I go in." He was trying to make it sound like a joke, but it really wasn't.

Natasha turned to him, grasped him by the shoulders, looked him in the eyes and said, "In a strange way, I think you're perversely correct. It's very Australian, that self-deprecating quality. But it's wrong as well. Nathanael, in the Jewish law, if someone touched a leper, he was polluted by that and couldn't attend the temple until he had been officially declared clean."

He felt his face twist and he tried not to let it move, in case his real mixed feelings about this church thing showed through. "What does this have to do with...? Are you saying I'm a leper? You're saying I shouldn't go in?"

Natasha put her index finger on his lips. "No. I'm saying the opposite. You see, it was different after Jesus came. When Jesus touched a leper, the good Lord didn't become polluted. The leper was cleansed instead. We're all lepers, Nathan, morally speaking, in relation to a perfect God. The church won't suffer pollution from you coming into it. If you let Jesus touch you, He will cleanse you instead."

He nodded, none too confidently.

He thought about that day in the office - Natasha's conscience had clearly been troubled by Lisa's treatment of their prisoner and she had protested, and Natasha had declined to join in. But he had joined in quite happily, basically, by approving Lisa torturing the guy. He'd stood there and held the gun for her. Mostly mental torture, but still. He felt as though God ought to judge him, not only for that. For everything.

For his resistance, all his life, towards God.

Funnily enough, despite the fact that he still thought of himself as an atheist, Nathanael had begun to think it was possible, based on the historical evidence, that Jesus really had risen from the dead. After all, the outrageously swift early spread of Christianity, all those martyrs and suffering saints who hadn't seemed to fear death at all, that begged for a logical explanation!

In three hundred years the religion had taken over the entire Roman Empire.

Yes, he could see that the Muslims had taken off in the Middle East in a similar amount of time, but they basically said to all their proselytes, "If you don't believe we'll chop your head off." Understandable, the spread of early Islam.

The outrageous and curious thing about early Christianity though was that the Christians were complete pacifists. They basically said, "We do believe. In fact we believe so fervently that if you chop our heads off we don't care."

Something amazing must have happened, to start all that off. And take the eleven apostles, ten of them died as martyrs. If they had been liars about Jesus being resurrected, or even had significant doubts, then surely a couple of them at least would have come clean before they got executed. Nathanael knew this wasn't a new argument, it was in Pascal's Pensees, but still...

And the New Testament - his friend Bruce, a historian in London, had told him that the criteria for documents to be included in the New Testament was that they had to have apostolic authority. And an apostle was an eyewitness, in fact, Bruce had told him that was exactly how an apostle was defined in Acts of the Apostles, one of the New Testament books.

Yes, Nathanael decided that he believed that it all could be factual. God existed. But he wasn't sure that he personally actually believed in God still. He believed the facts, but did he have faith? What was faith?

He sighed. Here he was, he was going to hear about sin and an angry God, after all, this looked like basically a fundamentalist type of church, and Nathanael knew what a sinner he was. The preacher was going to stand there, listing Nathanael's sins, one after the other, sins he already knew about. He wanted to leave right away, actually, but he couldn't abandon Natasha.

She needed this.

It was his fault she needed to be here.

After all, he might have stopped Lisa from treating that guy that way.

Natasha hadn't kissed him since that night in the car. Was it because she knew what he was really like? He glanced at her and she smiled at him, which encouraged him more than a little. He felt a warm glow in his heart, and that surprised him too.

Nathanael certainly felt out of place standing in the pew next to Natasha. Many of the people here were Spanish. Her family came from India, or Sri Lanka maybe, he wasn't sure. Well, she was just as out of place here as he was.

At least if the service was in Spanish he wouldn't be able to understand it, thank God.

Thankfully the service started with some fairly

pleasant songs with a make-shift band, a guitar, a keyboard, a bass guitar and some kind of oboe or cor anglais and a clarinet, but the songs were in English, and as it happened the service continued in English.

Nathanael was suddenly completely sure that God would speak to him here, and he knew what God would say, that he, Nathanael, was condemned, that he was an unworthy sinner and a hypocrite just to be standing in a church, in other words, that he was going to hell.

But then the Bible reading began. An elderly Latino lady stood up and read in a clear voice, "Romans chapter eight verse one. There is therefore now no condemnation to them which are in Christ Jesus, who walk not after the flesh, but after the Spirit."

The preacher, a short, balding Latino guy wearing glasses and sporting a greying moustache that matched his neat grey suit, stood up and said, "Welcome to everybody today and especially our guests. I'm preaching this verse from Romans today. As you all know, life is full of troubles. As Ecclesiastes says, Vanity of vanities, saith the Preacher, vanity of vanities; all is vanity. The word vanity in the King James Bible is Hebel in the Hebrew, meaning mist, vapour, chaos, breath. Mist, mist. all is mist. Everything is vapour, vanity. This world of trying to get rich and building some kind of legacy and glitz and glamour and getting honour and praise from others, it's all mist, vapour, hebel.

"It says also, 'man is born unto trouble, as the sparks fly upward.' Our lives are brief as a breath. Why should an eternal God care about us? We have many troubles and many would say the presence of suffering in our lives is proof that God doesn't care, that we're stuck on an endless cycle of day to night to day to night to day, a wheel of sorrow and suffering, burdened with poverty, sickness, estrangement, loss, grief, and they would agree that even the glories of this life are emptiness, vanities, honour, reputation, esteem, riches and the like, all vanities. But friends, the worst of our troubles, the fountain of them all is condemnation. The burden of guilt and the belief that we are under the judgement of God. Well here's the good news: Jesus died to take away this burden of condemnation and guilt. On the cross he carried our guilt and our sins and our temptations and our sorrows and our shame and all the abuse we have ever inflicted on others or suffered at the hands of others, he took it all away, and now, my friends, if we believe in Jesus, we do not need to carry these burdens any longer. In Christ Jesus, my friends, the burden of condemnation is done away with."

Nathanael was amazed. The message was the reverse

of everything he had expected. In place of condemnation and a list of sins or commandments to follow, he had found a message of acceptance and forgiveness.

At that moment he realised why he like Natasha so much. That attractiveness in her - that acceptance, that goodness, that gentleness - it all had another, deeper source - her faith in God.

Her faith in Jesus.

That presence of God that he saw within her was the fountain of her goodness.

"Please bow your heads," said the preacher. "This is the time to give your hearts to Jesus if you haven't done so. Surrender your lives to him. Say to Jesus, and repeat after me, I'm sorry for all my sins, Lord Jesus. Please forgive me for them all. Thank you for dying for me on the cross. I give my life to you Lord Jesus Christ, I surrender control of my life to you, I will let you be King, God. Please come into my heart and be King of my life."

To his great surprise, Nathanael found himself praying the prayer. A great, flowing river of peace filled his heart, and he realised he had never in his life felt real peace or satisfaction before this.

Despite the events of the last few days, the last year,

this, he realised, was a truly momentous happening. Far more momentous than anything that had ever happened to him before.

* * *

Straight after the last hymn Natasha went up to the front and spoke to the minister. Nathanael followed her.

"Pastor Carlos," she said, "Do you think hacking is wrong?"

"Well, it's just a different sort of spying isn't it? God specifically appointed Joshua to spy on the Canaanites when the Jews were travelling into the promised land."

"But it's against the law? Aren't Christians required to follow the law?"

"Well, Natasha, it depends on why the hacker is doing it and for whom. Are they hacking someone's computer to spy on them for selfish reasons? Or are they exposing wrong-doing? Bringing things to light that the general public ought to know? Whistleblowers are protected under the law, and even when hackers are not exposing a corrupt society, God sees the motives of their hearts and will not condemn them, if they are Christians. The reason behind what they're doing, what the Bible would say is the motive of the heart, is what makes all the difference.

"A few years ago in Britain a hacker exposed a scientific organisation by releasing their emails. Those scientists were receiving billions of dollars in government funding, and these emails had been requested under FOI, which the organisation kept refusing to release. Turns out they were essentially committing fraud and perverting the peer review process and even talking about destroying data. Releasing their emails was well deserved and the right thing to do in that case. And, I might add, Bradley Manning, Edward Snowden, Julian Assange, are actually heroes and one day will be acknowledged. It's not unpatriotic to desire that your country could do better at living up to its ideals. Citizens need to know what the government is up to, Natasha. Sometimes hackers are doing a service, not a disservice."

"Thanks," said Natasha, and Nathanael thought she looked rather buoyed up by his answer.

"But if I were a hacker," continued Pastor Carlos carefully, rather obviously trying not to imply that Natasha might be talking about herself, "I would not rely on my own wisdom. I would ask Jesus for guidance and help. I would ask the Father to guide me and help me to act justly and not in my own self interest, or for fame or notoriety."

"To be a white hat," said Natasha.

"Not just a white hat," said Pastor Carlos. He smiled, his teeth white against his brown skin, his eyes twinkling bright as diamonds. "But wearing white robes as well. Robes that have been washed clean in the blood of Jesus. This is what all Christians have, they don't have to depend on their own goodness or righteousness. Because they have the righteousness of Jesus Christ." He laughed a breathy laugh, then said joyfully, "It's such wonderful good news."

Afterwards, during morning tea, Natasha said to Nathanael, "You became a Christian at that service, didn't you?"

He nodded. "I gave my heart to Jesus during the prayer. How did you know?"

She said, "I believe I could actually see, in a spiritual way, the peace coming down upon you. You look different, Nathanael, more radiant."

"I feel a wholeness in my life, like the part of me that was always missing is there now."

She nodded. "Where Jesus is, Nathanael, there is wholeness. That's his gift to us. The gift of the cross."

"What now?" he sighed.

She took his hand and reached up and kissed him, very passionately.

He kissed her back, right there in the middle of the

morning tea, for about ten seconds.

"Wow," Nathanael said. He was feeling stunned. "Well, you're certainly giving me a reason to persevere. Would you still be interested in me if I hadn't, you know, said that prayer just now?"

"I was already interested. Very interested. You are the one person I could turn to in my difficulty. You have so many inherent virtues, you're competent, brave, kind. And I know you love me. But I could never marry a non-Christian, Nathanael. No, I just couldn't even date one. It's against God's word."

Whew, he exhaled, she had said the word, 'marry', and he wasn't sure that he wanted to go anywhere near even the thought of marriage so soon after his divorce.

He felt dizzy.

But then again, Natasha was a more forgiving person than his ex-wife had been. Way more forgiving.

That had to be a plus.

She might just be able to put up with his foibles.

And she was a bit younger, too. Quite a lot.

And kind of prettier.

Way prettier, actually, than that shrew.

And everything had changed now. He knew it had.

He was a Christian now.

He could barely believe he had taken that step and didn't really know how it had happened.

Marriage.

He nodded to himself.

It might not be such a bad thing.

Natasha's sister Michelle waltzed up to them and said, "I barely recognised you two in that get up. Sunglasses and hats, Natasha. It's pretty trippy, seeing you here, girl, dressed like that. Very trippy indeed. What's the deal?"

Natasha said, "That whole business with i-ogle is still going on. Please don't talk on the phone about seeing us here or put anything on social media or into a search engine."

"I won't," nodded Michelle, and Nathanael thought there was a tone of 'how stupid do you think I am?' in her voice. She pleaded, "But when will it be over, Natasha? When can things go back to normal?"

"I don't know," said Natasha. "Hopefully soon. But until then Nathanael and I need to keep out of sight. Alright?"

Michelle nodded again. "It's been hard, Natasha, not hearing from you. But I understand. But you can stay here at church for lunch, can't you?"

It turned out that the church had a shared lunch after

morning tea and Nathanael and Natasha stayed to eat. At one o'clock Natasha's phone alarm went off and they both quickly said their goodbyes to Michelle and Pastor Carlos and bundled themselves into the SUV to go meet Lisa at her office.

As Nathanael started the engine, Natasha's phone buzzed.

"It's the TOR message board," she said, opening up her phone. "It's a message from Aaron."

```
Brisa is dead.
```

Natasha's voice broke, "His cat died."

Nathanael said, "Oh no. He was clearly pretty fond of that cat."

Reading the rest of the message, Natasha said, "Gee that's odd."

```
An anchovy pizza was delivered, my
favourite, but I got suspicious because no one
had ordered it. Neither Mum nor Dad nor me.
Despite Mum's protestations of waste I put it
in the garbage but somehow Brisa got hold of
it; she's like that, a naughty cat, really,
always getting into trouble. She started
vomiting and three hours later she was lying
```

dead on the examination table and the vet said
he'd never seen anything like it. He said it
looked like radiation poisoning.

     Tread carefully.

     Squid555

LISA'S OFFICE, SOUTH MOUNTAIN BUSINESS PARK, PHOENIX, ARIZONA

They all held their breath as Lisa opened up her laptop.

"Look," she said, clicking on the security camera feed. It showed some men with a small digger, digging up a portion of the carpark near Lisa's cafe. "The FBI are starting to dig up the pavement outside the server farm. It's only a matter of time before they find the optic fibre cables. Then we're done."

Natasha said, "What about the worm? Is it working?"

Lisa clicked on something else and said dramatically, "Yeah! Look, the worm is more successful than I anticipated. Seven versions of the document have downloaded so far. Another one is on its way. Let's see what we have so far."

She opened up the first document.

It read:

BEL ALGORITHM PROJECT HISTORY

PROJECT DESCRIPTION:

The BEL Algorithm is designed to deal with the most pervasive modern problem in politics - the 24 hour news cycle. Politicians as never before are confrontedPΣ÷"æFÙ¨Ñã]£¾ØN/A¬ΨxØ¿êÛÜ'Ψ8N/A¬±í½CN/AdÌN/A¶Ü¬°ÙΞN/A=LoíΨwFΞ¾ýòN/AÓÖN/AIÁ†ôìN/Aš²JN¡*N/A$Ì²òNN/AΞÌ=ìN/AšÕìN/AÚØN/Ae¿N/AN/AÔu&N/Aª¥ãΩN/AÚ]N/A,ã»¡ÌEΨšN/AC±N/ARÑ¬ÜCN/Adð®ΔNN/A8¿Ê¡eN/Acÿ[9¾d<ìN/A†ÙÒQh½N/APΣ|u±QN/AX¡²'c&ÒœN/AQcN/AN/A&ÙN/AíÿXéN/AÙÜØ¶F<N/Aêý8²Õ¡N/AÛ¾ôÛ¡=EN/AN/A],ÑLN/A'Õ9N/A¬,ìN/A8£ÊXðN/A'hÿd¡&¶êN/A]ÿhN/A£N/API&ªN/A¿hN/AúqÓN/AN/AÑw¡"

The rest of the document was encrypted.

Lisa swore rather effectively. "It's just one of the encrypted copies. One of the others will be complete."

She opened up another document.

BEL Algorithm Project History

PROJECT DESCRIPTION:

The BEL Algorithm is designed to deal with the most pervasive modern problem in politics - the 24 hour news cycle. Politicians as never before are confronted with an unfair microscopic moment-by-moment examination of every single thing they say or do, the kind of analysis no human being could possibly endure without slipping up. In most normal social circles, 'faux-pas' may cause problems for a week or two (unless it has been filmed and shared publicly on facebook, effectively a rarity). In politics, a faux-pas can ruin a whole career.

In other words, there seems to be no way back in the public perception when a politician says or does something inappropriate or embarrassing.

And the fact is, that every human being acts in a socially inappropriate way on occasion. Today we have virtually perfect news coverage of public events.

Technology has made it possible to capture nearly every moment of a public person's public life. ÎoãÒæF[¨ê$Æ£ÊœÑE¼ΣJŽN/AEÜ²-N/AN/A¥|N/A®9N/AΞRIN/AÖÑJ8²¿ãN/AÜÖN/A'"{]ðÛ|ΨÿãN/AΞýN/A¬oª½N/A±Ù*N/AªCvqN/AýΔŽN/AEN/A¥¬'"ô]ðÛ|¾ýCN/AN/A¼v¿N/AíÕòìN/Acô±¶®EΨΔNN/Acô*šΨΩ"J¼&»¡N/AÛÜò-&e»|ð[N/AŒ5ÁIN/AÌ£ÒN/A(ŽΨØN/Au±'"EN/A{Ê¥CÉeN/AdìN/A$RðN/A¶Ó¬*J$oôìN/Ai5'êÉN/A²CN/AN¿±ΩN/AÈÑΩNI¬†C$N/AN/AúÌ=N/A¼ìc†N/A¿]N/A<,cE*N/AP†N/A5<¡N/A8±¬¶²ΞN/A]Ø±íN/AÔΨ¬*N/A$ýN/A

She looked through all the copies they had. So far, none of them had the missing middle section unencrypted.

"We're stuffed," said Lisa. "Look, let's give up, I think they've encrypted the last part, it's always encrypted, we'll never get a copy that shows that middle section unencrypted."

Nathanael said, "Just show me those again. With the creation dates."

Lisa said, "Alright, but there's no point. I'm a computer programmer. I know these things." But she opened each document and showed him where the encryption was, the beginning varied, but the second half of the document was always encrypted.

Nathanael said, "There's a pattern here. Look."

He wrote down the creation time of each file and counted the number of characters that had appeared correctly before the encryption started on each one.

1:20am - 207 characters

7:28pm - 466 characters

1:35pm - 726 characters

7:43am - 985 characters

1:50am - 1244 characters

8:58pm - 1504 characters

2:05pm - 1763 characters

Nathanael said, "Look. There's about eighteen hours eight minutes between each one. It's on a predictable cycle, each time the encryption starts a little later in the document, and exactly where it starts is actually increasing by a linear amount. In fact it's... Either 259 or 260 characters later each time."

"You're right," said Lisa. "Pretty smart. Of course I didn't open them in order, actually, or I'm sure I would have noticed that myself. I think what's happening is that the server decrypts the document every time its about to deliver it online. It could be happening hundreds or even thousands of times every second. We could try and reset the position, I guess, but why mess with success? What we're getting here is the partial decryption each time, like when a wheel on a bicycle looks like its going backwards when it's really going forwards."

"I don't get the connection," said Nathanael. "But what it does mean is that we can predict the next few documents that we will receive. And we know we have up to I'd say about 1900 characters already in Natasha's copy." He quickly noted down a few figures and said, "The next few files will be something like this:"

9:12am - 2022 characters (this is the one coming down now)

2:19am - 2281 characters

9:26pm - 2540 characters

2:33pm - 2799 characters

Nathanael said, "So I'd estimate from what's missing Natasha's original that by the time we have the next four documents, we will have the whole thing."

"Another couple of days," said Lisa. "They've taken possession of my coffee shop, you know. Thankfully it's not in my name. And I was always careful about surveillance around there, it's why I chose that area. I'm pretty sure they don't know who I am. And they still haven't got into the server room. The external power is still on, and the diesel generators are still primed to kick in at full throttle when the power goes off. But, you know, so long as they don't cut the optic fibre cables…"

She looked at her computer again. Something was flashing in the notifications and she opened it.

"Oh. The diesel generators have kicked in now. They've cut off the power. Still, so long as they don't get into the server room or cut the fibres in the next two days I think we have a good chance of getting the whole thing."

Natasha said, "How long will the diesel generators keep your server farm running for?"

"At least seventy two hours. Long enough, barring them actually getting in and the whole thing melting down. Ha! We should definitely be able to get the whole document by the time we're in New York, around the time we're sitting there waiting to watch Leo Bos's first speech! By the way, how are you getting to New York? How long will it take you to drive? I presume you're not flying."

"No, we're driving," said Nathanael. "We have to keep clear of surveillance cameras and passport checks."

Natasha said, "It will take us about thirty eight hours to drive, not counting any sleep time we have."

She handed over two of the tickets to Natasha. "Well you've got to get going, then, don't you? If you leave now you'll be there before dawn Tuesday. Here's your tickets to Leo's speech by the way. Your alter egos are members."

Nathanael looked at the tickets. The name on his ticket was William Bell and the name on Natasha's was Olivia Dunham. He looked at Lisa and raised his eyebrows.

Lisa shrugged. "Alright, alright, hopefully there are no Fringe fans checking tickets at the gate. I'm flying, by the way. You two enjoy the drive, my old bones won't take a thirty eight hour road trip, I'd be so stiff by the end of it you might as well carry a plank of wood out the car at the end. I'll meet you out the front of the park at eleven o'clock. The speeches start at four, but we'll need a good position, right up the front. We need to see what's really happening. We need to see what the news cameras don't tell."

INTERSTATE FORTY HIGHWAY, PHOENIX, ARIZONA

They watched a dust devil whirl the Arizona sand up into the sky. It crossed the highway about twenty yards in front of them, making a truck driver swerve slightly and lose control. Nathanael slowed down until the truck was back in its lane.

It was about the only interesting thing that happened for quite a few hours.

The drive from Phoenix took them through a lot of Arizona country, desert with low shrubs as far as the eye could see. But it wasn't Australian desert, it was different somehow, Nathanael reflected as he drove. The soil was not as red, that was one thing. And the plants were all different.

But he knew Arizona well now.

Nathanael had volunteered to drive for most of the first part of the journey. Natasha had protested but he had said, "I'm used to long drives. Living in Australia, you know, a hundred kilometres is just next door. We don't have a town every three minutes like you guys."

Natasha rolled her eyes. "Every three minutes."

Nathanael pointed out, "And I memorise number plates."

Nathanael wondered about that. Surely Raymond Adamant knew that that gunman was out of touch, or maybe the gunman had contacted Adamant already. Either way, he was certain Adamant would be looking for them now, well probably the NSA was.

But what could he and Natasha do about security cameras and highway surveillance cameras? He was wearing sunglasses and a hat, Natasha had on a head scarf. That was about all they could do. Disguise themselves a bit. But who knows what they could do with facial recognition these days? Apparently the computer programs were getting pretty good at identifying faces even despite such obvious disguises.

Albuquerque was a surprise; it seemed a much less significant town than Nathanael had thought it would be. Maybe Nathanael thought it was significant because of that song, "By the time I get to Phoenix," which was before his time but his Mum used to have it on record and used to listen to it.

It started getting dark as they were going through New Mexico. There seemed to be more hills here, more like benign shapes on the horizon, really.

The highways became particularly monotonous after that. Nathanael kept an eye on number plates but he knew the traffic was very steady so he was bound to see the same plate a few times on the same highway.

Texas was flat again. Nathanael thought Amarillo didn't seem like a bad place to live, or what he could see at night.

They swapped driving a few times, each of them dozing while the other took the wheel. For the first day, though, Nathanael drove a lot longer.

Oklahoma was flat, too. Really flat. But there

were more trees and rivers and it was more fertile, from what Nathanael could see from the highway at four a.m. in the morning.

Then Natasha took over driving again and he fell asleep.

Natasha woke Nathanael up when they were driving through St Louis, because she had decided to pull off the highway. It was daytime now and he was feeling stiff and sore but he had had quite a decent sleep, actually, all things considered. He stretched as well as he could while still in the car.

The part of St Louis they ended up driving through reminded Nathanael of an Australian country town more than a city because all the buildings were on huge blocks of land with wide roads and lots of vacant blocks. It was about eleven in the morning and they hadn't eaten breakfast so she was looking for a café to have brunch in. She found one.

They chose quiches from the display cabinet and watched the staff prepare them in the microwave.

Nathanael took the wheel again and soon enough they reached the state lines for Illinois. It was a much greener state than the others, or perhaps it was just the fact they were going through in the day time. They passed through the city of Indianopolis at about two o'clock in the afternoon.

They stopped again for coffee and a snack in Columbus, at a place called Harvey's Coffee Bistro. As usual, they were very careful what they ordered, only ordering things from the display cabinet that they could see being prepared. It was about five o'clock when they left.

Afterwards Nathanael began reading number plates again. There were none that were the same as any back in Phoenix, he was completely certain of it.

But that didn't guarantee they weren't being followed or watched.

After all, there were cameras all over the place on the freeways, surveillance cameras in every store and gas station that presumably the NSA could hack, and then there were cameras in cars and trucks and even on motorcycles. And then there were mobile phones everywhere. And the NSA was perfectly capable of hacking any one of these and looking through the cameras.

And don't forget the now ubiquitous drones, both government owned and kids' toys and snooping neighbours' drones, all of which could give the NSA pictures, wandering about in the skies like thistle seeds floating on the wind.

Thistle seeds that were looking for them. Bentham's Panopticon was real now, and it was everywhere.

The last twelve hours of their journey were taxing. It was just a matter of enduring. When Nathanael thought about that part of the drive afterwards all he could remember was the incessant freeway street lights passing, the headlights on the other cars in the rear view mirror, a long row of brake lights looming gradually in front of him, the road ceaselessly repeating like some eighties vector graphics video game.

Then a dreamless sleep while Natasha drove that left him feeling unrefreshed when he awoke, then driving some more, then another restless, uncomfortable doze.

The biggest worry he had, that brought him up short, because he was driving when they passed through and he'd forgotten about them, was the toll booths. He paid using a credit card purchased in Phoenix, for which he had given a false ID, but for all he knew they had photographed him in that store as well as here and who knows? A false ID might well raise its own red flag.

He thought to himself, if they were caught, it would be because of the toll booths, but then they were through without incident and he wondered if he was getting unnecessarily paranoid.

It was about five o'clock in the morning when they finally arrived in New York city. It was still dark. The city seemed monumentally huge, the buildings stretched up and for the first time in his life Nathanael understood why the term skyscraper had been invented.

They found a small café to have breakfast and sat silently drinking coffee while their order was being prepared. They hadn't been too careful about what they were eating because they were too tired to worry, but Natasha mentioned it after they had ordered so they watched the guy take the ingredients out of the fridge and he cooked the meal in front of them, so they didn't worry, they just ate.

As they were driving through Brooklyn they went past the Adamant building. Nathanael pointed it out to Natasha.

She said wryly, "So that's where our great enemy lives. Strangely ironic. Nathanael, I read about this tower. There was a big controversy when Adamant's father built it. They demolished a historic building and the planning permission was hard to come by. Most of the councillors did not want the character of the area destroyed by a skyscraper. But somehow Adamant got it through. No one really knows how. Lots of people suspect the councillors were bribed or coerced."

Nathanael said, "What do you think?"

Natasha shook her head. "I wouldn't know. I think Raymond Adamant is mostly full of hot air."

ADAMANT BUILDING, NEW YORK, NEW YORK

Raymond Adamant had been trying to ring Liverpool since at least last Friday; he had lost track because of the preparations for Leo Bos's first public appearance as the contender for the nominations. Maybe it was longer. He chided himself over losing track of that irritating business; it might have been longer than four days.

It was Tuesday now.

Raymond was sitting at his desk, staring out at clouds that were gathering above the New York skyline, thinking of Liverpool's evident absence.

It's so hard to get good help these days.

He had thought maybe Liverpool had taken the weekend off, after all, Raymond knew the man had a family living somewhere round Arizona or something. You know, he might have wanted to watch his son's baseball game or something. Raymond suspected the whole reason Liverpool had taken on this job was to fund a new house or his son's college education or something.

Some people treated family like a god, it was everything to them. Raymond had never seen the point.

Was Liverpool's house in Phoenix as well? He had had him checked out thoroughly by the NSA, easy as pie, when he employed him. He couldn't remember.

But now he was starting to think the guy was missing. Should he get the NSA involved? Why not, they wouldn't care if Raymond Adamant was employing a hit man, they were too involved now, too. It would implicate them thoroughly if he went down.

Who was he kidding? They probably already knew.

Raymond wondered about the other guys. He hadn't wanted to involve them. A bit too messy, this whole Plutonium topping on a pizza thing, had too much potential for causing bad publicity, or at least, conspiracy theories online, which might in the end point back to him.

But maybe they had better poisons than Plutonium? After all, they had done that job in that particular way to make sure all the hackers knew to steer clear of those documents.

He picked up the other phone, the one that wasn't tied to him in any way, and rang the number he had memorised a while back. He had a good memory for numbers.

"Hello?"

Raymond said, "Hi. Are you that Doomsayer guy?"

"Yes I am."

"Stupid name. But you did a job for me a little while ago. A guy called OxyMoron. Just wondering if you could do some more work for me?"

"Yeah? Who?"

"Three people I'm looking at. Guy called Nathanael Wayfarer, a girl called Natasha Chase. And a bloke. I call him Liverpool."

"Yeh, yeh, petty crimes, works the seedy side of Pheonix. I know of him."

"He's an assassin. Well a wanna-be assassin, anyhow. I don't think he's ever killed anyone yet. But he won't be the one who'll give you the trouble."

"Really? Even though..."

"Yeh. He's a little short on smarts. You know? Elevator doesn't quite reach the top floor. One sandwich short of a picnic. No, it's the other two. They're smart and pretty good at evading anyone who wants to get at them. And I want you to get anyone who's working with them, too."

"Well, fine. I'll do what I can. If we can find them, we'll do them."

"No, look, you'll do more than that. I've got access, if you know what I mean. Access."

"Okay. I know what you mean. Access to the system. Well, that would make all the difference."

Raymond looked at his computer screen. "Give me a secure onion address and I'll get my friends to send whatever they can get your way."

"No problem. Look, this will be expensive. You know that."

"Money is not an issue. But privacy is. I want it all done on the quiet. No publicity, not like the other one."

"Okay. Listen, use this site: <u>breathe@ doomsayers7e2y3t89.onion</u>, write it down, doomsayers, one word. Breathe with an e, not breath. Use Tor, don't try and do it on the normal internet, mind, it won't work. I'll give you an invoice and you send through half as a deposit. Then the other half once we've delivered. And an additional fee for any extra players. Oh, it'll be a separate invoice for each job, by the way."

Raymond said, "Alright but you don't get the other half till you've done all three," and put the phone down.

He looked at the time on the clock on the mantlepiece in his office. Well, he guesstimated this would take about an hour to organise. He had to send through whatever he had on Nathanael and Natasha (he thought of them by their first names now, they had caused him so much trouble.) And he had to find Liverpool's real name, it was in a folder somewhere on his computer.

Ah, there. In the folder marked, "Hitter". He was

proud of coming up with that name for the folder because he'd avoided using the term "Hit man". He'd get it all organised quickly, he thought, less than forty minutes.

Leo had his first speech this afternoon and Raymond wanted to be there nice and early.

He wanted to know whether the BEL Algorithm actually worked.

CHAPTER 8 - LISA GREETS A PIZZA

Nathanael and Natasha parked outside a random hotel on Manhattan Island and went in. The prices were a bit steep but the room turned out to be reasonably plush, and they even had Netflix and Fox available on a sixty inch screen, which was the centrepiece of the room. But they were both too tired to watch television.

Natasha set an alarm on her mobile and after showering and changing they both slumped onto the King-sized water bed. Natasha sort of draped her arm over Nathanael, and he went to sleep thinking how nice it was that her arm was there.

At a few minutes before ten o'clock in the morning the alarm went off. Nathanael wanted to switch it off and go back to sleep. Instead Natasha got up and forced him out of bed as well.

After Nathanael quickly changed his shirt they set off for Four Freedoms Park on Roosevelt Island.

They walked down 34th street, a tree-lined street that Natasha thought she had seen in a movie before, and they recognised a few landmarks. When they reached the jetty they caught the Astoria ferry to Roosevelt Island.

On disembarking they were met by airport style security, complete with armed police and a walk-through x-ray machine, which stressed Natasha out, Nathanael could see that. But no one stopped them or asked for identification, and they accepted the names on the tickets without comment.

After that, though, the walk to the park was relaxing and reminded Nathanael of a spot on the southern shore of the Swan River in Fremantle back in Western Australia. They had the East River on their left and green, leafy gardens and relatively tasteful architecture on their right.

It was a beautiful, sunny day and there was a crowd of people, families and individuals, some with flags and banners, walking along the path towards the park - clearly Natasha and Nathanael were not the only ones who had thought of getting there relatively early.

For a little while Nathanael had almost forgotten that they were worried about surveillance, but then he caught himself looking warily at anyone who came within a few yards of them - a habit that he realised was ruining his enjoyment. But there were a lot of people around - it would have been difficult for anyone to do anything to them in a crowd.

Natasha was worried too. She said, "I keep looking around for someone watching us or someone with a syringe or something. I feel sort of hyper-aware of everyone and I flinch if someone walks too close."

"Me too," said Nathanael. "It's post traumatic stress disorder, basically, isn't it? With everything that we've been going through, we can't relax. We've got to keep aware and alert, and everything becomes a potential threat. It is natural, really, though, a part of our innate defence mechanisms." He exhaled deeply. "It's an undeniable fact that it will take us both a while to adjust to normal life again." He breathed another puff of air out and said, "Of course, that's assuming we win out in this." He paused for another moment. "Do you know, though, it's strange. I'm not afraid of death now. I always have been, in my life, you know? But now I have a sense of an underlying peace, a sense of... Jesus' presence with me."

Natasha nodded. "I know what you mean."

Nathanael continued. "And I've been wanting to read the Bible. That's kind of weird, because it was a chore beforehand."

Natasha said, "I don't know where you found time."

"Just while you were driving, I was reading it on my phone. I've got an app."

Natasha said guiltily, "I should read mine more often."

They reached the park. It was surrounded by a makeshift fence and armed guards. They went through security again, and a volunteer marked their tickets but didn't bother checking any other identification.

Once they were through, though, they found Lisa quickly. She was standing near the entrance wearing a "Leo Bos for President" T-shirt and she had some more T-shirts and some hats for Natasha and Nathanael as well.

The very front, right near the stage, was already taken by supporters, mostly young couples with families and what looked like a few newly married gay couples, sitting on blankets. They were all well prepared and had coffee flasks and picnic baskets and coolers and looked as though they had been there all day.

Nathanael approached one of the families and offered two hundred dollars for his spot. The father looked at it and shook his head. "We've been waiting here since nine o'clock this morning. Well actually, since six o'clock but security wouldn't let us through until nine. Money can't buy this spot. We love Leo Bos." Nathanael took out another hundred and the man looked at his wife and said, "That would pay for the air conditioner in the lounge to be fixed," and she said, "Alright. I feel bad about receiving money for this, though," and Nathanael said, "Well, donate some of it to the party." And they looked at each other and it was clear that was the last thing they would do.

So Natasha, Nathanael and Lisa ensconced themselves right next to the stage. Lisa had brought a blanket for them to sit on and had her laptop with her.

Nathanael slept for most of the afternoon, with Natasha cradled next to him. Despite the warm day, he was tired enough to have a sound sleep.

Lisa woke them up at about three fifty five. "Leo Bos's here," she said. They watched the motorcade arriving at the security gate behind the stage. There was a gap between the poster and the stage at eye-level and they had a tantalising glimpse of Leo Bos getting out of the car and walking over.

Everybody was wearing the campaign hats they had given them at the gate except for Natasha and Lisa, but Nathanael had found the battery in his campaign hat and had ripped it out. He had offered to do the same for Natasha but she had refused to wear the hat no matter what.

Leo Bos walked onto stage and a great cheer started, right at the back of the park, and travelled all the way along until the entire park was cheering. Suddenly everyone was standing up, clapping.

"Pretty good," said Lisa, "The man's got a standing ovation and he hasn't even said anything yet. Maybe those hats are working. By the way, Natasha, your mobile - that fancy one with 4K and three microphones - does it connect to the internet?"

"Not any more," said Natasha. "I took out the chip when all this started. It only connects if I've got a cable connecting it to something else that's connected. I can still set up a hotspot though."

"Smart girl," said Lisa. "You've got it with you?"

"Yes," said Natasha. "I should film this, don't you think?"

Lisa gave her the thumbs up. "Exactly what I was thinking."

Natasha took out her mobile and started filming.

Leo Bos came to the podium and the cheering became deafening.

He waved for people to be quiet, then said, "Sit down, sit down, this isn't going to be a short speech." Nobody sat, they just continued cheering. He said, "Thank you. Thank you so much for being here. It's so wonderful to be with you all." They began sitting down. "To be here in New York, a city like no other, a progressive city that has always embraced the cause of climate mitigation and a city that has always supported me in my campaign to save our planet." The crowd cheered again. "Roosevelt Park. It's such a symbol of our nation. Roosevelt - you know he was an environmentalist?" They cheered. "Indeed, he was. He said, 'The conservation of our natural resources and their proper use constitute the fundamental problem which underlies almost every other problem of our national life.' And one of our natural resources is the air, is it not?" The crowd quietened then. "Oxygen. The stuff of life. And CO2 is death."

Nathanael rolled his eyes. "CO2 is life for plants. What an idiot."

Leo Bos straightened himself at the microphone. "But you know, there are other issues than this one. Our economy. Our present president promised to take care of things, to improve things for ordinary people, to create jobs, to rescue the economy. Now unemployment has gone down, but only at the same rate as it has been going down since two thousand and eight. So did he keep his promise?"

The crowd cried, "No!"

Nathanael looked around. The crowd was decidedly middle-to-upper class, there was obviously no one here whose job had been in any danger during the global downturn.

Leo Bos continued. "No, he didn't keep his promise, you are right. And the thing is, we can balance the needs of the economy with the needs of the environment. Surely," at this moment static came out of the speaker, but it looked as though Leo Bos was still speaking, and then suddenly his voice came through again, "be pleased if we can balance these two responsibilities and would ensure that America prospers." The crowd, just as unsure as Nathanael and Natasha about what Leo actually said, cheered nonetheless.

Leo waited a short while for the cheering to die down. Then he said, "Of course, New York has recently had problems with the climate - am I right? JFK airport, shut down for days because of unseasonable snow. Climate change affecting you people. Well, I promise to deal with these problems if I am elected as President, not just in the long term. We will defeat climate change!" Strangely, nobody cheered. But Leo continued, "Extra funding for the airport to deal with unexpected weather events. More snowploughs. More staff on the ground. Heated runways, at Federal expense, if that's what it takes!" Then something strange happened. Leo Bos's mouth was moving and Nathanael could hear him saying something about people flying and that's no good, but what came through the speakers was, "We will do whatever it takes." No one seemed to have noticed and the crowd roared their approval.

Leo hesitated for a moment, clearly as puzzled as Nathanael was by what had happened, and he looked out at the crowd with a look that reminded Nathanael of a deer caught in headlights, before he continued his speech. "Ahem. As Roosevelt himself said, 'Far better is it to dare mighty things, to win glorious triumphs, even though checkered by failure, than to rank with those poor spirits who neither enjoy nor suffer much, because they live in a gray twilight that knows not victory nor defeat.' And you and I my friends are going to dare great and mighty things when I, Aloquacious Aeolus Bos Junior, am elected to the White House."

After he had spoken other people came forward with testimonials, past Presidents, a Secretary of State and a few Generals. But the main part of the day was finished, and as the speeches continued people started to peter out gradually.

When Leo left, though, the crowd revived and cheered him just as loudly as they had at the start.

A HOTEL, MANHATTAN ISLAND, NEW YORK

Lisa came with them back to their hotel. They walked again, but Nathanael was tired by now and it was getting late and the walk didn't seem as enjoyable, so when they were about half way down thirty fourth street they hailed a cab and sat in comfort the rest of their journey back. When they reached the hotel Lisa booked a room in the same corridor as they were in and they waited for the elevator.

In the foyer, a grey haired man was talking with one of the maids. Nathanael distinctly heard him say, "Yes, she brought it down here to the bar. Can you put it back in the room when you clean it? Yes, it's her only spare. Very important, she could… Can't do without it. Thank you."

He wondered vaguely what they were talking about but then the elevator bell dinged and they were on their way up to their floor.

Once she had put her few possessions in to her own room, Lisa retired back to their room, bringing her laptop.

"What did you think?" said Lisa.

Nathanael said, "There were a few funny glitches in the speech between the audio coming through the speakers and what Leo actually said. Did either of you notice?"

Natasha was wearing her skeptical look, the same look she used to wear when Nathanael expressed his agnostic convictions. She said, "When?"

Lisa said, "Not really."

Nathanael said, "I saw it, I really did. It's true," He

felt embarrassed at having to insist, as though they didn't believe him. "When that static came over, remember that? But that wasn't the main one. Later on, afterwards, I am completely sure Leo Bos actually said something different from what was coming through the speakers."

Lisa looked at the sixty inch television screen and said, "Look, that television is pretty small. Come back to my room."

They followed her back to her room.

There was a hundred inch television screen in her room, right in the centre of the room.

Lisa opened up her laptop bag and took out a smaller black bag and unzipped it. She pulled out various connectors and cables and chose some. "With these I would think we can get everything up on the screen. First, though, let me download your video, Natasha, from your phone. Let's watch that first and we'll see if we can see what Nathanael is talking about."

In a few minutes she had uploaded Natasha's 4K video to her laptop and had the laptop plugged into the television. A few minutes after that, the speech was showing on the large television.

"This is the first bit," said Nathanael when the

speech was about four minutes in. Natasha's video clearly showed Leo saying something while the static came through the speakers, but what it was, who could say? None of them could read lips well enough to see.

Lisa opened and closed a few windows, and a few seconds later had her Tor browser running and was surfing through i-ogle's video uploads. People were already uploading the speech, and Lisa quickly opened it and went to the same location, 4'33", and she then pressed play on both videos as simultaneously as she could.

She did a good job. The two videos were synced pretty well, and they could hear Leo saying, "We can balance the needs of the economy with the needs of the environment. Surely," and at this moment static came from the video Natasha had recorded, but the other one had words, then they both synced again with, "be pleased if we can balance these two responsibilities and would ensure that America prospers."

"Hold on," said Lisa. "I'm muting yours. It must have been the speakers that malfunctioned, but they probably had a feed straight out of the mixing desk."

On the video that someone had just uploaded to i-ogle video, Leo was saying the same thing to start with, but the rest of the sentence was clearly audible.

"We can balance the needs of the economy with the needs of the environment. Surely Gaia the goddess of the earth would bless us and the water nymphs and wood nymphs of the environment would be pleased if we can balance these two responsibilities and would ensure that America prospers."

Lisa said, "Did he just mention Gaia and wood nymphs?"

Nathanael and Natasha nodded.

Lisa said, "Geez, he is an air-head. Let's watch that again. I'm not even sure I heard him say that."

She rewound the video back a few seconds.

Something very disconcerting happened then. The sentence started exactly the same. "We can balance the needs of the economy with the needs of the environment." But then it continued completely differently from what they had heard the first time. "Surely the God of our founding fathers would bless us if we could. Surely the Creator would be pleased if we can balance these two sacred responsibilities and would ensure that America prospers."

Lisa said, "I feel like I'm living in the matrix. That was one hell of a glitch." She said, "Just let me check something."

She went to a file somewhere on her computer and

clicked it. "I have a pretty big cloud account and I tend to like to keep track of what's happening on my computer. When I opened the laptop up for this session I started recording a continuous video feed of everything that happens on the screen, just in case anything weird happened. Like that."

She clicked the file.

Leo Bos was saying, "Surely Gaia the goddess of the earth would bless us and the water nymphs and wood nymphs of the environment would be pleased if we can balance these two responsibilities."

"Well there you are," she said. "We three aren't completely delusional. It's what he said the first time." She closed the continuous feed and went back to the two videos.

"Where was the other glitch, Nathanael?"

"Closer to the ten minute mark, I think."

Lisa forwarded the video to nine minutes fifty and clicked play.

Leo Bos was saying, "Heated runways, at Federal expense, if that's what it takes!" Then Leo Bos's mouth was moving and they could hear the two at once, him saying something about people flying and that's no good, and something different coming through the speakers. "We will do whatever it takes."

She quickly started the other video at the same spot.

Leo Bos was saying, "Heated runways, at Federal expense, if that's what it takes! People like you people, flying to and fro are part of the problem, especially when you're too poor to afford carbon credits. It's no good. You have to change your ways."

She ran it back, but it didn't play for a moment and the webpage went blank except for, "server not available," in the middle in grey writing. She refreshed the video and it returned.

"Here we go down the rabbit hole," said Lisa, and pressed play.

Leo Bos was saying, "Heated runways, at Federal expense, if that's what it takes! We will do whatever it takes. We will do whatever it takes!" And the crowd on the video roared their approval.

They compared it with the video Natasha had taken, with both running silently in slow motion. It was very clear that the video image of Leo Bos was saying different words in both videos, in fact, he was also doing different gestures, gestures that reflected the high impact of the version that wasn't real.

"Holy cow," said Lisa. "I think they're editing Leo Bos. And obviously some of that editing is taking place in real time. That's pretty wacko. This is pretty high on the bizarro scale, peeps."

Her laptop dinged. "Hold on," said Lisa.

Lisa clicked on something, she was accessing the café server. The live camera feed came up showing several points of view from the café security cameras. Some men in orange safety jackets cutting through the metal wall of the server with some sort of reciprocating saw.

Lisa said, "They cut the power a while ago but the server is still operating on diesel, but I'm not sure how much longer the diesel will hold out. The cameras are on a separate circuit - they'll keep going, ad infinitum, so long as there's some sort of internet access. We've got - what? Three minutes to go? It's two twenty nine now. If we can just get the last version of the document downloaded before they get in. That's the one."

The men appeared to be cutting through very carefully, obviously trying to avoid trip wires or whatever mechanism Lisa had installed to sabotage anyone who entered the room.

The circle they were cutting was slowly being closed. They watched as the men cut another inch, then another.

The clock was ticking.

Lisa said, "It's two thirty. But it still hasn't downloaded

yet. It'll be here soon."

Finally the circle they were cutting closed. They carefully pulled the steel circle away from the wall. Lisa switched cameras. The camera in the corridor showed looking in through the hole, into the server farm. She switched again. The camera in the server farm showed the computers were all still working.

The hole was big enough for a person to go through, but they didn't seem to be doing that.

One of the men had a large reacher grabber tool. He slowly reached in towards one of the servers.

The tool grabbed the server and he slowly lifted it up. At that moment, an icon started flashing in the corner of Lisa's computer screen.

Lisa clicked the icon. "This is it," she said. "Dammit. I don't think we're going to make it." The clock showed 2:31.

A notification window came up next to the icon with writing on it, "ALERT! ALERT! Unauthorised server access identified. Security protocol commencing. Complete shutdown. To cancel type password:_________"

Lisa did not type the password. "I can't cancel it," she pleaded, "Otherwise they've got me."

The notification changed, "Security protocol in

process. Complete shutdown and self-destruct beginning."

Through the security camera inside the room they could see the computers in the server racks. One after another smoke began trickling out then pouring out from them and they could see the wires and cables around them melting. The man pulled the grabber tool out quickly and they got out of the way and some guys in jeans and t-shirts, probably computer experts, Nathanael thought, clambered in through the hole to try and salvage some of the units. But by now there was smoke billowing out, filling the room.

Lisa switched cameras. The units were beginning to melt. There was not a single one they could see that was intact. The guys in jeans were coughing and spluttering, going through the units trying desperately to find at least one that hadn't been fried. There were none.

Then a guy pointed to one that hadn't melted yet, a single unit, in the corner of the room. Lisa said, "That's the computer that sends the camera images onto the net. That one will be last to go."

Smoke began trickling out from the top, a thin stream, and the picture flickered. Digital artefacts began to appear and then the picture froze.

A single message appeared on the notification

window.

"SHUTDOWN COMPLETED. ALL UNITS DESTROYED."

"Well, that's it," Lisa said to Nathanael and Natasha. "They broke into the café server and it self-destructed."

So that's that, we won't get the document now, thought Nathanael.

Lisa said, "Well, we're stuffed then, aren't we."

The clock changed to 2:33.

Another message appeared.

"BACKUP INTACT. ALL PROCESSES TRANSFERRING TO SOUTH MOUNTAIN FACILITY"

"Oh, look at that," said Natasha. "You had a contingency plan."

Lisa said, "I did. To be honest I thought it had failed. It never worked in any of the test runs. I don't believe it. If we're lucky the document will still download."

"ALL PROCESSES TRANSFERRED. OPENING ACCESS POINT."

Another window opened, like the one earlier that Lisa had used to access the i-ogle servers. It had basically picked up where the other one had left off.

Natasha said, "You're well organised, Lisa."

Lisa nodded. "It's a fluke. Honestly, it's a complete miracle."

Natasha said, "I knew God was in this."

Lisa looked at her and said, "I never expected that backup to kick in, Natasha, but it did. Thankfully I don't think they got around to cutting the optic fibres, that must be what saved it. Look here. We've got the whole document now."

She opened the latest version. It had everything up to the very end, the part that Natasha's version had included. Lisa did a quick copy and paste and created a new document that had no encryption whatsoever.

She put the whole document up on the big television screen.

BEL Algorithm Project History

PROJECT DESCRIPTION:

The BEL Algorithm is designed to deal with the most pervasive modern problem in politics - the 24 hour news cycle. Politicians as never before are confronted with an unfair microscopic moment-by-moment examination of every single thing they say or do, the kind of analysis no human being could possibly endure without slipping up. In most normal social circles, 'faux-pas' may cause problems for a week or two (unless it has been filmed and shared publicly on facebook, effectively a rarity). In politics, a faux-pas can ruin a whole career.

In other words, there seems to be no way back in the public perception when a politician says or does something inappropriate or embarrassing.

And the fact is, that every human being acts in a socially inappropriate way on occasion. Today we have virtually perfect news coverage of public events. Technology has made it possible to capture nearly every moment of a public person's public life.

And as St Augustine said, it is the function of perfection to make one know one's imperfection. Too many promising Presidential candidates have had their hopes ruined by the momentary lapse in good judgement, the type of lapse we all commit from time to time. Thus the 24 hour news cycle works against inculcating excellence in our political leaders. What our political analysts have called the Camelot Effect, referring to the popularity of the presidential reign of John F Kennedy. may no longer be possible without some sort of intervention to control the negative effect of the 24 hour news cycle on public perception.

The type of intervention that the BEL Algorithm may be able to provide.

Considering that i-ogle controls at least 60% of legitimate internet media, and the fact that i-ogle has the most extensive computing power on the planet, the possibility exists of controlling the representation of a politician by editing and interpolating a different representation before the record reaches the mainstream.

Of course, in accordance with the i-ogle policy of "do only good" such an editing system would only be used to prevent embarrassing incidents in an otherwise excellent politician from reaching the mainstream, or to enhance the Camelot Effect using scientific principles (something political advertising already attempts to achieve).

I) THE BODY OF BEL – CREATION OF PLAUSIBLE REAL TIME INTERPOLATION

1) Creation of completely plausible fictional facial images

7) Creation of completely plausible 3D facial images of real people.

8) Creation of plausible animated figures using the facial images.

9) The Persinger effect in physical appearance: Research into how best to represent figures, capturing/recreating the sort of images that evoke temporal lobe responses (awe, devotion, adoration, fear). In other words, creating the Camelot Effect.

10) Real time hi-res interpolation of animated figures into real-life video.(All states completed)

II) THE MIND OF BEL - SOURCING POLITICAL PREDICTIONS BY DATA MINING AND PROCESSING.

1) A Distributed Asynchronous Database (DAD) linking every possible data resource to create a model of political interactions in the real world.

11) Neural Analysis Merging Extended Systems. (NAMES) Uses information clustering to summarise what DAD has learned.

12) Long Iterative Temporal Term Logistic Electoral Markov Universal

Mapping (LITTLE MUM) Use long term logistic Markov decision processes to predict likely and possible electoral and population responses to various possible speeches and actions of politicians.

13) The Persinger effect: Research into how political figures might express the Zeitgeist and in so doing evoke temporal lobe responses.

14) Use NAMES, MUM, DAD in concert to work out what a politician ought to do (in process now) These three together create BEL.

III) BEL - COMBINING MIND AND BODY INTO A TOOL FOR REAL TIME PUBLICITY MANAGEMENT.

1) Real time identification of likely inappropriate outcomes - using BEL to identify when a politician says or does something that is likely to have long term negative electoral effects, i.e. on polling, or even politically speaking long term negative effects on the populace on important

issues such as climate change, immigration, social justice, etc etc.

15) Interpolated Policy Response. Replacing the inappropriate behaviour/speech with BEL interpolated into the live video feed, saying/doing something the program works out is more likely to have a positive response or effect on the populace.

IV) MANAGING DISSENTING VOICES

1) Just as content can be interpolated, it can be removed. Remove content as soon as it goes up.

16) The original content on mobile phone apps could be edited or managed, to avoid dissenting images being disseminated.

17) Prevent people from talking about this on Facebook etc. Apps or viruses on mobile phones important in this regard.

18) iPhones in particular will need added effort as they are harder to hack.

V) OTHER USEFUL TECHNIQUES

1) Remote Magnetic Neurostimulation? Unlikely to work.

19) More efficient perhaps to insert neurostimulators into campaign hats (Sell both the pro and anti hats) using magnets. Have flashing lights on the hats to justify the electrical components.

20) Creating awe using low frequency vibration (already used in motion pictures)

They read through the whole document.

Natasha was first to finish. She said, "So what they're doing is interpolating some sort of computerised animated Leo Bos from time to time. To insert the computerised Leo Bos into the live feed, ultimately, is the aim, although they don't seem to have quite got it working live yet."

Lisa shrugged. "Well they got the audio working, just not the vision. They had something different coming out of the speakers, didn't they? That must have been the BEL Algorithm speaking, cause it surely wasn't Leo Bos."

Nathanael said, "So it's some sort of Artificial Intelligence? Trying to make up for Leo Bos's mistakes, before they can be disseminated on the net?"

Lisa said, "That's exactly what it is. Strange stuff."

Natasha said, "Is it really unethical? I mean, if you post a document on your blog you can edit it afterwards, change it as much as you like. Isn't it the same as that?"

Lisa said, "I think it's lying. I mean, people have a right to know who it is they're electing, don't they?"

Nathanael said, "It is lying. But it's more than that. Anyone, not just a presidential candidate, could have what they just said changed by i-ogle, moments or minutes afterwards, and no one would be able to prove that it wasn't. It completely removes the integrity of video as proof of anything."

Natasha said, "Can they really control the flow of information, to that degree, though? I mean, there must be hundreds of videos of Leo Bos speaking at that rally being uploaded and shared every minute. Are they going to edit each one?"

Lisa said, "Well they managed to edit the one we were watching, which I chose fairly randomly from about twenty examples on the first page of i-ogle video, each from a different point of view. And you realise i-ogle video hosts eighty seven percent of recent video uploads. Youtube only has a fraction of that, these days, they've lost their market share to i-ogle. It was i-ogle's promise of instant monetisation I think, though that seems to have been completely left by the wayside since Adamant took over."

ADAMANT BUILDING, NEW YORK, NEW YORK

Leo Bos was standing at the reception next to Adamant.

Leo said to Raymond, "What happened today?"

"Well, there was a few glitches. That's all. Usual sort of thing."

"No," said Leo. "If you're not honest with me I can use my own ways of finding out."

Raymond said, "What do you mean?" It irritated Leo because Raymond feigned complete ignorance. He was lying.

"I mean," said Leo, emphatically hitting his fist against the table, "I mean that the version on i-ogle video was different from what I actually said. In two places. One was when I was telling those stupid sheep to stop flying - I mean, flying is fine for climate conferences - but really, going to see Aunt Betty in England? Skype her for God's sake. The other incident was before that, when that static came over the speaker, coincidentally in the very bit you didn' t like much. My bit about the goddess of the earth, Gaia."

Adamant said, "You can't talk about Gaia. It's a false god. The majority of people in the great US of A still believe in the God of the Bible and the founding fathers. Well, I suppose they were deists mostly, but they think they're the same."

"I said what I said," said Leo, thumping his fist on the table again. "I said what I said and I didn't say what I didn't say. Or who is going to be President, here? Are you? Are you Presidential material? And how on earth did you edit it so quickly?"

Adamant answered, "That's what I was telling you about. That's the whole point of our project, Leo! The BEL Algorithm. It's a life-saver for you. Didn't you listen to a thing I said, when we were eating at that restaurant? This is what is happening, Leo, our computer program, the BEL Algorithm, decided that your speech would not come across so well in one or two places. So, during the time lag, the computer program itself edited the video. Clever, hey?"

"And what about all those people who have the real video?"

Adamant answered, "I don't like to boast about our engineers. But they're light years ahead in this stuff. No, it edits all of those too. Every video in the whole world of that event can be changed, within minutes. Any device that's connected to the internet in any way, shape or form, the BEL Algorithm will examine, hack whatever device uploaded it and change the video before anyone realises what happened."

"Yeah but I said what I said."

"Don't you want to be popular, Leo?"

"Yeah but I still said what I actually said, not what's on that video. Don't you care about honesty? Truth?"

"Our philosophy is do only good stuff. Of course I care. Truth is a good thing. I just value popularity a little more if it leads to a good political outcome. Don't you? Don't you want to be popular? Isn't that what this is all about, this whole presidential bid, being the popular kid on the block?"

Leo sucked his lips in for a moment. "Yes, I guess it is. But is it worth it if I have to lie?"

"Of course it's worth it," said Adamant. "You lie all the time. Come on, this is fame that we're talking about. Reputation. You becoming the President of the United States."

"Hell," said Leo, feeling as though he was sinking into the ground. "This is deep. I'm in deep."

"Well, get a good sleep, Leo," said Adamant. "We've got another speech for you to deliver tomorrow. We're going for the primaries. Let's go, come on, Leo, get to bed and get your beauty sleep. We've got a big day tomorrow."

A HOTEL, MANHATTAN ISLAND, NEW YORK

They were exhausted and hungry and had not eaten anything since breakfast and it was now about ten o'clock at night.

Lisa rang up the hotel lobby and ordered a pizza.

A knock came at the door. Lisa answered and collected the pizza from a young teenager. She paid him in cash and brought the pizza in and opened up the box.

It smelled delicious.

Nathanael was the one who remembered, "We're not supposed to eat food we haven't seen being prepared or chosen from a selection available to the general public."

Natasha said, "Yeh, I told you already, Lisa. That's what happened to OxyMoron. He ordered pizza."

Lisa said, "But it smells so good. Smell it. Could that really be poisonous or radioactive or something? Look at it. Nothing glowing on top. Wouldn't it glow?"

She turned the light off. Nothing on the pizza was glowing. She flicked the light back on.

Nathanael shook his head doubtfully. "I don't think plutonium necessarily glows. Only if the particles are very small and its a particular oxide or something. Normally it's just a grey, silvery metal."

Lisa said, "Well I don't see any tiny bits of grey metal on there either. Just pepperoni and ham and cheese and pineapple and cheese."

She took a piece and brought it up to her mouth.

Natasha said, "No!" But Lisa took a bite. "Look," she said. "I'm not dying. I'm fine. Have some yourselves."

Natasha picked up a piece. Nathanael took her hand and made her put it down again. "It's not wise," he said. "We know what happened to the hacker." He tried to make Lisa put her piece down but she shook off his hand and swore at him. "If you keep that up I'll call hotel security. I'm having my pizza and there's no freaking thing you're going to do about it."

Lisa ate the rest of the piece and picked up another. She said, "Mmm, this is delicious," as she ate her second piece.

Natasha looked at her doubtfully. "She looks fine, Nathanael."

He said, "The effects are not necessarily immediate. It took Alexander Litvinenko several days to die."

Lisa said, "Well I'm completely fine. Just shut up about it and let me enjoy my pizza. Talk about paranoid."

"Come on," said Nathanael. "Let's go back to our room."

Natasha looked at the pizza longingly. But Nathanael said, "We'll go down to the lobby and get some chips from a vendor machine or something. This is not a good idea."

Natasha said, "Come on, you're just being paranoid now."

Nathanael took her arm rather forcefully and made her leave the room. As they walked out, she tore her arm away from his grip and said, "You know, this is the kind of thing I hate men doing."

Nonetheless she went with him down the corridor and as they approached their room Natasha saw a chip vending machine around the corner, so they got some Doritos and Coke and went back to her room.

As they were crunching on the chips, Natasha complained, "Look, these are really not filling me up. That pizza looked really good. I think we should go back and have some."

Nathanael shook his head. "No."

They went to their beds after that, with Natasha still complaining.

At about three o'clock in the morning, there was a knock on the door. Nathanael went and looked through the spy-hole.

It was Lisa.

He opened the door.

She looked very pale and was leaning on the door frame for support.

"Nathanael," she said. "I am sick. I've got diarrhoea, I've been vomiting. It's probably just food poisoning, isn't it?"

He said, "These were the exact symptoms Litvinenko had." He went to the phone and said, "I'm going to call an ambulance."

"No wait," said Lisa. "Forget it. I'll call one from my room. You two shouldn't be involved."

Nathanael said, "I'm coming back with you to make sure you do."

He supported her on the way back.

When they got there she said, "Help me to the bathroom. Quickly!" He half carried her to the bathroom and before she reached the toilet bowl she vomited on the bathroom floor. She slumped onto the toilet seat and pulled her pants down, right in front of him, and started going. He averted his eyes.

The diarrhoea sounded like a water hose hitting the toilet water.

"It's pretty bad," she said apologetically. "It's rather embarrassing."

Once she had finished Nathanael helped her back to bed. While he cleaned up some of the mess in her bathroom she made the emergency call. "Hello? Yes, it's a medical emergency. I don't know. It might be food poisoning. But it seems worse than that. It might be radiation exposure. Vomiting. Extreme diarrhoea. Why? Someone's trying to kill me. It's not just paranoia. I've never had diarrhoea like this before. It happened to someone I know."

Nathanael came back in to the room. Lisa said, "Make sure you haven't left any fingerprints." She reached down and got her handbag, lay back exhaustedly, then took a microfibre cloth out of her handbag.

She said, "Quick, wipe everything down in the bathroom. And anything you were touching in here, glasses, cups, the television. Look for hairs. Get rid of any evidence you and Natasha were here. And don't touch the pizza box."

He did everything she said. The pizza box was next to her bed, open, with half the pizza left uneaten.

Lisa let out some invectives then said. "I've survived through the Aaron Kershowitz affair, evaded the authorities for years, even grown my business until I owned three buildings and whole companies, and I've kept on hacking the whole time without once getting caught. And it's a piece of pizza that gets me." She laughed bitterly. "I've been really stupid, haven't I? I'm sorry about threatening to call hotel security. You were trying to protect me. Look, take my laptop, in case I don't make it. Give it to Natasha. It's got access to everything. The password is beoWulf4624 with a capital W and a lower case b at the start. Easy enough to remember."

"What about the server farms?"

"That's the password for everything, the server farms, the software I wrote, the whole lot." She quickly opened her email client and typed an email then pressed send. "There, I've emailed the security guys at my company server farm to give you complete access. I trust you and Natasha."

He looked at the laptop.

She shouted, "Go, you idiot! Go! Before the paramedics get here."

He picked up the laptop and left.

When he got to their room Natasha was sitting on the bed, wheezing. She had a blue asthma puffer in her hand and was breathing out, about to inhale it.

Nathanael saw it immediately, or rather, he saw what he didn't see. He dropped Lisa's computer on the bed, leaped across the room, over the bed in one bound and knocked the puffer out of Natasha's hand so forcefully that it must have hurt her hand, because she grabbed her wrist and held it close to her, and kept going. He smashed into the wardrobe so hard that it left a huge crack in the wooden door.

Natasha looked at him with wide-eyed fear and started wheezing even more, with every tormented breath forcing out another word, "Why - did - you - do - that? You're-trying-to-kill-me!"

He found Natasha's computer bag beside the bed and rummaged in it, pulling out one of the puffers with the black dot that he had marked on it and threw it over to her.

Natasha gratefully pressed the button so that the relieving mist filled her throat and opened her airways and she breathed again. Once she had recovered sufficiently she turned to Nathanael and said in a short tone of voice, "What was that all about?"

He picked up the other puffer from the ground.

"No dot on this one," he said.

"Oh," said Natasha, and swore. "So where did that come from?"

"I don't know," said Nathanael.

"How is Lisa? Is she okay?"

"No. She's very ill. She called 911 and they're on their way. She gave me this." He pulled the laptop over to Natasha. "The password is beoWulf4624, capital W, lower case b."

Natasha opened the laptop and tried it. "It works! I'm into her server."

Nathanael was thoughtful for a minute. "You know, I did see a man in the foyer a little while ago, telling a maid to put something in someone's room, that she needed it, might die without it. I reckon that was your puffer."

Then she swore again. "I almost had some of that pizza. And you stopped me. Than the puffer. You might have saved my life twice tonight. Sheesh." She looked at him with tears in her eyes, and laid the laptop back on the bed next to him. "Thanks. I'm not sure I'm ready to join Lisa just yet."

Nathanael pressed his lips together then said, "She's not dead yet, Natasha. Who knows, it might just be food poisoning. And that asthma puffer could be completely innocent. You know, these sorts of coincidences happen from time to time."

Natasha shook her head. "I don't think it's just a coincidence, Nathanael. I think they're after us and I think they knew we were in the room with her and they tried to get us too with plutonium. And with the asthma puffer."

He took the puffer that didn't have a button on it and carefully wrapped it in newspaper. He stepped on it, breaking it with a crack, so nobody else would use it, being careful not to inhale, and disposed of it in the rubbish bin in the hallway, still holding his breath.

A few minutes later they heard ambulance sirens coming closer on the street and then footsteps going along the corridor outside their room, with voices going past saying, "Intravenous antibiotics, three hundred milligrams. Antimicrobial, five..."

Natasha said, "It's my fault. I should have stopped her eating it."

Nathanael said, "It's not your fault. We tried to stop her and she threatened to call the hotel security. She insisted. She refused to listen. And she's in good hands now." He hesitated. "Maybe we should pray for her?"

They prayed for her.

Natasha said, "I don't know how we can keep going. I feel so afraid, so pressured by all of this. How can we keep going, Nathanael?"

Nathanael embraced and held her. Then she prayed and pleaded, "Dear Lord Jesus, please help us get through this. I want to have a life again, a better life. I'm not even sure what's true any more. Please help us."

He surprised himself by saying, "Amen."

Nathanael held her for a long time after that.

Finally, when she had relaxed, he said, "I am sure all of this is really happening, Natasha. It's not our imagination. But at least we know that it's going on. There are things we can do to protect ourselves, Natasha." He picked up Lisa's laptop and closed it. "Let's get out of this hotel now; they know we're here. We've got to make some different plans, get rid of the SUV, make ourselves scarce." He swore. "We weren't careful enough and they found us."

Natasha held his shoulder, stopping him, "Wait, before we do that. Let's find out where Leo Bos is doing his next speech. That's where we need to be."

Nathanael took her hands in his and said, "I don't want anything to happen to you. I'm feeling now that I don't care about what happens, I don't want you to be harmed. Maybe we can leave this to other people."

Natasha shook her head. "Nathanael, I was wrong before. Hacking is not necessarily a bad thing. I've been praying about it. I believe this is what Jesus wants me to do. And I want to do God's will in this matter, whatever it costs."

Nathanael frowned, an expression of anguish crossing his face. "I don't want to lose you. Not now."

She said, "You won't. But doing this means I might have to risk you losing me, losing you. Whoever gives up their life for Jesus' sake, will find it. Whoever keeps their life will lose it."

"That's precisely what I'm trying to avoid. Giving up our lives."

"Nathanael, that's the only way anyone can find their life, by being prepared to lose it in serving God. I realised that while we were praying, while you were holding me. I felt strength flowing into me. Now, just let me use that laptop, for goodness' sake." She took Lisa's laptop out of his hands. "I've got to get on the net. She's got Tor Browser, everything is very secure, supposedly, but we'll find out somehow, I believe. I'm just going to quickly find out where Leo Bos's next appearance is. We have to get proof of what they're doing." She started packing her bags. "I think Iowa will be first."

"It is all very dodgy," he admitted. "I'll help you - I'll do the packing."

<u>*DES MOINES, IOWA*</u>

Leo Bos arrived by plane at Des Moines International Airport, Iowa at eleven thirty in the morning on Monday. He wasn't speaking at the rally till Tuesday, but he had to meet some of the town leaders and potential investors first, at a dinner specially put on for the really big donors and supporters.

All his luggage was taken care of and thankfully Raymond Adamant was covering all the costs. From the airport he found himself bundled into the usual black limousine. His security detail had already mapped out and secured the route to the Des Moines Hilton; the thing is you never know when some climate denialist or nutjob might be out to get him, and in any case the route was far quicker when they blocked the roads off so he was comforted that they didn't have to brave the traffic.

They had already organised for his lunch to be brought up to his room, a Thai beef salad. Leo liked to have a bit of alone time before speeches and appearances and even his security detail had agreed to leave the room for the hour, while he ate lunch and had a quick nap.

<u>*I-80 WEST HIGHWAY*</u>

Nathanael used up another twenty thousand of his hard-earned cash to buy another vehicle. It was a nondescript white Mazda 5 door sedan. They managed to put it in Natasha's mother's name, which Natasha thought might be a good way of at least delaying the surveillance, if not avoiding it.

They sold the SUV to a different car dealer for about five thousand, which left Nathanael only fifteen thousand worse off, if you didn't count the actual value of the SUV.

Nathanael was driving.

Nathanael glanced over at Natasha. She was working on Lisa's computer. "So what are you going to do?"

She typed the password again and the windows opened up.

Natasha said, "It works still. I'm in to the main server, at the company building. I'm going to see if I can get Lisa's big server to actually hack into the Bel Algorithm process itself. I mean, they're using a large amount of video bandwidth and processing power, if I can come up with the right hack I might be able to actually break into their method of controlling what Leo Bos's supposedly live feed actually shows."

"Well I'd better keep driving then."

Natasha said, "For a while, okay? And after that I'll be creating a nice little mobile app too, that infects anything that connects to my open hotspot."

CHAPTER 9 CONFUSION AND CONCLUSION

Leo was having a quiet coffee at the bar downstairs when Raymond Adamant walked in and sat down next to him.

"Leo," he said, indicating the barman should bring him a drink at the same time, "The usual. Nice to see you're staying off the hard stuff."

Leo simply sighed. Yes, Raymond was helping and yes, Raymond had revived his dreams of being president, but this self-assured jackass was the last person Leo wanted to see right now.

"Good news," Raymond continued, "The programmers reckon they have BEL program working properly now."

"Which means?" said Leo, rather skeptical as to whether it really was good news.

"If you stuff up in one of your speeches-"

"You mean, say something you don't like?"

"It's not just me, Leo. We have programmed the broad demographic most likely to vote for you into BEL. For instance, very few of them will want to hear about Gaia or wood nymphs."

Leo sneered. "You have to bring that up don't you?"

"Well, most of them are either nominally Christian or atheist left-wingers. Alright, there might be a few nutcase greens who like hearing about Gaia, but they're in the minority. Pleasing a tiny demographic and losing the rest is stupid."

"So what happens if I 'stuff up'?"

"The BEL program kicks in and takes over the live video feed. If it can it will interpolate static or the new version of the words into the speaker feed (we've inserted a short delay line in the audio feed to make that possible.). Basically, if you stuff up, BEL takes over and creates a different, entirely plausible version of what you're saying and feeds it into the live video feed."

"What if I don't want this? What if I want to get elected on my platform, not on this stupid computer's platform?"

"You signed the contract."

"So... That's the deal, is it? You won't give me any money if I don't toe the line?"

"Essentially. Yes."

"So, none of it depends on what I do at all? I'm going to get elected anyway? And I'm tied into this contract that makes me the puppet of your AI program?"

"You're putting the whole thing in a more negative frame than you should, Leo. The glass is half full, not half empty. You're going to be President of the United States of America. Look on the bright side."

Leo sipped his coffee. The barman deposited Raymond's drink.

"It won't be President Leo Bos," he said. "It will be A.I. Leo Bos who's gonna be the one who's elected."

"A.I. BEL," said Raymond, and raised a glass of scotch to his own joke, which Leo did not think was very funny at all.

SIMON ESTES AMPHITHEATER, 75 E LOCUST ST, DES MOINES

Natasha had managed to hack the guest list for the third annual Iowa Sweet Corn Feed, and they had two seats on a table very near the front.

The dinner conversation revolved around money, shares, dividends and markets, until one of the clearly well-heeled ladies, bedecked in a loose shoulder-strap black designer dress, a pearl necklace, and rather large diamond earrings said, "I know it's disingenuous and highly socially unacceptable, if not entirely immodest, for me to even mention this, but I'd love to know how much you all donated to Leo's campaign to get seats at this table?"

The man she was talking to, an older man in a Zegna suit with a gold chain round his neck and a genuine Blancpain

Le Brassus watch, said, "Oh, about nine hundred." Natasha didn't think that was a lot, really, nine hundred dollars.

"Oh," the woman smirked, "You gave more than us, then. We only put in half a million."

Oh, he meant nine hundred thousand, Natasha thought.

They went around the circle, and each of the ten people there had put in at least five hundred thousand into the campaign.

Then the lady asked Natasha, "So how much did you and your de facto husband put in?"

Natasha said, "Oh, I wouldn't like to say."

Nathanael said, "We wouldn't want to embarrass anyone by telling the truth about that."

The lady said, "You know, I didn't see you at the benefit dinner last night."

"Oh, we were there," said Natasha, who had prepared for this contingency. "The Beluga was delightful, apparently, though I didn't have any, I don't like seafood."

The lady raised her eyebrows. Natasha had looked it up, the Beluga menu required a donation of more than a million dollars.

"It was. And where did you make your money?"

Natasha thought the lady wasn't certain what to make of them; she could see that they were dressing down, but she was wondering if this was because they were poor or because they were so rich they didn't care what anyone thought of them.

Nathanael said, "Oh, gambling. Casinos. Natasha's got her own money, she's into computers. I'm Nathanael." He offered his hand to shake but she ignored it.

She fiddled with her pearls and said, "I'm Dorothea Deborah Doty. People call me Dot. Or DDT, it's a joke. I didn't think you were old money. Mind you, one never knows these days. My family has been part of the New England aristocracy since the very moment the Pilgrims landed on Plymouth Rock." She looked over her nose at Nathanael. "How very Australian that is - to make your money on casinos. Did you know Kerry?"

"No," said Nathanael. "Before my time."

"A pig of a man but perfectly delightful."

At that moment a hush descended on the crowd and Leo Bos appeared on a small stage only a few metres away from them.

Most of the people at their table brought out their mobile phones and so did Natasha. She started filming Leo.

He was doing the standard speech, "I am grateful to be here and thank you for welcoming me so generously. I didn't want to miss it. Do you know, corn is part of something bigger," and so on, but it was half way through the speech that it all went a bit strange.

It began with one or two words, innocuous insertions. "As you know I've been a keen advocate for action on grommet change." Natasha was sure he was saying, 'grommet', but the word that came out of the speakers was 'climate'.

He continued, "The weather is changing - you just have to look out the winnebago to see that things aren't what they used to be - storms, hurricanes, sharknados, extraordinary weather platterns, ice in July, unseasonably golden weather."

'Winnebago,' came out of the speakers as 'window,' 'sharknado' came out as 'tornado', 'platterns' as patterns, 'golden' as 'cold'.

The speech coming through the speakers was conventional but what Leo was actually saying continued getting more and more bizarre.

By the end of the speech, the message coming through the speakers was, "We will stand together to face the challenges of the future, join me as I face this election on the platform of change! And I want to see you all at Gray's Lake Park tomorrow." but Natasha was sure Leo was actually mouthing absolute nonsense, "Wentiponti is stymie tonka truck to plonk the bottomly melanges of the funky punkwonker. Janus is the too façile freakish faces of the redaction of the dysfunction of strange! Handle the trifectless gondolas of the hallowed marrow barrow wights."

Natasha looked around at the other people at her table. They all looked shell-shocked. Dorothea Deborah Doty was looking into her wine-glass and swirling it around, as though looking for drug residue or some sign it had been contaminated. The man sitting next to her had actually taken out a small pamphlet from his wallet, that had, "Possible side effects," written in red and was studying it avidly.

She looked around at the other people in the room. No one was particularly perturbed at any of the other tables, but they were all further away, too far to notice, perhaps, what Leo was really saying.

When Leo finished he put it away, quickly looking around to see if anyone had noticed, but Natasha pretended not to have seen.

They all clapped and loudly espoused the virtues of Leo's speech and suddenly you would not have known that there was anything wrong.

Natasha realised every single one of the donors at her table thought they had <u>imagined</u> Leo's strange interpolations.

She laughed quite freely at them. It was like that fairy tale, "The Emperor's New Clothes." Then she remembered there was something she had to do.

Natasha got her mobile and opened up the app she had created during the drive to Des Moines. It created an open wireless hotspot and every mobile device within 10 metres connected automatically unless the owner had disabled that feature, and Natasha's app downloaded itself onto their phone.

<u>*PRIVATE GREEN ROOM, SIMON ESTES AMPHITHEATER, 75 E LOCUST ST, DES MOINES*</u>

Adamant pointed his finger at Leo's chest. "What did you think you were doing?"

Leo shrugged and an expression of defiant despair twisted his features. "I just wanted to check something. I wanted to know what would happen if I went off-script. It's marvellous, isn't it? My voice through the speaker just goes right on saying what's in the speech! And sometimes even improves on it! I can just say anything, any old garbage, but the speech just goes right on regardless!"

Adamant said, "Don't you realise the big donors' table was right near the stage? They could hear you."

Leo said, "Well of course they could. My voice was being amplified through the speakers."

Adamant said, "Well if you'd used that tiny pea-brained size piece of grey matter in your skull you would know that they were sitting just in front of the speaker, which was facing away from them. They could hear the <u>real</u> you. And some of them had their phones out."

"Yeah, well, you said you could edit the videos."

"We can. On you-tube. On their phones, too, if they're running iOS or Android, but not if they're not connected to the net. And our security blocked out all data and mobile signals in that building."

"Well I'm not responsible for that. That's all your responsibility, not mine."

Adamant sighed. Leo was right.

He said, "Don't do it again."

"Sure, I won't," said Leo in such a snarky tone that Adamant knew he was lying.

Still, their system was foolproof. His i-ogle people had been monitoring the net. So far, no one had uploaded any video of the event and there was no chatter, mind you, he didn't expect any of that to start in earnest until the guests had left the building.

Adamant said, "Well, don't do that at Gray's Lake Park tomorrow. I don't know how the BEL Algorithm system will cope with live interviews if you're playing childish games like that."

ADAMANT'S JET, FALLINGSTAR FIELDS PRIVATE AIRPORT, DES MOINES

Adamant was relaxing in his private cabin on the Boeing, sipping some port, when the call came through.

He normally wouldn't have taken it in his down-time but it was the i-ogle engineer who had been supervising the IT component at the Amphitheater.

Adamant said, "Yes?"

The engineer said, "It's Eugene here. Just something funny I noticed - you know the big donors' table?"

Adamant said, "Yeah?"

Eugene said, "Well, not one of their cell phones showed up on the way out."

"What do you mean?"

"Well, I monitor all the mobile devices coming in, to

the point they're sitting down at their tables, and then we turn the networks off. And, you know, they were so close to the stage, I wouldn't have been surprised if those people caught Leo airing his frustration, shall we say, on their phones. I wanted to make sure we deleted all that."

"And?"

"And not one of their phones showed up on the way out, when they were walking out of the building and we started up the networks again."

"Perhaps they all had them turned off? They were mostly fairly old, weren't they?"

"Yeah, except for that young couple, the dark skinned lady and the tall man, but their phones didn't show up anyway on the way in as far as I could tell. I don't think they had their phones on them. But all the others' phones were off on the way out. You might be right. They were old. But all of them?"

Adamant scratched his head. It didn't sound that bad. Just a coincidence. "But if they try to upload anything onto i-ogle video, you'll get it?"

"Oh, yeah, we've actually got a great visual algorithm search. Behind the stage is a pattern that our visual algorithm will immediately identify, so long as the resolution is at least

Standard Definition."

"Good," said Adamant, not really knowing what Standard Definition was. "Then don't worry about it."

HYATT HOTEL, DES MOINES

Dorothea Deborah Doty was looking at her phone. For some reason she couldn't get onto i-oglebook. And she had so wanted to post that strange video of Leo Bos saying gobbledygook during his speech, but the swear word phone wasn't connecting.

She thought for a moment and got her tablet. It had an internet connection, didn't it? And a camera too, she was sure it did.

She fiddled for a while and found the camera.

With the tablet she filmed the mobile playing the video. Alright it was a bit small on the screen, but the sound had come through the bluetooth good, you could actually hear Leo Bos saying completely different stuff to what was coming through the venue speakers.

Goodness, she had thought she was losing her marbles when that had happened. At first she had thought it must be early dementia, but then she thought, maybe someone put Psilocybin into my wine, or something? It seemed like the most peculiar delusion.

The fact seemed even more delusional, that it was real.

She looked at the post and typed in her comment.

"Watch this everybody - Leo is losing it, but the message goes on through the loudspeaker anyway! Sorry, couldn't make it any bigger, the phone screen is too small and mobile network is down. But you can hear it happening, its real, I was there."

And she pressed 'share'.

A HOTEL, DES MOINES, IOWA

Natasha did a search for "Leo Bos" on i-ogle video, and the video of the mobile phone came up immediately. Her ploy had worked. They had bypassed the i-ogle system for identifying the offending videos. She assumed it might be something like that, actually, after noting the strange pattern on the board behind Leo Bos.

She felt a pang of regret then.

"You know, Nathanael. What are we doing? What have I been doing? This is exactly what I was afraid of. Once I start hacking I get involved, it's exactly like a drug and I don't even think about the real consequences."

"What do you mean? Are you saying people's deaths are not bad consequences?"

"Leo Bos is one of the good guys, Nathanael, and

we're stopping him from being elected. Essentially we're interfering in the election. And we're stopping the good guys from being elected."

Nathanael rolled his eyes. "Natasha - they are trying to kill us. What on earth are you talking about? They are not good guys. They don't deserve to get elected."

"Look, I believe Adamant is trying to kill us. He's a billionaire. A nasty capitalist. But let's face it - Leo Bos is one of the good guys. Campaigning constantly on the side of the environment."

"While he jetsets around then goes home to his beachfront mansion that has all the lights on all night and uses ten times as much electricity as everyone else."

"We need Leo Bos as President to stop global warming."

Nathanael looked at her in disbelief. "You believe in global warming?"

Natasha looked at him in disbelief. "You don't?"

Nathanael said, "You've read FOI2009?"

"What's that?"

"That's the emails that were released from the climate centre in Hadley."

Natasha exhaled heavily, "Of course not. They were illegally hacked."

Nathanael was so flabbergasted he couldn't think of anything to say.

Natasha continued, "Well I'd given up hacking because I was a Christian. Doesn't seem right to read hacked emails then, does it? And that's the climate centre, Nathanael, the centre of IPCC research. They're trying to stop the world from being destroyed."

Nathanael said, "And it hasn't occurred to you that there might be another side to this question? Those emails were hacked after legitimate FOI requests were repeatedly refused. There is another side to it all."

Natasha said, "There simply couldn't be. This is global warming we're talking about. I almost think everything Adamant is doing might be justified if we can stop global warming. And we do need to get the present incumbent out of office. I mean, he's a climate denier."

Nathanael said, "A climate skeptic, Natasha. Look, maybe you just need to have a slightly open mind on this issue. Look up Patrick Moore, or Anthony Watts, or Joanne Nova, my compatriot. Look at the other side of the issue."

Natasha said, "I really think you're deluded if you think there is another side. CO2 stores heat, case closed. Arrhenius showed that in the nineteenth century. I'm surprised you're such a scientific luddite."

Nathanael felt his ire rising. Natasha was a climate believer, he couldn't believe it. He purposely softened his voice, he didn't want the anger to show, and he silently prayed.

Then he said, "Can I borrow the laptop?"

She put Lisa's laptop in front of him. He said, "Look, I'm just opening up a few pages on Lisa's TOR browser. You read these if you want to and then see what you think about climate skepticism and climate belief. And what about the recent cold weather? That's not global warming."

"Climate change, Nathanael. It can get colder or hotter."

"I'm going to bed. I'm not going to argue about it if you aren't going to even read anything from the other side of the issue." He opened up the web pages.

Natasha actually sneered and said, "I'm not reading those."

Then he thought for a moment and put his hand on her arm in what he thought was a conciliatory gesture. She pulled her hand away.

He said in his softest, gentlest voice, "Natasha, I wouldn't mind too much which side of politics these people were on. They're trying to kill you. And I care about you. Love you, maybe. I don't want you to die."

She admitted, "I love you, maybe, too. And the video thing is pretty bad, isn't it?"

"It's about lies. They're lying through their back teeth. They've got this whole system which is meant to manage the public appearances of the future President of the United States, for God's sake, and it's all about lies and more lies, and even more lies. They're purveying false video, no less, come on Natasha, it doesn't matter who does it, it could be someone on the other side of politics, but if we don't keep going we are allowing them to get away with lies. We have to expose it." He thought for a moment. "I think Leo Bos might be entrapped in this too - a victim of some sort of agreement he's made with Adamant. He could be the victim here. Why do you think he's mocking the whole thing?"

She looked at him and sighed. "You're right. He could be. And it doesn't matter which side of politics this is on, it's wrong. Sorry Nathanael. Do you know, let's pray. I feel as though it's gotten beyond us, and this disagreement feels like something almost..." She sighed. "Almost designed to rip us apart. And I think near to succeeding."

At one time previously he would not have wanted to be anywhere near Natasha when she was praying. Now, he found he wanted to. "I'd be happy to pray."

"Dear Father," said Natasha, "Please help us with this whole thing, please help us make it work. And protect us and everyone else involved. In Jesus Christ's name, Amen."

"Amen," said Nathanael.

LIPOVNIK, SLOVAKIA

It happened so quickly, Peter hardly even knew how. Peter and Meth were watching the Flintstones, "Frédi és Béni", and Meth was explaining the dubbed Hungarian puns to him. "They are speaking in - what's it called? - when the words end the same."

Peter said, "Rhyme."

Meth laughed. "It's funny."

Peter was feeling uncharacteristically happy in that moment; he had actually forgotten what happiness felt like. He looked at the boy laughing at Frédi és Béni and felt happy about their decisions.

Peter was realising that God had looked after them. The God of his fathers. Or the God of these faithful Hungarians' Jesus Christ, he didn't know, he didn't care, all he knew was that there was a God and He was good and He heard prayers.

The doorbell rang. Probably a delivery or someone asking Martinus to do a job for him or something.

Martinus answered.

The man at the door said something that surprised Peter for a moment, "Are they here?", because he could understand it. Had his Hungarian improved that much?

But then he realised it was English.

They had spoken in English.

It took a moment to process what that meant.

He said, rather than shouted, "Hurry, get up, Meth! We have to go!" But his voice was so full of anguish that the boy leaped out of his chair and leaped across the floor to the room to get his luggage, but by the time they had reached their room the men were already in the house, standing there with guns pointed at them.

Peter said, "What do you want? What do you want with us?"

One of the men said, "You're coming with us."

ADAMANT'S JET, FALLINGSTAR FIELDS PRIVATE AIRPORT, DES MOINES

Adamant was asleep in bed when the phone rang.

It was about 2 am. He answered the phone.

"What is it?"

"It's Eugene again sir. I'm afraid we have a bit of a problem."

"What?"

"Well, those phones - they were not turned off. I think some hacker might have disabled their data connection, somehow, some sort of virus."

"So? Is that a reason to ring me at 2 am?"

"They shared the videos of Leo's temper tantrum, speaking garbage. But they filmed the screen of their phones, using other devices, so the resolution was too small."

"What?"

"Our search missed them. The algorithm missed the videos. It allowed them to be shared."

"Well - change those ones."

"It's too late, now, sir. We tried. But they're all over the net. Not just i-ogle but youtube and Vimeo and everybody else. It's too ubiquitous now. Even we have our limits. People have downloaded them, copied them, made screenshots and audioshots, it's everywhere."

"Who did this?"

"That's the other thing. That woman at the table - we think she was Natasha Chase. The hacker."

Adamant put the phone down.

He called up a particular number on his unregistered mobile.

"Doomsayer?"

"Yes, speaking."

"That hacker, Natasha, and her friend Nathanael are going to be at the Gray's Lake Park in Des Moines tomorrow. They've caused me a lot of misery. I want them gone. You do that and you get paid. If you don't do it tomorrow the deal's off."

GRAY'S LAKE PARK, DES MOINES

Natasha and Nathanael arrived at the Gray's Lake Park at six in the morning. Security didn't stop them or even search their bags, to their surprise. It was almost as if someone had wanted them to get through.

After the videos going viral, they both had thought the i-ogle people would know who they were by now, and would stop them getting in.

They paid their way to the front of the crowd once again, right by the stage.

A journalist was going to interview Leo Bos during this appearance and Natasha was going to hack the system now. She had worked it all out.

She had her laptop in front of her, fully charged, operating on mobile data.

The crowd was milling around and they had a long wait. Natasha opened her computer. A notification pinged in the corner of the screen. Lisa's server had done its job.

But there was a problem. She still didn't have access to the program itself. There was one password missing.

A TOR Messenger message turned up in the corner.

'The password is AE0LUSZER0, with the two O's being zeros. Cheers, TG'

Natasha said, "Who the heck is TG?"

She typed a reply, "Who r u?"

'You'll find out. TG. PS keep up the good work.'

Natasha clicked a link and a screen opened up with the title:

'BEL ALGORITHM CONTROLLER.'

Underneath was a menu with various options.

```
'Edit feed

Interpolate text

Bypass

BEL Feed'
```

She had a pretty good idea of what they all meant.

Natasha pressed, "Bypass," and she knew that whatever happened now, it would be Leo Bos talking and not the BEL Algorithm.

A CAR PARKED IN THE PUBLIC CAR PARK, GRAY'S LAKE PARK, DES MOINES

Doomsayer was of course not his real name. His name was actually Harvey Albert Smithson and he was a little, balding man of fifty three who had never accomplished anything in life before starting his present career because he looked so very harmless. Of course, when your job was to assassinate people, looking harmless was a complete advantage.

It was a curse beforehand. With his computer skills he had tried to join the FBI, but they had overlooked him because he was eminently overlookable. He was so below average in appearance as to be almost completely invisible.

He had tried working in industry but other people were always stealing his ideas and passing them off as their own. He simply hadn't had the self confidence to fight, to stick up for himself. So again, he was always being neglected, overlooked, let go, fired, even thought quite often he had been the one who had saved the firm or done the good deed.

Harvey had tried starting his own firm, but he was so lacklustre in appearance that no one ever hired him.

And of course, romance was completely out of the question. In every date he'd ever been on the woman had spent the whole time texting with someone else, someone more noticeable.

That was when his fascination with the darknet had begun. It was porn at first, but when that got boring he had discovered a peculiar liking in himself for the macabre and the horrible. He never realised before that videos of real violence could be so, so enjoyable to watch.

He wondered in his idle moments if it was because he hated everyone so much, because they had all neglected him and ignored him, everyone had, all his life, and that was why he hated them so much and enjoyed watching them suffer.

Plutonium was his favourite. He had found a video of Litvinenko dying, put up by some nurse at the hospital, he guessed, and it was so dreadfully slow and painful. During radiation poisoning all the cells in the body start to disintegrate - and cells, you know, are highly articulate machines with many moving parts - marvellous things, even a cilia has seventeen moving parts - the cells fall apart slowly. A steady, painful, infinitesimally slow death of suffocation, actually. Struggling to breathe, as all the other organs malfunction and die.

He knew Adamant wanted him to use something else. But Plutonium on Pizza was his favourite recipe. And the fact is if Adamant wanted him to rush then Harvey had to use whatever he had on hand, the resources readily available.

He ordered the pizza in her name. Natasha Chase. But he sent the confirmation message to Nathanael Wayfarer's phone, "Dear Natasha Chase, the pizza you ordered is on the way." And he sent the opposite message to Natasha's phone, "Dear Nathanael Wayfarer, the pizza you ordered is on the way."

With any luck they wouldn't check. They'd just start eating.

Then he followed the pizza van on his computer and planned his route, to anticipate the van on its second to last delivery. The delivery before the final destination, so to speak.

He got his lead-lined gloves ready and put them on the passenger seat of the car.

So many people would be videoing this one.

What pleasure it would give him to watch Natasha Chase and Nathanael Wayfarer dying slowly, from different points of view, again and again and again.

GRAY'S LAKE PARK, DES MOINES

Leo Bos was due to arrive in about five minutes.

Natasha was really excited, so excited she didn't even see the text message.

Nathanael caught something of her excitement and when he saw the text message he forgot his paranoia for a moment in the exhilaration, and didn't even think twice about the fact that a pizza was coming.

At last, Natasha was ready. She had taken control of the BEL Algorithm.

Leo arrived with his entourage about ten minutes late. It took a long time for him to exit the car this time. They could see that Adamant was with him. Adamant was talking to him, seemed to be trying to convince him of something. Nathanael watched their body language. Leo Bos had conceded. He had agreed at last, to whatever Adamant was demanding.

Nathanael said, "I think Leo Bos has agreed not to say anything out of turn this time."

Natasha looked around. "There's a huge crowd here today. Maybe they're here to try and catch him doing something weird again."

Leo walked up to stage slowly this time, he seemed discouraged. He turned back to Adamant, who nodded encouragingly and said something.

Nathanael could just about imagine Adamant saying, "Other nominees have survived worse disasters in the past. Go ahead, we've got this. You are still going to be President."

And although it had been on all the video channels and various extreme right wing and extreme left wing blogs, the news of Leo's strange behaviour had not made it onto the mainstream media yet. Even Fox hadn't mentioned it, which was surprising - perhaps they thought it was fake news and didn't want to be caught out disseminating something fake, which would diminish their credibility?

Fox never worried about that before, Nathanael thought, why start now? Maybe Adamant had them by the short and curlies.

Of course none of the media were particularly trustworthy these days and on some issues Fox were the only one carrying both sides. What an age we live in, he thought.

Adamant said something more to Leo and Leo listened and nodded and replied and turned around and went back up towards the stage, walking slowly and carefully.

There was a woman on the stage now, some kind of town mayor or councillor or something, and she was introducing him.

Leo came up and lots of people cheered him, especially the ones carrying flags or sitting down.

But a lot more were standing up, holding up their mobile phones, videoing the stage.

They wanted to see it happen, Nathanael thought. They had all seen the video. They wanted to see Leo make a fool of himself.

At that very moment the pizza guy was going through security. The people he was delivering to had thoughtfully included their photographs on the SMS, with a note, 'we'll be right near the front.'

The councillor introduced the journalist, a veteran Sixty Minutes reporter.

She stepped forward and sat down next to Leo. Everyone clapped her and the whole crowd surged forwards, impatient for Leo to speak.

As usual, her questions were innocuous. She supported him, Nathanael thought. She would not be examining any of his beliefs or issues or policies in great depth or detail.

Typical.

During her first question someone shoved his arm. "Sorry. Pizza for two?"

Nathanael said, "Thanks," thinking, oh yeah, that's the pizza Natasha ordered. He opened it up and took out a slice and looked up at the pizza guy. "Thanks," he said again.

The pizza guy said, "No worries," and sighed. "I don't know how I'm going to get out of this crowd again." It was much more packed in now than when he had come in.

The reporter was still going on with a long eulogy about Leo Bos and his accomplishments.

Finally she was clearly about to ask the first question.

The pizza smelled so good. Nathanael brought it up to his mouth.

Natasha said, "Did you order this?"

He said, "No, you did," and opened his mouth to take the first bite.

She knocked his hand and the pizza piece fell back into the box.

The pizza guy was still standing near them trying to

move. He saw what was happening and snapped, "That's a good pizza. What are you doing?"

Natasha said, "It's poisoned."

A look of outrage crossed his face. "It is not. How dare you say that. John makes each one with his own hands, and he's a responsible guy, always washes his hands and uses gloves and all the ingredients are good and fresh. Luigi's Pizzas are good pizzas. How dare you. I would have a piece of this myself."

Nathanael closed the box and held it away from him. "No, don't."

The crowd was so thick that were pressed in to the stage. All of them had cameras, and by now a lot of them were trained in on the drama going on at the foot of the stage.

Nathanael said again, "Don't touch the pizza, it's poisoned. I'm trying to save you."

The pizza guy looked at all the people filming this lie, all the people on facebook who would see them fighting over the pizza which was not poisoned, all the people who would stop eating Luigi's Pizza because of this absolute slanderous untruthfulness and his face went red, completely red. He reached again to grab the pizza box, but Nathanael held it away from him.

People all around them were filming them, now, not the stage with Leo Bos upon it.

The pizza guy fumed, snorted air through his nose and like a young red bull about to attack a red cloak waving in the wind, lunged for the pizza box and missed. Then he seemed to really lose it. "That's good pizza," he bellowed, "And I'm gonna prove it!" With a sudden burst of insane energy he plunged forwards, tore the box out of Nathanael's hands and propelled himself up towards the stage.

Leo Bos was about to answer the first question when he saw the pizza guy clambering up like a monkey onto a Thai temple.

The pizza guy opened the box right in front of him and said, "Pizza for you, Mister Bos?"

The security were at the edge of the stage and were so stunned they hadn't reacted yet.

Leo Bos said, "Yeah, sure." And reached for the pizza.

Natasha shouted out, "Don't! It's poisoned!"

Leo took a very, very small bite and pretended to swallow and said, "No, look, it's fine. I'm fine. Thank you, son."

As the security guys rushed on and took the pizza

guy off, he was shouting, "Luigi's Pizza Bar! Luigi's Pizza Bar! Best pizzas in Des Moines."

"Just a small incident," said Leo. "Nothing to worry about. Just a kind-hearted pizza delivery boy giving me some pizza."

The interview continued.

Leo responded to the first question. "Yes, the new film was a big achievement. And I should probably be promoting it. But do you know it is more important to me that I continue with this presidential campaign. I think making a difference is even more important than publicising the issues, don't you?"

The questions and answers continued in a fairly innocuous fashion for about fifteen minutes, but then the reporter said, "Mister Bos, what about that incident yesterday, with the videos? What was that about?"

Leo swallowed and had clearly started breathing in short, hysterical breaths. He said, "What? This question wasn't on the list?"

"The videos, Leo," said the reporter.

He hesitated again and then said, "Purple pumpernickle politicking the grapeseed fickle sumperkind populistic cannaballoons." He looked over at Adamant. "Isn't it working? That thing? Pollsting fabulantastic poltoons of tavernistic poclownish fotherickers. Fabble fabble fabble. Bloopy bloopy bloop. Fackernickle bump fackernickle country matters country matters Hamlet. Is this coming through? Clompitty clomp." The whole crowd was laughing hysterically now.

Natasha was fiddling around on the software.

She had found another menu. "Audio feed."

Strangely enough, there was a facility on the software to interpolate other audio feeds.

She had noticed that the mobile phone networks were switched off, except for the network that the BEL algorithm was working on.

But one mobile phone, apparently, alone of all the phones in the place, had access to this network.

She selected it and connected it to the audio feed.

Leo Bos was still going, saying, "Fotherdike Fotherdick Fother fokker fokker biscuit nickle bike quidditchy quiddypickle twenty two harry potter potty pooster." But Leo Bos's voice disappeared from the speakers and the speakers now projected Raymond Adamant's voice over the whole crowd.

"Well, get it working again. What do you mean, someone's hacked it? How could they do that? Hold on, I have another call." A ring tone sounded and then a voice said, "It's Doomsayer here. The pizza has been delivered."

"And it's deadly?" said Adamant.

"Plutonium topping. If you had even a tiny mouthful you would be very sick. A whole piece of pizza will kill an elephant. I delivered it."

"Yes," said Adamant, "You delivered it. To Leo Bos."

The audio feed cut out then. Natasha tried clicking on things, she tried to get it back, but nothing worked. Clearly the i-ogle guys had managed to wrest back control from her.

But the speakers had gone completely dead.

Leo Bos was standing, wide eyed and afraid, in the middle of the stage.

No one in the audience was talking at all.

There was a bunch of FBI men standing guarding the rear entrance, highly visible in their black suits with a bump where their guns were strapped. Several of them started talking.

Raymond Adamant, standing just to the left of the stage, surrounded by his own security, looked up. He looked at the FBI and saw them watching him, looked at the crowd, saw them all watching him. All those mobile phones. All those videos. Every eye, every camera in the whole place, was on him.

A gentle breeze was blowing across the park and all that anyone could hear for a moment was the wind in the trees. It was a sound that was surprisingly normal, a reminder somehow that there was a whole world of nature that didn't even care for Raymond Adamant or Leo Bos.

Then the FBI moved forwards showing their badges. "FBI! Don't move! Step away. We're taking him in."

Raymond Adamant's security guards moved away from him with hands elevated, reached into their jackets, pulled out their guns and put them on the ground discreetly and put up their hands again, but the police didn't touch them.

They came and arrested Raymond Adamant, cuffed him and dragged him away, struggling and cursing and threatening them with lawyers.

A bunch of paramedics moved up onto stage who had clearly been stationed at some ambulance point or something. They quietly spoke to Leo Bos. He went with them to the ambulance, his hands visibly shaking.

Natasha started silently packing up her laptop, feeling everything was finished, and Nathanael packed up their blanket and the rest of their stuff, but just as they stood up a black-suited man came up and said, "Hello. Are you the girl that shouted out that the pizza piece was poisoned?" He was almost certainly FBI, his clothes, his demeanour told her that.

Natasha thought about lying. She had crossed a lot of lines recently. If she told the FBI the truth about this she would have to tell them everything. But hopefully they could see that she was a white hat; no, more than that, a white robe hacker.

She said, "Yes, I am."

He pulled out a badge and said, "FBI. Look we'd love it if you could come down and explain to us how you knew that. No coercion, mind you, you probably saved Leo Bos's life, but you are a witness in a federal crime."

She said, "I'll come down."

Nathanael said, "I'm coming with her. I'll testify too. Look, do you think we could have some sort of guarantee of immunity with this?"

"I'll talk to my superiors. I can't see why not. You saved Leo Bos's life. That's gotta be worth something. He's one of the good guys."

<u>*FBI OFFICE, UNDISCLOSED LOCATION, DES MOINES*</u>

They had taken Adamant's spare phone out of his hand, after he had tried to lose it on the way into the building. It had been in his back pocket and he had reached in, despite the cuffs, and had pulled it half way out.

But now it rang.

The phone was locked.

It was an iPhone and they didn't know the code.

"Just a moment," said Natasha.

She pulled out her laptop and surfed the net, looking for videos.

She found several high resolution videos showing Adamant, from a crowd member less than five yards away from him. He was taking his phone out of his pocket. He tapped in his security code, but the picture was too small.

Natasha zoomed the video and clicked something. The picture enhanced.

She rewound the video again then played it in slow motion.

"5, 4, 7, 3," she said, telling the FBI guy what numbers Adamant was pressing.

The FBI guy typed the code in and pressed 'speaker phone'.

Another FBI agent had a piece of pizza in his hand.

The one with the phone brought it over to Adamant.

The phone rang.

A third forced Adamant's mouth open and the other guy put the piece of pizza next to his mouth and nodded, saying, "Answer the phone, or eat."

The FBI agent holding the phone pressed the green button.

A voice said, "Adamant?"

"Yes?" said Adamant. Natasha thought Adamant seemed to be praying.

The voice said, "You want us to kill that guy, Peter?"

"No, of course not. I wouldn't want-"

"But you told us to kill him. He's the guy you wanted us to kill and take his boy, this weird baby kid who talks like an adult. We've got him here. We're about to kill him. What do you want us to do?"

"No. I told you I never-"

"You're full of horse manure. Alright we're letting them both go. Don't expect a refund. If someone pays for a hit then pulls out we still get our money. And by the way, we are not doing any more jobs for you. The whole deal's off." The phone clicked off and Adamant groaned and closed his eyes.

The FBI agent holding the pizza put it in his own mouth and ate it and said, "Yum. Now why would anyone be afraid of a good piece of pizza?"

Another FBI guy brought out Adamant's other phone.

He tried the same passcode. It opened.

He started going through document attachments in the email inbox and said, "Look, here's an interesting one. An agreement between Adamant Corp and someone called Deep State. Says that is the Code Name for the Interagency Interoperations Cooperative Resources Committee."

The phone rang right at that moment. The FBI agent put it on speaker phone.

A voice said, "Mister Adamant, just a courtesy call to say that the agreement between us is terminated, as per clause 9. Goodbye." The phone call clicked off.

****

The FBI gave them each an agreement to sign that guaranteed freedom from prosecution for both of them and for Lisa, who was apparently still alive and had left intensive care for the general ward a few hours before. It was not plutonium but some other poison, blowfish venom or something, on her pizza.

Giving their statements took about four hours.

Natasha handed over Lisa's computer at the end of it and the FBI brought them some burgers and chips to eat from some local fast food place. Natasha said, "Not pizza, if you don't mind."

As they ate one of the FBI guys that hadn't interviewed them came over and said, "Well done," to Natasha. He shook both their hands and said, "I really wanted to meet the people who saved Leo Bos's life."

Natasha ate the burger and sighed.

The whole thing was over now.

Then she remembered, there was still one mystery left to solve.

Who was TG?

EPILOGUE - TG

The FBI actually paid for their plane tickets back to Phoenix in gratitude for their help on the case. They left the following afternoon, after collecting the luggage and selling the new car.

Natasha's sister Michelle met them at Phoenix Sky Harbor. She said, "Look, how are you both? Too tired for lunch?"

"No," said Natasha, "Famished. Those were like hyper-economy seats and there was no food included. Apparently that's all the government can afford."

Michelle said, "Well, I've booked us some seats at a nearby restaurant."

So about twenty minutes later they found themselves at an Indian restaurant with a curry smorgasboard. Michelle said, "Well, Nathanael, if you're going to be part of the family, we have to administer the chilli test to see if you can take the hard stuff."

Natasha said, "That's right. Vindaloo for you."

Nathanael said, "Look, curry is my next-to-favourite thing."

Natasha squeezed up to him, "What's your favourite?"

"Oh, Jesus," he said. Then laughed, "And you. And

you. All part of the same package."

It was a lovely day and the restaurant had an outdoors section but while they were eating a sudden gust of wind came and knocked Nathanael's paratha bread onto the pavement.

Michelle said, "Ha. Aeolus is busy today."

Natasha said, "He's the Greek god of wind, isn't he? I looked it up."

Nathanael picked up his paratha and brushed it off. "Not a problem. Zero harm done."

Michelle mumbled, "Nathanael one, Aeolus zero," and Natasha laughed and then wondered why the phrase seemed so familiar and appropriate.

She glanced at Michelle questioningly, who suddenly got a look on her face like a deer in headlights and let out a string of invective.

"Michelle. That was the password TG sent us. How did you know?"

Michelle grimaced. "I guess I'm going to have to tell you, aren't I?" She rolled her eyes and ate another mouthful of curry.

Natasha fumbled, dropped her knife on the floor, gasped audibly. Her hand travelled up involuntarily to cover her mouth.

Even Nathanael's face switched from a habitual expression of slight quizzical curiosity to wide eyed amazement.

Natasha glanced at him for a moment, chuckled because she wasn't sure she had ever seen Nathanael so truly surprised, then she gasped once again. Speaking in short, staccato bursts, she said, "You couldn't be. Michelle. Could you? I didn't even know you knew the least little thing about hacking. You're really TG? No, it's impossible. Is it?"

"Trippy Girl," said Michelle, grinning like the Cheshire Cat. "That's me."

THE BLEND ALGORITHM

Book 2 in the Nathanael Wayfarer series by Andrew Partington

APPENDIX - THE SCIENCE

As in my first novel in this series, "The Adamantine Disclosure," there is real science behind the events and situations. I've tried to reflect the complexity of real life, particularly in the disjunct between people's expressed opinions and their actions, as well as in many other little ways; but whether I'm a fox or a hedgehog in Isaiah Berlin's terms, I do not know.

VIDEO EDITING & ARTIFICIAL INTELLIGENCE

Perhaps the prospect that an AI could edit video in real time seems a long way off, but with the enormous computing power that the largest internet giants such as google and Amazon have today, it is certainly not beyond the realms of possibility. And when you think about the credible special effects in movies today, it must make one start thinking that the time is coming when a video of something will no longer constitute proof that it actually happened.

Deep Learning AI is now reaching a stage where computer generated faces are indistinguishable from real photographs, for instance, NVIDIA has developed an AI that scans celebrity faces and puts the pieces back together to make extremely realistic human faces, as well as images of objects:

https://youtu.be/XOxxPcy5Gr4

The "uncanny valley" effect (which is when computer generated faces look creepy and inhuman) seems to be completely missing from these results.

https://www.youtube.com/watch?v=6cZIaUEmnLI

Google themselves are at the forefront of facial recognition, Artificial Intelligence research, and 'deep learning' algorithms.

http://fortune.com/2015/03/17/google-facenet-artificial-intelligence/

https://ai.googleblog.com

CLIMATE SKEPTICISM AND HACKING

Another point in the story worth noting is Nathanael's skepticism about global warming, something that both reflects his slightly autistic approach to facts and his total disregard of society's good opinion, but I will just say that Nathanael's climate skepticism might be something a rational person would think well worth looking into. These two websites, mentioned in the novel, are worth reading for a scientifically literate take on climate different from the mainstream media's offerings:

https://wattsupwiththat.com

https://joannenova.com.au

And Judith Curry the scientist is surely the most

balanced and highly educated voice in the climate debate today.

https://judithcurry.com

And CO2 is very good for plants (do I even have to mention that?) as the satellites show:

https://judithcurry.com/2018/09/19/the-most-amazing-greening-on-earth/#more-24382

The hacking incident mentioned by Pastor Carlos is perhaps a reference to the hacking of the emails from the Climate Research Unit in Hadley - but you can decide for yourself, the similarities may only be superficial - Climategate was big news back in 2009, though, and the consequences of this hack are still being worked through today.

That these hacked emails were in fact previously requested on a FOI request that seemed quite reasonable considering that the CRU is completely government funded and under British law ought to be amenable to FOI requests is something few people realise.

https://wattsupwiththat.com/2009/11/19/breaking-news-story-hadley-cru-has-apparently-been-hacked-hundreds-of-files-released/

Speaking of hackers, certainly Edward Snowden and Bradley (now Chelsea) Manning were both whistleblowers rather than traitors, Snowden the one who made us aware of the extent of government surveillance (the NSA have access to everything, we really do live in the Panopticon in these days), and Manning releasing videos of the misdeeds of American soldiers in the Middle East. Julian Assange, being a journalist, did not deserve to be abandoned by the Australian government. Indeed, it can only show the complicity of the Australian authorities that his situation has still not improved.

In this age when google has abandoned their motto, "Do no evil" (https://www.gizmodo.com.au/2018/05/google-removes-dont-be-evil-clause-from-its-code-of-conduct/) and everyone is concerned about fake news, when the global warming believers are accusing the skeptics of being like holocaust deniers it might be worth remembering CS Lewis' words about reserving our judgement until we know all the facts:

"...in other words, you must show that a man is wrong before you start explaining why he is wrong. The modern method is to assume without discussion that he is wrong and then distract attention from this (the only real issue) by busily explaining how he became so silly."

Well, things have certainly gotten worse. These days people bandy about accusations such as 'denier' implying that the global warming skeptic is somehow implicated in the Holocaust, without even trying to explain anything at all.

OTHER FACTS

Many of the geographical and local features are as accurate as I can make them. Szalonna, the Mesquite Public Library, Dreamy Draw Drive, all of these places are real but I have been to none of them (although I have been to Arizona and along some of the highways mentioned) but if I have written anything inaccurate about these places I apologise.

The places Leo Bos makes his speeches have also been used by previous Presidential hopefuls. Many of the other facts were also researched, but I'm sure some inaccuracies will turn up, at some point, and mistakes, so for these also I apologise in advance.

ACKNOWLEDGEMENTS

Thanks to Cas Pearson for editing the first draft so meticulously. Really appreciate it! Thanks also to various friends and also brothers and sisters in Christ who read and enjoyed "The Adamantine Disclosure" for their enthusiastic responses, which helped me keep on writing! And thanks to Richard Braham, whose hints about entering writing prizes spurred me on to finish this book quickly (I didn't win the prize though, never mind.)

Thanks also to those who in my difficult twenties helped me to persevere through a serious and debilitating depression, because without that help and listening patience and the wisdom of those people who persistently pointed to Jesus, I am sure I wouldn't be here now. Doctor Lachlan Dunjey comes to mind! Peter Kan, as well, who is no longer with us. And my parents, who thankfully are still with us despite what seemed to be a close call this year; they have stood beside me through many difficulties.